GHOST FLIGHT

WINNER of a 2025 International Impact Book Award. A 2026 Indies Today Award Finalist. A 2025 BookLife Fiction Prize Quarterfinalist. A 2025 New York Book Festival General Fiction Award Honorable Mention. A 2025 Shelf Unbound Best Indie Book Award Top 100 Notable Book.

'A sharp and well-observed portrait of lives at the crossroads' *Kirkus Reviews* (GET IT Verdict)

'A rarity...Asprakis's skill at tapping into life's beauty and pain lingers long after the book's final page' the BookLife Prize

'A haunting and heartbreaking story' Rebekah Gregoriades for *Cyprus Mail*

'A tender journey through memory...showcasing once again [Asprakis's] deep understanding of

EVA ASPRAKIS

Eva Asprakis is a contemporary fiction author whose acclaimed novels explore complex family dynamics, sexuality and womanhood, and the search for identity and belonging. She has won numerous literary awards, including the 2024 Ink Book Prize for Fiction and a 2025 International Impact Book Award. Born in London, England, she has spent her adult life in Nicosia, Cyprus, where she continues to live and write.

Thirty-Eight Days of Rain
Love and Only Water

GHOST FLIGHT

Eva Asprakis

For Max

*Commemoration is resistance to defeat the ugliness
of death.*
Michalis Hadjipantelas, Helios Airways Air Disaster Memorial, 11 August 2024

<h1 style="text-align:center">One</h1>

PETROS WILL RETURN TIME and again to his place on bended knee, gazing up at her. Melina. The only woman he has ever loved, with the flesh like baked apples and the soft-lashed brown eyes. A day has passed, and he can still hear the silence that came after his question, still feel the cavity in his chest that could only be filled by her answer. Nai. She cried honest tears, then. And now here she stands, admitting a lie. Petros stares at her.

"Say something," she pleads.

His scoff echoes through their kitchen. It is a small space, with wood-veneer cupboards and laminated countertops whose sealant still smells chemical. They have worked hard for this house, Melina as a junior-school teacher and Petros as an electrician. He was telling her what he wanted to do with the lighting when she broke the news.

"Please, Petro . . ."

"How could you?" he asks.

"How could I what? Invite our oldest friend to dinner?" She tilts her head.

"Aristos is not our friend," Petros growls. "He made that clear when he left for London."

"That was seven years ago," Melina says.

"And has he called us since?"

She drops his gaze.

"How could you?" Petros repeats, under his breath.

He watches Melina step closer in her flat brown shoes.

"I knew what you'd say if I told you he'd called. But you wouldn't have meant it," she adds, before he can respond. "You'd have regretted not hearing him out."

Petros inhales the smell of charred halloumi, and counts four plates awaiting portions of makarónia tou foúrnou from the oven.

"And it's too late to cancel," he says.

Melina gives him a remorseful look. "He'll be here any minute. With a new girlfriend, apparently."

Her engagement ring flashes as she turns away, a small diamond in a silver fist. It spoke to Petros, as someone who had clutched his love so tightly and for so long. He blinks the afterimage from his eyes. Before tonight he had never known Melina to lie, had never imagined her capable of it. But perhaps he had grown too comfortable.

***

The taxi swings around a corner. On the left-hand side of the road, Wendy observes, just like in England. She sinks back in her seat. There is something disappointing about this, despite the driver's speeding, a lack of the alienness or adventure that she had hoped to find here.

She braces her palm against the front seat as the driver breaks. He gesticulates, wildly, disturbing the string of beads that hangs from his rear-view mirror. There is a snort. Wendy looks to the man beside her, whose dark eyes are shining red.

"Welcome to Cyprus," Aristos mutters.

"Thanks," Wendy says. She denotes her sarcasm with a grimace, something she never had to do for her English ex.

Aristos's lips twist up at the corner. The signal turns amber, then green, showing him in new lights before the car surges onwards. He fires off a round of syllables, and the driver nods.

"What was that?" Wendy asks.

"I just told him to stop at a bakery, so we can pick up a sweet," Aristos says. "You'll choose."

Wendy catches the driver's eye in the rear-view mirror. His beads swing, pendulum-like, around another bend.

"Is that the kind of boyfriend you're going to be?" she asks Aristos, teasingly. "Sending me on errands for you? I know nothing about the sweets here."

"Is this the kind of girlfriend you're going to be?" Aristos returns. "Wanting my help with the smallest decisions? A sweet is a sweet, isn't it?"

They regard one another. This phase of any relationship is a contest, Wendy knows, with each party straining not to blink and admit dissatisfaction to the other first. She holds her eyebrows high.

"Come on," Aristos grins, as they roll into an unpaved car park. "We'll go together."

***

Melina is taking her pasta bake from the oven when the doorbell rings. She catches her wrist putting it down, and massages the burn through her oven gloves as she makes for the front door.

"I'll get it," she calls.

Her fiancé is silent. The web of his disdain blows off her as she admits the night air.

"Kalispéra, Melina," Aristos greets her.

"Ariste . . ."

It is the first time in seven years, yet his hooked nose and heavy brows appear unchanged. Perhaps his cheeks have hollowed, or has he taken to a cleaner shave? Before she can decide, Melina loses focus.

"Ah," Aristos says, following her gaze over his shoulder. "This is my girlfriend, Wendy."

Darkness parts for the creature, half a head taller than he is. She is wearing tattered jeans and a graphic T-shirt, with what could be yesterday's eyeliner. Her pallor strikes Melina. Her ashen hair, her flame-blue eyes. Aristos is the one who left Cyprus, and yet Melina feels that it is Wendy who is returning

4

to her. She opens her arms as wide as she can before her oven gloves tug.

"Welcome," she blushes. "It's nice to meet you."

Thinly, Wendy smiles.

"We brought dáktyla," Aristos says, proffering a white cardboard box.

"Efcharistó," Melina thanks him, folding herself against the door. "Come in."

"Thank you," Wendy says, with the flat accent that is at once so foreign and so familiar.

Melina lowers her eyes. She pretends not to feel Aristos's frown as she rubs at the burn on her wrist, which has flared red.

***

The first thing that Aristos notices is the smell. It curls from his friends' kitchen, just as it did from his parents' when he was a child. Sautéed onions, garlic and pork mince, sprinkled with dried mint and cinnamon while a pot of pasta boiled to mush. There was the melting of butter – together with flour and milk – and the tang of halloumi. *Makarónia tou foúrnou.* The dish is another old familiar, lined up to greet him after Melina.

Instinctively, Aristos approaches the rectangle of light across the front room. A figure blocks it, stopping him still.

"Petro," he musters, jarred. "*Kalispéra.*"

Petros is taller than he remembers, with broader shoulders and a fuller beard. Around his neck is a crucifix, not unlike the one Melina is wearing. Aristos feels an absence where his own used to hang.

Affecting a grin, he extends his hand. "Long time no see," he says, in his best British accent.

Behind him, Wendy snickers.

Petros's eyes slide over Aristos's shoulder.

"This is Wendy," Aristos says, drawing his hand back, "my girlfriend."

"Hi," Wendy says, as he loops his arm around her.

She feels insubstantial to him, suddenly, with her teetering height and her untoned limbs, like a runway-side pole whose windsock could blow a new way at any time.

"*Chaíro polý*," Petros responds, stony-faced. "Nice to meet you."

"Let's sit down, shall we?" Melina calls.

Following Petros into the kitchen, they arrange themselves around a table. Aristos surveys the room. A modest rectangle, with cupboards of the dark wood found everywhere in Cyprus. It is as oppressive as ever, clinging to walls and hulking across floors with the mandates of shutters and sideboards. It vanquishes the light.

With a thud, Melina presents her pasta bake.

"Smells good," Aristos says.

"Like home, *nai*?" she smiles, through the rising steam.

She goes and comes back with floral plates, a village salad. And no oven gloves, for the first time since Aristos's arrival. He is opening his mouth to chide Petros, who has only poured a beer for himself, when he sees the ring.

"Ariste, how hungry are you?" Melina asks, lifting a serving spoon.

"*Perímene*," Aristos says.

He turns her left wrist, and a diamond catches the light.

"Are you engaged?"

Taking a seat across the table, Petros looks at Melina. She opens and closes her mouth before conveying his smile to Aristos.

"Petros proposed last night," she confesses.

"Last night? Well, that's . . . Congratulations!"

Shunting his chair back, Aristos takes Melina into his arms. He breathes the cooking scents caught in her hair, and wills his heart not to hammer at her chest.

"And your fiancé has cracked open a beer," he tuts. "We should be drinking champagne . . ."

"Petro," Melina pleads.

Standing up, Petros slopes back towards the fridge.

"Congrats," Wendy says, from her seat. "Can I see the ring?"

Melina blinks. "Of course."

She is tense, too, Aristos senses. Though it comforts him, he knows that Wendy's cool tone can make her seem barbed.

Melina edges around the table, jogging it with her hip. She holds her hand out at arm's length, and Wendy leans no closer to inspect it.

"*Kókkino í lefkó*?" Petros asks.

Aristos turns his head. "What?"

"Red or white?" Petros repeats, jerking the fridge door open wider. "Wine."

"Ah." Aristos translates the question for Wendy.

"White, please," she says. Then, to Melina, "It's pretty."

Blushing her thanks, Melina resumes her place at the head of the table.

"Thanks, mate," Aristos says, as two wine glasses land before him.

Petros places a third in front of Melina, leaning to kiss her.

"So, how did it happen?" Aristos asks, sitting back down.

China clinks as Melina picks up a plate.

"He took me to a beach near our old village," she says, breaking the béchamel-and-cheese surface of the *makarónia*, "where we used to go for plane-watching."

"Plane-watching?" Wendy repeats.

"Yeah." Aristos shoots her a look. "Thank God they found each other, right?"

Wendy laughs, taking her plate. Melina picks up another.

"It was very romantic," she says, dishing out a larger portion. She places it down in front of Aristos.

"I'd expect nothing less, from our Petros. *Stin agápi*," Aristos says, when Melina has made up the final two plates. "To love."

They raise their glasses together, Petros with force. The quiet is loud in the wake of the crash. Aristos picks up his knife.

"You're our first guests," Melina says, with another apologetic smile.

Aristos glances sideways. It is as though he and Melina are alone at the table, with its other occupants cutting silently into their meals. Petros not willing to speak English, apparently, and Wendy not speaking at all. Shouldn't she be the one complimenting this nice food and asking about this new house? She isn't shy. That, Aristos knows. But perhaps he is expecting too much of his first dinner date in seven years.

"So, when's the big day?" he asks, in his brightest voice.

"We're thinking next summer," Melina says, parcelling *makarónia* onto her fork.

"And how long have you two been together now? Ten years, is it?"

"No." Petros scores his knife across his plate. "*Énteka*."

"Eleven," Melina translates, wincing.

"Wow. So, you guys have been, like, each other's whole lives," Wendy responds.

Melina's smile fades.

"Yeah. Since before they were a couple, even," Aristos says. "It's a heartwarming story . . ."

Petros's cutlery clatters to his plate.

"Petro," Melina starts.

Pasta turns to mush in Aristos's mouth, what remains of the wine sloshes around in the bottle, and Petros shakes his head.

"*Eftá chrónia*," he snarls, "seven years. With no emails, no phone calls. And he thinks he can speak on our relationship?"

"Well, look. I'm not holding my breath for the best man gig," Aristos concedes.

Petros rounds on him. "You just left. Practically lived between our houses through high school and the army, telling us we were your family," he motions, from himself to Melina. "Making promises you weren't going to keep . . ."

"I said nothing I didn't mean," Aristos says, "at the time. I wasn't planning to leave."

"No, of course not. A student visa just fell into your lap." Petros glares at him. "You know," he goes on, for the first time in English, "Agathi still hasn't moved on from 'The Great Aristos'."

"*Éla re*, Petro," Aristos says, conscious of Wendy at the edge of his vision. "I don't know about that."

"I do," Petros maintains. "We talked about it this afternoon."

A weight drops through Aristos's stomach.

"You still see her?" he asks Melina.

"Well, I don't really," she mumbles, tucking her hair back. "But Petros . . ."

Aristos stares across the table.

"Who's Agathi?" Wendy asks.

Aristos fingers the stem of his wine glass as Petros explains. Agathi was Aristos's girlfriend, from age sixteen to twenty. She thought they were going to spend their lives together. He told her that they were. And then he left, without warning.

"It destroyed her," Petros says.

There is no stopping him. To defend himself, Aristos would have to tell the truth, and he is no freer to do that now than he was then. There is a reason why he left his friends no time to question his move. Hand trembling, he lifts his glass.

"Melina and I had to adopt her, basically. She was broken," Petros goes on.

"She was young. We all were," Aristos says, gulping back sour wine. "She's not your maid of honour, is she?" he asks Melina, with a grimace.

Her smile is fleeting.

Petros looks at her, and his frown softens. "Have you thought any more about a *kouméra*, Melina *mou*?"

Melina stops with her fork halfway to her mouth. "Well. How about you, Wendy?"

"Me?" Wendy says, eyebrows arched.

"Yes."

"Be your maid of honour?" she and Petros chorus, an inharmonious choir of English and Greek.

"Yes," Melina repeats. "Why not? It's been lovely meeting you," she says, to Wendy. And to Petros, "I think this could be a nice way for the rest of us to get reacquainted."

Aristos gives her a nod, his throat bulging with so many grateful tears that he dares not thank her aloud. In any case, there is something about her apparent aversion to Agathi, and the troubled look upon Petros's face, that gives him pause. Perhaps Melina has not made this offer for entirely selfless reasons.

Accident Investigation Report

Date: 9 May 2004

Time: 14:50 AST

Aircraft Type: ATR 72-212

Operator: Executive Airlines, doing business as American Eagle

Flight Number: 5401

Occupants: 26

Fatalities: 0

Aircraft Damage: Substantial

Synopsis:

On Sunday 9 May 2004, Executive Airlines (doing business as American Eagle) flight 5401 skipped once, bounced twice, and then crashed during its landing at Luis Munoz Marin International Airport, San Juan, Puerto Rico. The aircraft came to a stop on a grassy area approximately 217 ft left of the runway centreline and 4 317 ft beyond the runway threshold.

The captain was seriously injured. The first officer, 2 flight attendants and 16 of the 22 passengers received minor injuries. The aircraft was substantially damaged.

Two

HE LIKES HER BECAUSE she is incurious. Critical, considered, but with no interest in other people or their pasts. He understood this at once, and it captivated him.

He was entering her house when they met. Then her bed. There was no flash of shock in her eyes, just a cool blue knowing.

They introduced themselves afterwards, with their backs to the brick wall of that house in Hampstead, that night in March. Smoking, both of them, her a roll-up and him a straight. He was lighting up when the door bumped shut on his back, in a rush to escape their sins. Then he saw her fingers, bone-white and thin, scattering loose leaf tobacco. He shivered, too, as he lowered his lighter, restoring the darkness and cold. He couldn't leave. Couldn't shake the steadiness of those same hands inside the house, where their owner had stroked and scratched at him with a carnal joy so unabashed it had seemed almost wicked. Those same fingers, struggling to assemble a cigarette, had strayed into places that had made him gasp and jerk away, only to sag back. The girl had given a triumphant laugh, then, and he hadn't cared who else was watching. He didn't know them, and they didn't know him. The anonymity of it was ecstasy.

Her lips parted, audibly, and still no words emerged. He could just make out her tongue, dragging across a rolling paper before she sealed her cigarette. His shame gave way to indignance, and then to awe. She was unlike any woman that he had known, happy to let him come and go from her bed with no questions asked. A new desire tugged at him.

"What's your name?" he asked.

Her lighter sparked into flame. He glimpsed her thin lips and the silver stud in her left nostril, reflecting orange. Then nothing.

"Wendy," she said.

"I'm Aristos."

In the darkness, Wendy's face was blank.

"Or Arty," Aristos blinked. "People call me Arty, here."

The end of her cigarette burned brighter as she inhaled.

"Arty," she repeated, lowering it. "You know, I'm an artist."

"Ah, really?"

"Mmn."

"Wow." Aristos dragged a breath through his cigarette.

"You're not from here," Wendy said.

"No."

She exhaled. And resumed her silence, Aristos marvelled, without asking him anything further.

A car swept past, its yellow beams like searchlights. Flattening himself to the wall, Aristos strained to make Wendy out in the shadows. A flash of peroxide-blonde hair shorn off at the shoulder, with silver rungs laddering the helix of her ear, and then she was gone again. Ash blew at his shins in the wake of the vehicle.

"Can I have your number?" he asked.

The shadows lurched as Wendy turned towards the house, then towards him again. Streets away, a motorbike carved through the night.

"Fuck it," she said, stowing her cigarette between her lips. "Yeah."

Her face shone in the light of her phone, with its slide-out keyboard.

"Ready?" she asked.

Aristos fumbled for his own phone, letting his cigarette burn down between his fingers.

"Thanks," he said, saving her details under, 'Wendy (pottery class)'. "I'll see you, then."

"All right," came her response.

Even as he walked away, his footsteps echoing down the street with its large houses and leafy pavements, Aristos kept looking over his shoulder. He couldn't believe that this girl would let him go, asking nothing more of him. And yet her door thudded shut.

Perhaps that was why he called her the next week, and the week after that. Perhaps it was why he bought her dinner, drinks and a plane ticket in such rapid succession, and why she is lying beside him now, in Cyprus.

Aristos sits up to survey their hotel room. His head feels heavy, his tongue rough. There were three of them drinking wine last night. Three bottles of it, though he cannot recall Melina refilling her glass more than once. Petros stuck to beer. Aristos closes his eyes, to squeeze them dry of the image in his mind's eye. How changed he must have looked, draining glass after glass with his British girlfriend.

Despite the cringing of the mattress, Wendy doesn't stir. The breath passes through her nose, not snagging even on the stud in her left nostril. Envy tugs at Aristos. He hasn't slept so well since he left Cyprus. Now he is back, between a ceiling like a blank page and clean-smelling sheets, as though he could cleave himself from his history here with the booking of a standard room.

"Wendy," he murmurs.

She gives a muffled groan.

"Wendy . . ."

He nudges her, for a view through her eyes. Her newness to him, and to his country, is the only thing that has given him the courage to come back.

Slowly, she rolls onto her ear. Fixes him with a smile.

"Morning," she says.

"Sleep well?"

"Mmn."

Her shoulder is cool to the touch, her collarbone jutting out like the wing of an aeroplane in bank. Aristos grazes his fingernails down her arm. He feels his eyes glinting back at hers, as though they have met mid-exchange. Before she can look away – before this first and most glorious phase of their relationship can end – he pulls her towards him. She reaches into that place again, when she is kneeling between his legs. He makes an animal sound. He clamps down on his tongue. Wendy laughs and he wants to hit her, but he lets her go on.

"So, yeah. Morning," she repeats, afterwards.

They are lying shoulder to shoulder, their chests rising and falling fast. Aristos snorts.

"Is that what you woke me up for?"

"No. It was good, though," he admits.

"It was, wasn't it?"

"That thing you do . . ."

Eyeing him, knowingly, Wendy stretches her arms up over-head. "There is something about driving a man mad. I missed it, in my last relationship . . ."

The skin stretches taut over her ribcage. Beyond the window, a child calls out across the beach.

Aristos shifts upright. "I thought we'd agreed that you weren't going to talk about that here."

"We can agree that you've asked me not to." Wendy drops her arms back to the bed.

Aristos stares at her.

"It's a change of pace from England, that's all."

"Well," he says, with a slow breath out, "I'm from Cyprus. It's a traditional place."

"Traditional?" She raises her eyebrows.

He swings his legs off the side of the bed.

"Given the way that we met, Arty—"

"Yes, well. We're here now."

The vinyl floor comes cold to the soles of his feet. In two strides, he crosses it and wishes that the space was larger. This was always his problem with Cyprus. Too confining. Overcrowded with people he knew too much about, and who knew too much about him. Snapping open their miniature kettle, Aristos fills it from a litre water bottle.

"Is there coffee?" Wendy asks.

He glances at the tray on the sideboard.

"There are sachets," he reports, rhyming the word with 'hatchets' before he remembers that the 'e-t' should be pronounced the French way, not the English.

Despite his seven years in London, Aristos still loses track. He casts a look over his shoulder, but Wendy doesn't correct him. She says that an instant coffee will do fine, as though she is quite used to receiving her beverages in bed. Then, with just as much nonchalance, she asks how he met Petros and Melina.

Aristos sinks back onto the edge of the mattress. "At *lyceum*," he says, balancing his own coffee on his bare knee, "high school. There was a group of us. Me, Petros, Melina and . . ."

"Agathi," Wendy says.

Aristos nods.

"So, Petros has stayed friends with Agathi, but Melina hasn't."

"You know as much as I do. Until last night, I hadn't spoken to any of them since the army."

Leaning back against the headboard, Wendy pulls her knees up to her chest. "You can talk to me about her, you know," she says. "We both have pasts, we're not sixteen."

Aristos looks sideways at her. "Like Petros and Melina were, you mean."

His girlfriend is sharp-eyed with mischief, making him feel giddy again. They spent their first weeks mocking her ex, and now it seems they will move on to his.

"It is strange, to stay with one person all your life," Aristos concedes. "You must always be asking 'what if'."

"Not you," Wendy smiles.

"No," he responds, feeling a coil of dread at odds with the pulse in his groin. "Not me."

In her kiss, he tastes coffee and the truth behind her sudden interest. It calms him. Wendy's questions do not come out of curiosity, but vanity. From their answers, she will take more about herself than she will about him or anyone else, for nothing broader seems to concern her. Not whether Agathi was pretty, with her round hips and dark hair, but whether she was prettier than Wendy. Not how Agathi was in bed – after a year of good, Christian waiting – but how she compared to Wendy.

Aristos sits upright. His new girlfriend has such pale eyelids that he can see their veins. He has known her for barely two months. He would never have met her, in that scandalous way, if it hadn't been for his mother calling and telling him that his father was sick. Really sick, Ariste. It was time to come home. Aristos's date for the night – some girl from his office – arrived no sooner than he had put down the phone. He drifted through their prearranged pottery class, feeling the helpless changeability of everything as the clay rounded and thinned between his palms. Dizzied, he lost track of his date. He sat on his stool, wide-eyed yet unseeing, until their teacher sidled over to him. She asked what was wrong and whether she couldn't make him feel better. She put her hand on his arm. He blinked. They were in Hampstead. Wendy was there. And then. He blinks. They are in Larnaca. His father is sick. Really sick, Ariste. It is time to go home, and yet Aristos itches to escape now as he did those few weeks ago. He has known Wendy for barely two months. He would never have met her, if not for that phone call. And yet he thinks that, of everyone in the world, he feels safest talking to her.

"They were never close," he recalls. "Agathi and Melina. It used to bother Agathi. She felt like Melina didn't want to be alone with her, or even look her in the eye, sometimes."

"Well, at least that should make my job easier," Wendy says.

Aristos looks at her.

"Taking Agathi's place," she explains.

"Ah." He exhales relief.

"Is there anything I should avoid doing?" Wendy asks, taking a sip of her coffee. "Anything that Agathi did, to annoy Melina?"

"Erm . . ."

As he considers this, Aristos feels her watching him over the rim of her mug. He lowers his gaze. The Melina that he knew seven years ago was, by all accounts, sweet. She spoke with an inside voice in every setting, was good with children and quick to smile at jokes that she didn't understand, if only to put their tellers at ease. She didn't have a bad word to say about anyone, nor did she seem very close to anyone, outside of Petros. She was so caring and yet so isolated.

Aristos fingers the handle of his mug. "I don't want to put ideas in your head, but back then I did wonder . . ." He trails off.

"If she had feelings for you," Wendy guesses.

Aristos shrugs. It is true that in his first months at high school, he believed he could have his pick of Agathi and Melina. Petros and Melina had met years earlier and were inseparable. Except that Petros cast long, wistful looks at Melina when she turned away. He smiled privately at her jokes, as though they were just for him. Melina must have known that he was in love with her – it was obvious – and yet she wouldn't submit to him. Until Aristos asked the bolder, more strikingly beautiful Agathi to be his girlfriend. Only then did Melina give in to Petros, and still she avoided seeing Agathi outside of the group.

"I'm sure there's nothing there now," Aristos adds, with a glance at Wendy.

Tipping her head back, Wendy swallows the last of her coffee and puts her mug down with a thud.

"You know I don't do jealousy," she says, pointedly, "so there's no need to worry."

Another reference to their first encounter, in all its sordid glory. Aristos grits his teeth through conflicting muscle contractions.

"Anyway," Wendy smiles, reaching for her tobacco. She pulls a rolling paper loose between her thin, white fingers. "Melina and I have a wedding to plan."

THREE

ON HIS FIRST SUNDAY in Cyprus for seven years, Aristos awakens to the ringing of church bells, and it is as though no time has passed. He rolls over, rubbing his eyes. Which is their nearest church here, Saint Lazarus? It must be, that limestone triumph containing the open tomb of its patron. Apparently, Jesus raised Lazarus from a premature death in Bethany, only for subsequent murder plots to chase the man from Judea to Cyprus. Aristos sits upright, the ringing echoed in his ears. This island as a place of sanctuary for anyone, he cannot imagine.

Coaxing Wendy out of bed, Aristos shaves and stands in the mirror, turning to survey his attire. Slim-fitting trousers and a white shirt, creased after its journey from London. Every garment he bought there was expensive, from Savile Row or Jermyn Street, despite his only having a student loan. He said no to nights out and trips home, smoking more than eating while he saved up towards each new tie. His fellow students didn't understand it, splashing their money on the tat at Camden Market, but Aristos would have paid any amount to avoid that Cypriot pocket of North London. Besides, if he had learned anything from his business management course – not to mention his parents – it was the importance of looking the part.

"Could do with an iron, really," Wendy says.

"There's no board," Aristos mutters, "but thanks for the criticism."

"What? I was talking about me, my top."

He looks at her, thin limbs all the whiter for the tattoos exposed by her T-shirt. It is one of the black, graphic kinds that she wears often, and rumpled.

"You know they'll want to take us to church? My parents," he adds, when her face remains blank.

"So . . . ?"

"The shorts."

"Oh. Okay, then," Wendy says, bending over her suitcase.

Aristos returns to his reflection as she gets changed, to the curved nose and thick brows so like his father's. He tries to focus on how short and tanned he looks next to his girlfriend, and on what his parents will think upon seeing him. Anything but what he will think of them.

"Better?" Wendy asks, presenting herself in a pair of ripped jeans.

"Yeah," Aristos concedes, with a glance at his watch. "Better."

It is a ten-minute taxi ride to Aradippou, the town just outside of Larnaca where Aristos grew up. It lies inland from their hotel, with no glittering views of the sea. Instead, cross-topped domes push up like molehills from every corner. The area is known for its copious churches and for the doubling of its population after 1974, when Greek-speaking Cypriots fled south from Turkish forces. Otherwise, it is unremarkable, with winding streets and sparse pavements, dogs of no discernible breed patrolling its chain-link fences. A large one darts out into the road, and their driver slams on the brakes, beeping. Beside Aristos, Wendy's gasp gives way to a grimace.

"Are you okay?" he asks her.

"Yeah. It's just . . . dogs."

"You don't like them?"

"I just wouldn't want the hassle," she says, as they roll past another 'beware' sign. "It looks like you have a lot of them here."

"I guess so," Aristos says.

Past the Church of Saint Lucas in its broad square, they come up an incline to his childhood home. The driver grunts his due, and Aristos pays it without taking his eyes off the property. A corner house, with black-railed balconies overlooking adjacent streets. Aristos leads Wendy to the matching rail around its perimeter. He braces himself for the squeak of the gate and gets a lump in his throat when it breaks the quiet. Hollow with pine-scent, just as he left it, everything here unoiled and ancient. Except for the house, a post-conflict build, which resembles its neighbours almost exactly.

On the doorstep, Aristos hesitates. He drops Wendy's hand to adjust his collar, looks at his shoes and then back at her. Is everything okay, she is asking him, in a faraway voice. Yes, fine. He is sure that he says this out loud, perhaps a little too harshly.

Then the door is folding inwards, revealing a slight woman with watchful eyes. They widen.

"Ariste . . ."

"Hello, Mamá . . ."

She clutches his hands, elbowing the door open wider. Aristos winces as his father looms up behind her, the world's longest shadow.

"*Geiá sas*, Ariste," the man greets him, formally.

His dark eyes slide to Wendy. With his heart beating in his ears, Aristos makes a grab at introducing them, his parents to his girlfriend and his girlfriend to his parents, Marios and Nausicaa. He feels false doing this, like there is a presence over his shoulder that could barge in and show him up with its more familiar terms. He wishes it would – introduce him, too – to the father that he hasn't called since he left for London. Nausicaa managed to visit him there only once, and Aristos could not bring himself to return the favour. Her knuckles are white with gripping his hands, her eyes wet with more emotion than she has ever articulated. She scarcely glances at Wendy. Aristos pulls back his hands.

"Please," his mother says, recovering her composure, "come in."

The door opens into the living room, with its high ceiling and marble-flecked floor. In the far corner is the L-shaped staircase, and directly ahead the door to the kitchen. Blinds cover every window. Doubtless, Aristos's mother will say that this is to keep the house cool while she scrubs and polishes, making the place smell sterile in her attempts to get out some stain. But it is only May. Overhead, the fans hang still.

"What shall I offer you, Wendy? Some water, or a coffee?"

"A coffee would be great, thanks."

Nausicaa nods. "Ariste?"

She is awaiting his answer too eagerly, with unblinking eyes and bated breath. It is a relief when she goes into the kitchen and sets the kettle rumbling. Marios stands silent until she returns.

As they take their seats upon the low sofas, set around a lace-covered coffee table, Aristos recalls the discomfort that drove him away. His mother starts them talking, about the weather and other things that feel too restrained for a set of parents and their child reunited after almost a decade. But it would be too abrasive for Aristos to comment on the thinning of his father's hair or the wrinkling of his mother's forehead, too much like addressing the chasm of time and distance that has opened up between them.

Meanwhile, Marios's sickness balloons, its rubber skin squeaking against the walls and prickling Aristos's hair with static. The pressure is enormous. Aristos wants to stab at it. But what would come out? After the rupture, there would be a sagging – the elasticity going out of everything, awful in its anticlimax – and the stench of death. Then the realisation of all the practical issues that would need solving, coming down like shards of confetti.

And so Aristos doesn't ask about his father's sickness. Instead, he lets his mother question Wendy, first about her 'boring', solely British background, then about her ambition to become a famous painter, and finally about how long she has been seeing Aristos.

"Two months?" Nausicaa balks, upon hearing the answer. She looks from Wendy to Aristos and back, brows raised. "And you agreed to move across the continent with him? He has proposed to you, I hope."

Wendy laughs.

"No need for any of that, Mamá. Cyprus is in the EU now, remember? Wendy is free to come and go as she likes," Aristos says.

Nausicaa glares at him, fingering her crucifix.

In defiance, Aristos reaches an arm around Wendy's waist. He is scolding himself for his regression – from twenty-seven to teenager, in under ten minutes – when his girlfriend tilts her head.

"It would be cool to have a wedding here, though," she says, as though moved to consider it. She looks around. "Do you have any photos from yours?"

Nausicaa falters. Her lips stop halfway to a smile, her fingers still on the chain of her crucifix. Aristos sees this. He knows the answer to Wendy's question, and yet his eyes follow hers to the walls. Blank, between the lowered blinds and religious icons. The largest of the latter depicts the Virgin Mary, caressing her son in silver and gold. Its metal taints the air. Weren't there any photographs of Aristos and his mother in such an embrace? He was eighteen when he asked her, newly free of his teenaged disinterest, and conscious of the families – their subtleties and their keepsakes – in his friends' homes. Like Melina's, his had Lefkara Lace webbing every table. Like Petros's, worry beads studding all the dishes. Like Agathi's, wooden chairs sporting rope seats. But unlike any of theirs, Aristos's parents displayed no picture frames. They reared away from his questioning this, his father clamping his mouth shut and his mother running hers.

"Well," Nausicaa waffled, "their parents were displaced, weren't they? From Achna. It must be important to them, to have those reminders of their old homes."

"Yeah, but . . ." Aristos frowned as it occurred to him that he didn't know. "Where did you live, before the invasion?"

Slamming a glass down, his father strode from the room.

"A village towards Limassol," his mother smiled, thinly, "called Tochni."

There is a knock at the door, rousing Aristos from his memory.

"Would you two mind taking these cups through to the kitchen?" Nausicaa asks, smoothing down her skirt. She gives Wendy a smile. "Marios will show you the way."

"Sure . . ."

Teeth gritted, Aristos follows his father across the floor. As though he hasn't walked it innumerable times, with the slapping feet of a toddler before their inevitable slips over, or the ceaselessly rumbling stomach of a growing boy. Wendy is the newcomer, not Aristos. He wants to impress this upon his mother. But when he looks at his feet, large upon the terrazzo tiles, he sees a stranger's.

"Just leave them here," Marios says, indicating the counter beside the kitchen sink.

With a clink, Wendy lowers her crockery. Aristos follows suit and finds his father watching him.

"You're a modern man, Ariste." Marios's smile is reptilian.

After the murmur of voices comes the clacking of heels, Nausicaa in her Sunday best.

"Marie," she says, in a rush of cool air.

Her skirt settles around her.

"There's someone at the door for you."

"Now?" Marios responds. "But we're about to leave. Who is it? Can't you tell them—"

She grips his elbow.

This gesture jars Aristos, so rarely did he see his parents touch as a child. Only in public, and then conservatively.

Nausicaa whispers, ". . . the CMP."

Marios's smile falls away. Aristos's stomach plummets after it, and he watches his father stride from the room.

"What's the CMP?" Wendy asks.

"Ach," Nausicaa says, as though just remembering her. She waves a hand. "Who knows, really? One of these 'charitable' groups. There were so many formed, after the invasion." She gives a terse chuckle.

"The Committee on Missing Persons," Aristos murmurs.

The women look at him.

"The Committee on Missing Persons in Cyprus," he repeats.

He hasn't said the name of this organisation aloud before, though he knows all about it. The work that it does, uncovering the names and fates of those – both and Greek and Turkish-speaking Cypriots – who went missing during the conflict. The way that it works, in a coordinated effort across the country's divide, with the participation of the UN. Aristos read about it compulsively during his twenty-six-months' military service. Then he went to London.

"Is that it?" Nausicaa asks. "I lose track. Maybe."

As she prattles on to Wendy, voices rise down the hall. Aristos lifts a blind so that when the front door slams shut, he can see the man retreating from it. The windowpanes tremble. With his back to the house, the man stops. He has hunched shoulders, his face turned up to the sun. Eyes closed, Aristos imagines, before the man turns around. Aristos jerks backwards.

"*Loipón*," comes Marios's voice, into the kitchen. "Now."

Turning around, Aristos sees his father as an echo of himself, a parallel life in which he hadn't left Cyprus. With the church bells ringing and the room reeling, he could have hit his head and imagined it all. His creeping suspicion and his self-imposed exile, his mother's desperate phone call and his unwilling return. Even the CMP investigator's raising a hand at him through the window.

"Time for church," Marios declares.

Nausicaa is nodding, fumbling for her handbag.

Swallowing his dread, Aristos shoots Wendy a smile. As he warned her, his parents are traditional people. There was always the Divine Liturgy on a Sunday and hell to pay if he dragged his heels there. Why should today have been any different?

Four

WITHIN WEEKS, ARISTOS AND Wendy are living in one of
the many apartments that his father owns. It is two-bed in the
centre of Larnaca, with high ceilings, glass sides and a view of
the sea. The day they moved in, Wendy asked Aristos where his
parents' money had come from. She sounded conflicted, both
incredulous and accustomed to such apparent wealth. Aristos
explained that his father had been lucky with stocks, invested
in seedy Camden and been lucky again when the area came
up. Now, Marios has an extensive property portfolio, and has
invited Aristos to get involved in 'the business' until he finds a
job.

After their run-in with the CMP investigator, Aristos wanted
to say no, fly back to London and his graduate work as an
auditor. To isolation and order. But he had come to Cyprus, and
couldn't keep his girlfriend cooped up in a hotel room forever.
The refusal crumbled on his tongue.

For all her incredulity, Wendy looks at peace in their broad
bed in their big apartment, her hair a spill across the pillow.
Her skin smells sweet for the night they have spent beneath the

sheets. Faintly sore, Aristos gets washed and dressed around her. Even when he pushes their wardrobe door shut – harder than he means to – she doesn't stir. Again, that flicker of envy. He leaves her asleep, closing the front door, softly, behind him.

He walks the fifteen minutes to his father's office, the penthouse apartment in a building that Marios owns out-right. Aristos can smell the woodiness of its many books from the stairwell. They line the walls upon mismatching shelves, as though Marios has collected them in maddened dashes, only realising once he has lumbered in with each new armful that he will need somewhere to store it. Slowly, Aristos enters. The place unsettles him. It is the only sign he has ever seen that his father might be a man of passion, poring over ancient Greek dramas and musings – by Aeschylus and Sophocles, Aristotle and Plato – where no one can disturb him. As a child, Aristos thought him stern. He hadn't imagined, before seeing these shelves, that there might be a depth to his father's silences. A privateness, yes, perhaps even a darkness. But not the tenderness implicit in books.

Down the hallway, a toilet flushes. Aristos turns from the shelves.

"You walked," his father observes, from the doorway.

Aristos follows his gaze to the damp patches beneath his shirt sleeves.

He tuts. "I got used to it, in London."

"*Nai*," Marios agrees, "too used to it."

He resumes his stride across the room, to a desk set in yet another window with the blind pulled over it. Down the hallway the pipes stop rattling.

"The weather is turning now," Aristos says, to dispel the silence. "I guess I should start—"

"And talking about the weather. You got used to that, too."

He blinks.

Sitting down, his father drags a file across the desk. "Since you're the expert, why don't you take a look at this?" He withdraws a page.

An email, Aristos sees, crossing the room.

"From our estate agent in Islington." Marios sits back.

Dabbing at his forehead, Aristos scans the text. It is not his first time seeing Latin letters since his departure from London. Last week, he ordered new blinds for a local property, bidding the curtain maker *geiá sas* and *efcharistó* before receiving his bill in English. Why? he asked his father. Because of the so-called 'Cypriot dialect', Marios sneered, people speaking a language that didn't exist in a written form. There were no Greek letters for the 'c-h' sounds with which so many Cypriots replaced their 'k's. They were a people confused, resorting to English for a lack of confidence in their own mother tongue. If they only spoke 'proper' Greek . . . Aristos paid the bill.

"So, all these people want to rent the apartment," he surmises, from the list of names.

"*Sostá*," his father confirms. "Now, you tell me. Whom should we rent it to?"

Rereading the email, Aristos considers their options. A working couple in their mid-twenties, three part-time students, and a businessman approaching sixty.

"The couple sound good. Reliable," he says, straightening.

"At their age?" Marios thrusts out his chin. "Before you know it, they'll have a baby. That could affect their income. And I've just redone the carpets. No."

Leaning closer, he points partway down the email. Their best option is the businessman, whose older age suggests that he will likely remain single and lead a quiet, tidy life.

"With no surprises," Marios concludes.

Aristos stares at him. This comment is so at odds with the shocking and messy life that he fears his father has led, he feels it echo off his forehead. This is the sick man – the 'really sick, Ariste', man – for whom he had to leave London?

"If you'd already decided," Aristos snaps, newly aware of his clinging shirt, "then why did you ask me?"

"Because," Marios barks. "You need to know how to handle these properties. When I'm gone, they'll all be yours."

Neither of them blinks, until a peel of laughter comes through from the floor below. Aristos busies his hands with tugging the ceiling fan into motion. Its current stirs his hair. Leaving the paper under a weight, his father stands up.

"If you could let the estate agent know whom we've chosen, I've got a meeting with our accountant," he says, tucking in his chair. "It shouldn't be longer than an hour."

"Okay," Aristos mumbles.

And Marios leaves him alone with the books.

In his absence, their smell is stifling. Aristos's eyes crawl the shelves. It overwhelms him to know that he will be the sole beneficiary of as much wisdom and warmth as there exists in these pages – more than he has ever received from his parents – as well as a fortune in assets. The latter, he wants. Of course he does, with his Savile Row aspirations. But he hates that his father can give it to him. That in exchange Aristos will have to take on this great project, gleaning from centuries-old words the secrets of his father's heart. Can he face it? No need to yet, he soothes himself. For now, Marios remains working and as dour as ever. Aristos can't believe that he is about to concede his possessions, not to death. Unless he is preparing to disappear someplace else.

Marios's father – gone too soon, a casualty of 1974 – was a prominent left-winger, outspoken against the British colonial rule that preceded the Turkish invasion. At night, British soldiers often burst into the house and beat him. Young Marios watched, wide-eyed, until his trembling and his night terrors became too much to bear. His parents sent him to Athens, where he went to school for several years.

Aristos has heard this story, from his grandmother, who shakes her head, and from his father, who smiles, wistfully, but never has he wondered what his father was smiling at. He creeps closer to a bookshelf. Running his fingertips over timeworn spines, he dares to imagine. His father abroad, while the British struggled, with increasing violence, to maintain control of a

Cyprus that fought to reject them like a poison from its body. Athens not perfect – far from it, in the wake of its own civil war – but there were no soldiers beating down Marios's door. The Greeks took pride in their country – irrespective of its political turmoil, they had invented democracy – and there were no outsiders reigning over them, destroying their sense of national self. Perhaps it was there that Marios had fallen in love with Greek culture and come to see it as something that all of Cyprus could benefit from drawing closer to, as he had. In his eyes, supporting an independent Cyprus could bring nothing but trouble.

At the end of the bookshelf, Aristos stops. He catches a fingernail on the cover of one *Greek Nature Stories*, and a bit of the leather flakes off. He steps back. How old is this book? For all he knows, there could be a piece of the nineteenth century under his fingernail. He is at once awed and appalled, holding his hand out in front of him. Is this how it feels to pause and consider the world as one's parent might? Aristos wonders. Perhaps he was wrong to stay away all those years, suspecting his father of an act that he resented but did not understand. Or perhaps he is wrong now, to seek grounds for excusing the unforgiveable.

Scraping the leather out from under his fingernail, Aristos flicks it to the floor. He remembers asking his parents, when he was young, if he could turn their spare bedroom into some kind of den. His father said no, because that bedroom wasn't spare. It would be for Aristos's younger sister or brother. Years later, Aristos asked his mother – in the tactless way of a child – what was holding his sibling up on their way into the world. His mother raised a hand to her heart and replied that when humans made plans, God laughed. And He punished them, she added, before her fingers found her crucifix. She gave Aristos a smile and a bowl of ice cream.

Now, Aristos is supposed to accept a part in his father's business as readily as he accepted that bowl, as consolation for his parents' secrecy and their starting every story from after 1974, as though their lives began then, just three years before his. He is supposed to nod along, and not cause a scene by running away or by running his mouth now that he has returned. He knows this. He wishes, against all virtue, that he could cease to know it.

Aristos turns around, and the fan blows his hair into his face. Pushing it back, he makes for the phone on his father's desk.

"Wendy," he breathes, into its mouthpiece.

"Hello? Arty, is that you?"

Wendy's voice comes groggily through the receiver, as though she has just woken up. Aristos glances at his watch.

"Any plans this afternoon?" he asks.

He smiles, closing his eyes, at her answer. Despite the lowered blinds, he can feel the sun warming his face as he pictures her, taking her sketchbook down to the sea and shading the day away with her pencil. Aristos doesn't know much about art – he struggles to see the worth in his father's most valuable paintings – but he believes that Wendy has a talent for it. She has shown interest, certainly, in seeing the few small galleries that he knows in the area. They have walked out of each one deflated, her retreating into quietude and him hanging his head, ashamed that his home country has no more to offer in the way of cultural centres. Larnaca was never going to be London. But Wendy would find some inspiration there, Aristos had assured her, even if she didn't speak Greek. She had an artist's view of the world, beyond the reaches of any language.

Aristos still pictures Wendy this way, as a creature not quite human. She is transcendent, looking through people with her pale eyes, moved only by the bold colours and textured brush-strokes of her paintings. She is animal, driven by base instinct and desire. At mealtimes, she eats wolfishly or not at all. In bed, she cries out and claws at him. Then she falls asleep. Whatever she dreams of, Aristos is sure that it is vivid. Both super and subhuman, Wendy has her head higher up in the clouds than anyone else he has met. Her dream matters more than her reality, or perhaps her reality exists only insofar as it caters to her dream. She will be a renowned artist. She will.

A magnetic force, this commitment of hers to some alternative world, when Aristos lives in one churning with dread. He wants to take shelter in Wendy's head, venturing out only as far as the flats of her canvases – where there is no sense of any past and no investigator darkening the door – to stretch his legs. He wants the kind of quiet, tidy life that his father looks for in tenants, with no upsets. Until now, Aristos hasn't suffered any, really. But he is exhausted with feeling lucky that this is the case, as though he is lurking in the foothills of chaos' mountains, inescapably.

"Are you still there?" Wendy's voice comes, into his ear.

Aristos opens his eyes. "I'm here. Sorry, just sending an email."

He powers on the office computer and watches it heave into life.

"Oh. So, yeah," Wendy goes on. "I'll probably spend a couple of hours doing that, and then come home."

"Good. That sounds good," Aristos repeats.

He is watching the icons appear one by one on his desktop, holding tight to the phone. An impatient silence comes through the receiver.

"Wendy?"

"Yeah?"

Aristos bites his tongue. It is all there, everything that he fears about his parents – his father, particularly – teetering on the tip. Like bile, he gulps it back.

"I like you."

"I like you, too," Wendy says.

And yet, Aristos puts down the phone with haste. The more they talk, he fears, the more her otherworldliness and the comfort it brings him will wear away.

Five

Aristos checks his watch. Five to four, it reads, and Petros and Melina are never late. Aristos hasn't hosted his friends for seven years, but he remembers. They were considerate, reliable. Everything that he ceased to be when he left them. The minute hand lurches forward, and he lowers his wrist.

He paces into the kitchen, a cherry-wood square cleared of all but four coffee cups. They are evenly spaced on the granite countertop, awaiting their fills from the kettle. It flashes silver as Aristos steps back. Should he set it to boil, or is now too soon? He could lay out some pastries, at least. He crosses the room, and the fridge yawns cold air into his face.

"Wendy," he calls, shutting its door. "Wendy . . ."

His girlfriend looks up as though out of a daze from her sprawl on the sofa, book in hand. *I Am Not Jackson Pollock*, its cover reads.

"What are we going to serve with this coffee?" Aristos asks her.

"I don't know."

"We have nothing in the fridge."

"Well, then I guess we're not going to serve anything."

Her smile is playful, yet the unconcern in her eyes makes him grit his teeth. Wendy is not like his mother, he reminds himself, a woman bound to the kitchen in service of her household, her church, or her time and place of being in the world. Aristos doubts that he would like her if she was. But he needs this afternoon to go well.

At the sound of the buzzer, he lets his friends into the building and awaits them, anxiously, at his front door.

"*Geiá sas*," Melina calls, her voice carrying up the stairwell.

She precedes Petros along the hallway, looking as glad as he does grudging, with a cardboard box in hand.

"For Wendy," she smiles, lifting the lid on its *dáktyla*.

"Ladies' fingers," Aristos says.

"She loved them before, right?"

A pulse in Aristos's ears. He looks from the pastries' syrupy dressing to his friend's smile. Just as sweet, it seems, with no intention of inuendo.

"Thanks," he manages, taking the box. He turns to Petros. "Hello, mate . . ."

A facade, all of it, the cocky grin and the posturing stance. Aristos is not this person any more. Petros shoulders past without meeting his eye. Melina squeezes his arm before stopping still in the living room doorway. Aristos strains to see beyond her. There, swinging her legs off the sofa and sauntering across the pale-oak floor, is Wendy. She greets Petros with a nod, her indifference perhaps the best match for his standoffishness. Then she looks to Melina.

The box of *dáktyla* creaks in Aristos's hand. He watches Melina's shoulders tense up before she meets Wendy in an embrace. Neither woman appears to know how many times they should kiss the other. As they exchange pleasantries, Aristos wonders if he was right about Melina, having feelings for him when they were teenagers. It would explain her anxiousness around his new girlfriend and – at least some of – Petros's rancour.

They settle around the coffee table, Wendy in the butterfly chair where, an hour ago, she knelt before Aristos. There was no time, he protested, they needed to get things ready. What things? Ach, so they failed to buy any pastries, fine. Melina has brought some. Eh, so Wendy is a thoughtless hostess, the first to sit down with her smudged eyeliner, okay. Aristos will fetch their guests' drinks. Melina offers him a hand.

"Amazing place," she says, coming after him into the kitchen.

"It's nice, huh?"

"*Polý oraío*. With that sea view . . ."

"Beautiful, right?"

"And this kitchen . . ."

As he lowers the *dáktyla* box, Aristos glances sideways. Melina is gazing up at his cupboards, her palms pressed to his countertop. This kitchen must be worth three times what hers is, and still her engagement ring taunts him. However small the diamond, he knows that Petros earned every cent of it.

"You must do some wonderful cooking in here."

"Me?" Even as Aristos raises his eyebrows, his bravado ebbs. "It hasn't been that long, has it, Melina *mou*?"

She laughs. "Okay. Wendy, then."

"Actually, no. She doesn't cook, either. Can't risk losing a finger, in her line of work."

"Ah, of course . . ."

Aristos leads their next round of chuckling before reopening the *dáktyla* box. The smell of cinnamon rises, as it did from his mother's dishes – sweet and savoury – when he was a child.

"You'd do more with this place that I ever could. You'd deserve it," Aristos mutters.

He is staring so hard into the box, at the shards of almond littering its corners, that he doesn't register Melina's gaze until he looks up.

"He's always been hard on you," she says, then. Of his father.

Aristos stops halfway to a frown. Of course Melina remembers. She and Petros were as much his confidantes as Agathi was – they had all four sat for hours and talked about everything – back when Aristos's worst fear was that it wouldn't matter what he did in life, because his father had enough money that no amount of success would impress him, nor any inertia distress him. Aristos was doomed to be disappointing, to the kind of severe man whose approval a boy couldn't help but crave. He shrugs, dropping Melina's gaze. Since then, he has spent so long running from the past he fears, lurking behind his father's glare, that he has put none of the thought his friends have into the future. And yet, Melina's hand rests upon his granite countertop.

"What about Petros? You know, he's still ignoring my calls."

"I know."

"So, you had to drag him here?"

She sighs. "In a word, yes. He's hurt. But, Ariste," she says, stepping closer, "that wouldn't be true if he didn't love you. Keep trying with him, please. He just needs time."

Her brown eyes are large with feeling, impossible to refuse. With a nod, Aristos flicks on the kettle, and its rumbling saves them from speaking again until they are carrying their coffees through to the living room.

"That view," Melina repeats, as the sea stretches out before them.

Setting the ladies' fingers down on the coffee table, Aristos resolves to better appreciate this aspect of his inheritance. The water glittering and shifting outside, like a creature alive as it catches the light. Then, an intake of breath.

He turns from the window, blinking, to see Petros raising his eyebrows.

"Wendy was just telling me about her new bar job," Petros says, pointedly, "where she doesn't have to speak Greek."

Melina squeezes his knee as she sits down. "That sounds ideal," she smiles, at Wendy.

"Yeah," Wendy says.

With so many customers being tourists and her colleagues coming from assorted backgrounds – mostly Russian and

Lebanese – her manager says that it is a more uniform look for them all to speak English.

"Which is fine by me," Wendy adds.

Petros's snort is one of contempt, catching in his nostrils. Melina's hand goes again to his knee.

Sinking into a second butterfly chair, Aristos reassumes the swagger of his former self. "You're not still on about the British, Petro?"

"The conflict they caused is still dividing our country," Petros says.

"Thank God for that divide," Aristos parrots his father, "keeping us safe from the Turks. But the British didn't ask them to invade."

"No," Petros says, drily. "The British just 'divided and ruled' us and the Turkish Cypriots for decades, and then left a power vacuum in their wake."

For the first time, he meets Aristos's eyes with his own. Sea-blue, unlike almost any Cypriot's. Petros is taller than average, too, with skin paler by just a shade. Still, that is enough.

"You know, I don't remember you hating the British so much before your dad left," Aristos says, in a low voice.

"I don't remember you loving them so much before you did." Petros looks to Wendy with scorn.

As though just stirring again, Wendy turns her head. Her eyebrows pose questions at odds with the silence, until Aristos musters a grin.

"Wow, Petro. This is the most you've spoken to me yet," he jibes. "We're making progress, huh?"

This time, Petros's scoff comes with a smirk. Barely perceptible, but it is there. A glimmer of hope, returning Aristos to their high-school days when he was the ringleader, joking and daring, while Petros laughed from a pace behind him.

A plane sears over the sea, moments from landing at Larnaca Airport. Petros and Melina smile at each other, before its British Airways logo comes into view. Aristos reaches for his coffee.

"I don't suppose you've been over the border yet, have you?" Melina asks, tucking back her hair.

"To the Turkish side?" Wendy responds.

"The occupied side," Aristos reminds her, his cup too warm in his palms. He lowers it.

"I didn't think you were allowed to go over," Wendy says.

"We weren't, until about a year ago," Melina explains, "when they opened a crossing point in Nicosia. A friend of Petros's just went. For the first time in his life, he got to see the house where he should have grown up . . ."

"Kyriakos," Petros nods.

Aristos flinches. This name throws him, to the day after they swore their army oaths, when a fellow conscript invited them to a barbeque. The conscript smiled, expansively, as his parents and sisters mingled with his friends. Aristos gripped his wine glass, his ears ringing with anxiety, until jealousy took hold. He had just begun to read about Tochni.

"That guy?" he sneers. "He's a weed."

"He's my *koumbáros*," Petros responds, evenly. "My best man."

Aristos clamps down on his tongue. As he watches, his friend glazes over again. Gets lost in the dream of an ancestral home, from which few displaced people ever wake.

"The new, Turkish Cypriot residents let him see inside his parents' house," Melina goes on, explaining to Wendy. "They'd had to flee, too, of course, from their home in the south. Kyriakos said that they cried *mazí*, together. It was very emotional."

"Oh." Wendy frowns at Aristos. "I thought the Turkish Cypriots were, like, the bad guys."

A ripple through the air as Aristos's friends turn to look at him. On their faces, the puzzlements of people with views born of their own tragedies, and grown in the years that Aristos has been away into living, breathing beings with which he cannot reason. How simple it must be to feel so perfectly wronged as Petros or Melina, who both grew up in displaced families. Aristos was not blessed with such clarity of hardship. His parents' village wasn't one that Greek-speaking Cypriots abandoned, after 1974, but from which Turkish-speaking Cypriots fled. They were chased out, and worse.

"Good riddance," Aristos mutters, unfailingly.

His friends blink at him. What do they want him to say, that he has cast Turkish-speaking Cypriots as the pantomime villains in his retelling of the conflict? Of course he has, not just when performing it for Wendy, but late at night when he has found himself alone in the cold, dark theatre of his mind.

At its back, the truth gleaming like an emergency-exit sign. If the Turkish-speaking Cypriots were not the 'bad guys', then Aristos's parents might have been. If Marios and Nausicaa left Tochni – that infamous village – for the reason that Aristos fears they did, then the Turkish-speaking Cypriots were evil. They had to be, or else his parents were indefensible.

"No, it's me. I'm the reprobate. And you're all heroes who voted for the Annan Plan, I'm sure," Aristos says.

Steam twists from the coffee table.

"The Annan Plan?" Wendy says.

"We had a referendum in April," Melina explains, "on whether or not to establish a United Republic of Cyprus, a federation of two states . . ."

"Of course I didn't vote for it," Petros sneers. "The Annan Plan would just have meant colonisation again, by Turkey."

Aristos lifts his coffee. "Melina?"

Head bowed, Melina shrugs. "Petros said we should vote against it, so . . ."

Apparently satisfied, Petros nods.

Aristos turns back to Wendy, unable to help himself. He maintains, "Turkey invaded us."

Melina says, "After Greece backed our military coup."

Petros says, "All because of the British."

"The northern coastline is beautiful, though. Almost untouched," Melina adds, with a smile. Fleeting, as though she wants to give Wendy more than she can, somehow. "It's worth going to visit."

"It sounds like it," Wendy says.

Aristos takes a sip of his coffee, turning his mouth acrid. He does not return his girlfriend's smile.

Six

Aristos is trembling as he unfolds his flip phone, whose Vodafone sim card he has yet to replace with one from Cyta. He has been in Cyprus two months, long enough for the July sun to tan his skin and slow his movements. He has fallen into a routine with working for his father, and reinstated his old habits of buying *loukanikópita* on his drives to the beaches of Paralimni and Protaras, letting the pastry flake onto his car seats before filling its footwells with sand. Yet there are things that Aristos will not commit to. Buying a car, rather than renting one. Changing his mobile number to one beginning with nine. To do so would be to admit that he had returned to Cyprus not just for now but for good, and how could he countenance that? On a morning like this.

Peering around his bedroom door, Aristos confirms that Wendy's chest is still rising and falling evenly. Then he calls his parents' house. He is halfway through leaving a message when his mother picks up.

"*Kaliméra*, Ariste."

He grits his teeth. "Ah. You are in."

"*Nai*," Nausicaa says.

She doesn't sound breathless, like she rushed for the phone. Because she let it go to voicemail, Aristos thinks, let its ringing resound until his voice came crackling out. He knows the reason for her wariness, and he cannot pretend otherwise any longer.

"Did you give my address to the CMP?"

A thud on the line.

"What?"

"Did you give my address," Aristos repeats, sidling up to his living room window, "to the Committee on Missing Persons?"

"Of course not," Nausicaa says. Her voice sounds closer now, like she is clutching the phone to her cheek. "Why would you ask me that?"

"That investigator just showed up here," Aristos hisses, watching the man with the hunched shoulders walk away from his building. "He was very polite, asking after you both. Said he'd had a tip-off about an incident in your old village."

Aristos's breath comes back at him off the window, just as the investigator turns around. Sunlight glints off his glasses. Aristos steps backwards. Heat presses in on him, trapped in his apartment overnight. He wants to open the windows and set the fans in motion, to drag in the new day's air. He wants the sea and the blue sky, the endless portions of stuffed peppers and scrambled eggs upon *tavérna* tables, to be the truth of Cyprus. But there is a shadow beneath the water, a cloud passing over the sun. Whatever his parents share with him – in properties or platters – Aristos cannot confess his fears. He stops short of naming the date and village about which the investigator questioned him, for the words '1974' and 'Tochni' sound dangerously close to 'Massacre'. He cannot disentangle them.

His mother must sense this. "I'm coming over," she says.

"Don't," Aristos responds, looking over his shoulder. "Wendy will be up any minute."

On his arms, goosebumps from the air-conditioned room where he left his girlfriend, just moments ago, to answer the front door. Down the hallway, Wendy lying in wait and all her alienness, a shuttle that could fly Aristos away again as long as she keeps cold and unchanged.

"I don't want her involved in this," he says.

"Fine. Then come and meet me," Nausicaa instructs him.

Her bakery of choice occupies a corner building, with golden bricks and wooden shutters, opposite the Church of Saint Lazarus. In the square, pigeons scatter after bits of tourists' bread. There is the smell of fresh loaves baking and of the sea just down the road. Already, a film of sweat plays upon Aristos's back. He goes to check his watch, only to recall that he left it beside Wendy when the doorbell rang, along with his shower and fresh collared shirt. He couldn't risk waking her just to change out of his gym clothes, and so he meets his mother feeling exposed. A coffee, at least, should still the spinning in his head.

Nausicaa stops his hand on the bakery door.

"What are you doing?"

"What did he say to you? The investigator," she asks.

Her scent is of lemon and vinegar – clean food and a clean house – too close to Aristos, pushing its way up his nostrils.

He leans away from her. "Why can't we talk inside?"

"Tell me," she pleads.

"*Entáxei*," he relents, just so that she will drop his wrist. Stop looking guilty of everything he has ever suspected.

Aristos is ready to bellow this at her, when the bakery door opens outwards. Following his mother across the road, he resumes murmuring.

"The investigator asked me what I knew about EOKA B."

"What did you tell him?" Nausicaa asks.

"That they were a paramilitary group in the seventies, who wanted to unite Cyprus with Greece."

"Well, I know that," she snaps. "I meant . . ."

Even as she lowers herself to the wall that surrounds the church, her hand rises to her crucifix. She drags it up and down, a section of the chain that is thin with wear, Aristos notices. He sits down beside her.

"He asked if Papá was involved with them."

"And?" Nausicaa whispers.

"I said I didn't know," Aristos tells her. "And the investigator said that if I ever felt more curious about things, I should give him a call. He's curious, too."

With a shaky breath out, Nausicaa lowers her hand. Behind her, a cat startles the pigeons skywards. Aristos squints after them, the sun staining his eyes.

And yet he sees clearly. "I shouldn't have come back here."

"Ariste, *agápi mou*," his mother implores him, reaching into her handbag. She presses ten pounds into his palm. "Let's have coffee before we talk any more. And some orange pie, please. I hear it's especially good here," she adds, with meaning.

Aristos stares at the banknote in his hand.

"*Portokalópita*," he repeats. "Really, Mamá?"

"What have I asked of you, in the last seven years?" Nausicaa presses him. "What will I ask of you in the next seven? When you're gone again."

She lowers her eyes, and the reality strikes him. He will go again, leaving as much hurt in his wake as he did before. Aristos was taxiing towards his first flight out as a high-school student, though he didn't know it at the time. He didn't hear his engines winding up towards wailing, or feel his body gathering speed, until he was coming away from the tarmac of his life with his stomach lurching. He was eighteen, in love with his girlfriend and embedded with his friends. He was questioning the history of Tochni and horrified by its answers. Then he was swearing his allegiance to Cyprus, an army conscript with no hope of escaping his country in the twenty-six months that he had to serve it.

The more suspicious Aristos became of his parents, the closer he pulled to his girlfriend and friends. He told Agathi that he would marry her. Told Petros that they would build their houses next door to each other. Told Melina that they would plan it so she and Agathi had their babies around the same time. Grinning, always, not betraying his desperation. Aristos declared that they would all four remain close – like the American sitcom characters they watched to help them learn English – living parallel lives in neighbouring quarters. They would be family. They had been family, as far as Aristos was concerned, since he had put his parents' evasiveness about their pre-conflict life together with his Tochni findings. He no longer saw his mother and father as God-fearing, but as people who lived in fear of a material force catching up with them, all their churchgoing a guise. He resented them and their religion.

In his nights off from the army, when his girlfriend was sleeping and he could not, Aristos submitted applications to universities overseas. He would study business management and make something of himself – if only to escape the fate of working for his father – in America or England, Bulgaria or France. Anywhere but Greece. In the fits of sleep that he did snatch, Aristos saw neighbour-on-neighbour attacks and reared awake gasping, unable to tell his girlfriend why. To confide his fears in anyone could have been to implicate his parents in a crime – of what? Being senseless killers, or simply citizens of their place and time? Aristos didn't know. He didn't know and he couldn't risk asking.

It was overnight that he broke the news of his moving to London, and his friends' hearts with it. Agathi was tearful, Petros terse. Melina looked shocked, though she coaxed the others into hearing Aristos out. He shrugged, trying to make out as though his departure were no big deal. Never mind the months that it had taken him to orchestrate, or the years that he had felt

Cyprus taking off his life in the meantime. Aristos would keep in touch, he said. And then he didn't. He boarded a plane and refused to look back.

Before him now, his mother looks small and older by years than every one that he stayed away. All she seemed able to ask him about, then, was whether he was eating enough and when he would settle down with 'some nice girl', if he was sure that it couldn't be Agathi. How sad that we speak like strangers to those with whom we are most familiar. If Aristos's parents suspected his reason for leaving, they didn't address it. His father never called. His mother did so anxiously. Aristos told her about the girls that he had taken out on dates, first from his course and later from his office, all of them too grounded and focused to provide the distraction that he craved. It was in a last-ditch effort to loosen one of them up that he had suggested that pottery class. His date became no more fluid, but there was something whimsical about the teacher, Yvonne. Something resolute in her proposition to him, even as she stammered it. Then there was Wendy, with whom, at last, Aristos felt abstracted enough from the world to face it.

"Please, Ariste," Nausicaa says.

Folding her cash into his pocket, Aristos crosses the road. The cobbles stumble beneath his feet. The bakery door falls away from his palm. Inside, cutlery clatters and jokes land, sending explosions of laughter up from a few, close-set tables. Aristos weaves his way around them, eyes on the faded-tile floor. In a voice that he barely recognises, he asks for two coffees.

"And a piece of *portokalópita*, please."

"*Portokalópita*? I think we have some in the oven, but . . ." The boy behind the counter looks sideways. "Elena," he calls, before the door at his back swings shut.

A sweet fragrance flies out.

"It doesn't matter," Aristos says, fumbling for his ten-pound note. "Just the coffees will do fine. To take away, please—"

"It's no problem," the boy insists, as his colleague reappears with her index finger held up. "The *portokalópita* will be out in one minute, okay?"

He turns his back before Aristos can say that he is too busy to wait for cake. A London baker would have presumed as much and had their confections out ready for the day's first commuters. Aristos knows this because he was one of them, tasting the dew-slicked metal of the city's train tracks on the air, with the weight of his workbag on his shoulder as the sun went up between tall buildings. London was larger and more alive than any part of Cyprus. What has he come back here for?

His eyes land on a takeaway box, bearing the same logo as that of Petros and Melina's *dáktyla*. Aristos's mouth waters with envy. How lucky his friends are, to have family bonds here that are built on love and not on money. How dignified, that they can think purely of grieving their parents' deaths, and not of gaining from them.

Aristos didn't come back to Cyprus for Marios. He knows now that he is as appalled by his father's past, still, as by the future sliding towards him as his health declines. Nor did Aristos come back for his friends, who remain sore from his time away. There is no professional scope here like there is in London. So what is there?

"*Oriste*, here you are. Your coffees and the orange pie," the boy behind the counter says.

Aristos looks up, just as the kitchen door swings open again. A third staff member emerges, balancing an oven tray upon gloved palms. She slots it into place beneath the glass countertop before lifting a hand to chase a runaway strand of her ponytail. The gesture is so familiar, Aristos catches his breath. Their eyes meet, and the girl's widen. Heat blooms in Aristos's chest, more intense than any of July's bombardments. He is burning with recognition, with remorse, with fury at his mother for engineering this encounter. It cannot be happening, he thinks, he must put an end to it.

And yet the girl's name comes to him, steeped in their history together, as the answer to his question. What has he come back here for? She blanches.

"Agathi . . ."

Seven

On Thursday the fifteenth of July, at twenty-past eight in the morning – when it smells of bed warmth and gym sweat and shaving foam, coffee and burned toast and toothpaste – Larnaca slips through time. An air-raid siren snakes through the air, a ribbon flicked from the wrist of 1974. It warns of a military coup, backed by the Greek junta. Aristos closes his eyes. At this moment, members of the National Guard are storming the Presidential Palace, and he does not exist. He is minus-three years old, his parents not long married.

"The Greek dictatorship has invaded Cyprus," President Makarios will inform the United Nations, having fled Nicosia, in four days' time.

A day after that, Turkish troops will land on Cyprus's northern shores, and the sirens will sound again.

The cries trail off a street at a time, rising and falling at odds with each other until they die away. Aristos reopens his eyes to 2004. He is standing in his bathroom mirror, toothbrush in hand. He slots it back into its cup, dripping. Feet come pounding across the floor, and Wendy's reflection appears behind his.

"What was that?" she asks.

Aristos wipes a streak of toothpaste from his lip. "The air-raid siren. They play it every year, to commemorate the coup. I should have warned you," he realises, as she sags against the doorframe.

"Oh."

"Sorry."

Wendy shakes her head, as though to deny her fright. It melts, visibly, into an awe not unlike arousal.

"So, that's what it would be like? In a war."

"I guess so," Aristos answers, "with the addition of bombs and tanks rolling in."

He winces at her laughter. It echoes off the tiled walls, unfiltered as the water supply. Wendy has no loyalty to this country and lost nothing to its conflict. Once a comfort, her being here now strikes Aristos as crass. With the siren ringing in his ears, he stares at her reflection. They both have histories, him as a Cypriot and her as a Brit, him as a man and her as a girl. Three years his junior and yet, Wendy has experienced all kinds of relationships, while Aristos has been sincere in only one.

He turns to face her. The vines of their pasts twist together around him, tight enough to make his eyes water. He sees hers turn brown, their lids grow heavy. Her lips swell. Her skin tans. Her hair pulls long and dark down her back, until she is no longer Wendy but Agathi, the girl with whom Aristos once believed he would spend his life. A sweet scent stirs in his nostrils. He blinks and then he is back with Wendy, his woman from another world. They were enthralled with each other, there. And now?

Gently, Aristos touches the pillow imprint upon Wendy's cheek. He recalls her peering out the window of the plane that he had booked them to Cyprus – before he could think better of it – then turning to face him.

"What did you say?"

They were taxiing onto the runway, about to take off, and Aristos's fears had caught up with him.

"I said, you should keep your history quiet in Cyprus. It's not something that will make you seem cool or interesting there."

Wendy's eyebrows shot upwards.

"My history," she repeated, raising her voice as the engines turned roaring. "Is that what you think I wanted? To seem 'cool' or 'interesting'?"

Aristos felt queasy as the earth shrank away from him, knowing that things would be different when he touched down in Larnaca. Just as they had been in London, he reminded himself, and that hadn't been all bad.

He runs the back of his forefinger across Wendy's lips. Perhaps a third flight would change things again, for the better. Grant Aristos a reprieve from Cyprus, with its howling and its harbouring of his ex-love, Agathi. His heart contracts at the thought of returning to the bakery where she works. Its orange pie is exceptional. His mother was right about that, though wrong to send him in there in the way that she did. After years of taking his teenaged withdrawal from her out on Agathi –

treating the girl coldly until Aristos left for London – Nausicaa seems to think that she can keep him here now, using his ex. It won't work. Aristos pictures that orange pie until the girl who served it to him blurs behind its burned top, its shredded-filo body and its syrupy aftertaste. That is what he wants from the bakery. That is all he wants from it, he tells himself, until his mouth is watering and he is hooking his finger inside Wendy's.

Wendy eyes him, coyly, before tightening her lips. Her tongue is warm, making him shiver despite the heat.

"Let's go somewhere," he says. "I want to take you away."

"Mmn . . ." Her lips smack as she slides them from his finger. "When?"

"Soon. I'll talk to Papá about it today," Aristos says, straightening his shirt collar.

Already, sweat lines his neck. Wendy smiles. The pillow imprint is fading from her cheek, her skin returning to its usual pallor. She has picked up no extra colour from her shifts at the beach bar, disappearing as though to nowhere in the afternoons and lying in bed until late each morning. In the hours between, when Aristos is at work, he cannot say what she does. Only that her sketchbook has sat unmoved on her bedside table for some weeks, and she has ceased to enquire about any galleries further afield than Larnaca. Perhaps she could do with a holiday, too.

"Where were you thinking we'd go?" she asks.

Heaving his schoolboy bravado up, across the ten years that have chastened him, Aristos smiles. "Wherever you want."

EIGHT

But of course it is Athens. Aristos's father owns several apartments in Kolonaki, for his love of the neighbourhood that runs like a river down Mount Lycabettus – the highest point in the city – and the view from the top. When Aristos was a child, Marios took him regularly and went even more often alone.

Emerging from the airport into a softer, thicker heat than Cyprus's, Wendy points to a sign for the *metró*. Aristos blinks. The wheels of her suitcase grind in his ears as she sets off, with the confidence of a first-time visitor who has never known the place any different, while he struggles to catch up. In preparation for the Olympic Games, Athens has extended a trainline – along with the olive-branch wreaths upon so many posters – out from the city centre. This station opened just last week and looks pristine.

'Welcome Home', its banners read, hung up ready for the innumerable tourists that will arrive next week.

Marios has quoted this slogan, constantly, in his excitement about the Games returning to their historic birthplace.

"You'll have to tell me what it's like there," he said, as he bid Aristos and Wendy *kaló taxídi*. "The energy . . ."

Then he went to a doctor's appointment, his second in a week.

They fight their way onboard a train, Wendy cursing the gulf between it and the platform before Aristos catches her suitcase. Their lips meet, taut with smiling, in time with the doors. Beyond them, the view slides from rocky to black to suburban, and a slew of passengers disembarks. Aristos takes a seat still warm from its last occupant, and the train dives back underground.

When they surface in Syntagma Square, he leads Wendy uphill to one of Marios's recently vacated apartments. In exchange for staying in it a few days, Aristos is supposed to report any damp patches or peeling walls, cracks that might need filling before a new tenant moves in.

"Dust," Wendy murmurs, lifting her foot from the parquet floor.

No sooner than she has lowered it, she is winding up the window shutters. Aristos follows her, eyes scrunched to the sunlight, onto a balcony overlooking their tree-lined street. A breeze lifts the smell of jasmine and sends the electricity lines – strung up like fairy lights – nodding. Down the hill, motorbikes roar.

"This place is amazing," Wendy says, with the sky in her eyes.

Aristos smiles. "You like it?"

A needless question. Athens is a metropolis, alive and vibrant, in which his girlfriend can happen as surely other things do.

She wants a drink before anything else. Still British after all, Aristos thinks, not unkindly. They descend to one of two café-bars in Kolonaki Square, open twenty-four hours and facing off from either side of a cobbled walkway, where customers can roll from coffee and cheese pies into beer and nuts as the day turns to night.

"Sit this side," Aristos says, indicating a chair with its back to the bar, "so you can see out."

Wendy stops with her hand on the opposite seat. "But you're sitting that side."

"Yeah, next to you," he tells her. "That's how they do it here."

"Oh. Okay . . ."

Side by side, they stare across the tabletop at passers-by. Kolonaki is a well-to-do area. The Mayfair of Athens, Aristos proclaims it, untapped by most tourists and home to old-money Athenians. The latter proceed stylishly, men in plaid suits and women in gowns, draped with watches and bracelets, pocket squares and silk scarves. Even the ladies with canes hobble past in high heels.

"Now I get it," Wendy says, turning her head as though after a tennis ball.

Aristos follows her gaze to a paisley blazer. He watches, sipping his retsina, as its owner waits to cross the road. Taxis swing by in beads of yellow, and the liquid seeps cool down Aristos's throat. He is two drinks in and just starting to feel loose, like he could expand to the edges of his seat and stay there for hours to come. He lets his head roll back. So cool, the girl beside him. He strokes her hair and marvels anew at its crispness. That's years of bleach for you, Wendy says. Beauty is pain, and other such platitudes.

"You know, they have this TV show here," Aristos says.

He explains the show's premise, a panel of women critiquing the looks of newsreaders and gameshow hosts. They are fiercely made-up, often sneering with contempt at their juniors while reserving their applause for older, less threatening ladies.

"I'm surprised you'd watch that," Wendy says, raising her eyebrows. "It sounds pretty gay."

Aristos shrugs. "What can I say? Maybe you're rubbing off on me after all."

She gives a shock of laughter, and he downs the rest of his wine grinning.

From there, they spin through the city, restored to the abandon that Cyprus had stripped from them. Kolonaki is home to so many small, private art collections that they don't make it to the National Gallery. Instead, Wendy ducks down the holes of every painting-hung basement that she sees. It is cool inside, with the breath of the air conditioning. The lifeblood of culture flowing a storey beneath the city's skin.

"I bet we were the only people in there today," Wendy boasts, as they climb back to street level.

She doesn't want to see the Parthenon, or the Ancient Agora or Hadrian's Library. Not up close, certainly, like all the people in suncream and hats. She doesn't want to have Athens present itself to her, with a site map and a postcard view, but to present herself to Athens. This means avoiding large crowds and anything signposted as 'traditional'. It means getting lost down narrow backstreets and looking to hilltop temples only for a sense of direction. Aristos suggests that they make a game of it, strumming through a copy of *Top 10 Athens* at a souvenir stall to decide where not to have dinner.

They eat cheese pies on the walls around churches, stamping their feet at encroaching pigeons. They put on airs with the clothes in designer boutiques, where women balk at Wendy's tattoos. In their apartment, after they have happened upon the Changing of the Guard at the Monument to the Unknown Soldier, Wendy asks Aristos to teach her the soldiers' dance. They march towards each other, straightening their legs and flexing their feet, and fall laughing to the floor. Aristos says, with a cough, that they should probably sweep it of dust. Instead, Wendy swings her leg over his lap, and he unhooks her bra.

On their last day, Aristos wakes up alone. Late afternoon. He feels heavy-headed from their night at a jazz bar, despite his nap. His ears ring with the tinkling of piano keys and the clinking of cocktail glasses until, with a beep, he turns off the air conditioning and drifts out towards the balcony. There, there is only the sound of his girlfriend sketching.

"Nice," he says, looking over her shoulder.

Wendy goes on, shading in a shape that he can't quite decipher, until it is as grey as the soles of their feet.

Then she shoots him a smile. "You don't know what you're talking about, do you?"

"No," he admits.

But her hair smells good, like a stranger's shampoo.

She closes her sketchbook. "Are you ready to go out again?"

"Yeah?" Aristos yawns, stretching his arms overhead. "I guess we should get a move on, if we want to do something with this last evening . . ."

Wendy is nodding, unfurling her legs from her plastic chair. "I want to get up there before we lose the light . . ."

"Where?" he asks, as his ears pop.

She jerks her head sideways. "Up the hill."

"Mount Lycabettus?"

"This one that we're on, yeah."

Aristos drops his arms. "It's very touristy," he starts.

But Wendy is resolute. She tucks her sketchbook under her arm, moved to it for the first time in weeks. She will not ignore the call of inspiration now, no matter how steep a climb it demands.

Aristos leads the way to the topmost street in Kolonaki, his heels hanging so heavily off the concrete steps up that he fears toppling backwards. Faced with the path that winds the rest of the way up Mount Lycabettus, he stops. He feels breathless, recalling the speed at which his father used to march him to the top. Up there is Marios's favourite view in the world, and he may only see it a few more times. The pine trees exhale death, like everything else that the man has touched. Only now, that death is his own, its stench so much fouler than that of the skeletons Aristos sees – rotting in shallow graves here and everywhere else – it brings tears to his eyes. How can he loathe and love, blame and mourn a person all at once?

Further along the street is a one-room station, where Wendy buys an evil-eye charm and Aristos two tickets for the *teleferik*. They sit hip to hip as it heaves them up the inside of Mount Lycabettus. Halfway up the tunnel, they pass the carriage coming down. Aristos stares through its windows and sees people staring back him, two trains on one track whose paths are destined to cross and recross. Daylight comes as a relief at the top, though it is fading.

Between groups of girls posing for photos in their halter-neck tops and miniskirts, and couples determined to make this spot 'theirs' by gazing only at each other, Wendy finds a way to the viewing point's edge. She opens her sketchbook – just for notes, she says – and dashes off a series of lines that Aristos cannot reconcile with the scene before them. The tide of the city sweeping in, from the sea to the mountains. The sun turning it a burnt orange, catching on satellite dishes and cars roofs as it sinks towards nightfall. So much motion, and yet so little noise. As hard as he tries to take it all in, Aristos can feel nothing more acutely than the church over his shoulder.

On the air, pine needles and cigarette smoke. Just like home, he thinks, that's what is making him uneasy. But weren't there moments in London – with its endless, foreign rainfall – when he felt this way, too? Staring at the back of Wendy's head, Aristos recalls the classmates and colleagues with whom he was friendly, first as a student, then as an auditor, and then not at all. He disappeared from those people's lives as soon as he did from their after-work drinks, not responding even to those who reached out afterwards. Because he had taken himself with him from Cyprus, hadn't he? He had moved to London not just to escape his parents, but to escape the way that they made him feel, and that feeling remained within him. Their secret, insidious. The longer he kept it, the surer Aristos became that he was lying to everyone, just by breathing. The more intimacy people asked of him, the shallower his breaths came, until he was so full of self-loathing that he could only blame them and turn away. From all except one.

A hush falls over the viewing point as the sun drops, at last, behind another mountain. While the other tourists crane tall and flash their cameras, Wendy is content simply to sag against Aristos. He grazes his fingernails down her arm.

"Can it always be like this?"

"Probably not," she says, as the darkness gathers.

Indeed. When they disembark their taxi home from Larnaca Airport, it is to find any illusion of untouchability crushed. Their balcony, with a dent in its railing that could see a car written off.

"What the fuck?" Aristos says, dropping his suitcase.

It rolls away from his fingertips, while Wendy watches with the same mild interest that she did the outfits in Kolonaki, and Aristos counts the balconies one, two, three floors up the building and to its left.

"What the fuck . . ."

"Nasty business you've had up there," a voice sounds, from behind him.

His ears gape. He turns to see his suitcase stopped, in the hand of a man with crinkly eyes, a kind smile. And hunched shoulders.

"That is your apartment, isn't it?" the man says.

As if he has never shown up on the doorstep, uninvited. Aristos snatches his suitcase, and the man extends his hand after it.

"I'm Costas, by the way. I don't think we've had the chance to introduce ourselves properly."

"*Geiá sas*, Costa," Aristos says, through gritted teeth. "How did you know you'd find me here today?"

"Well, I hoped I would," Costas responds, evenly. He peers around Aristos, smiling. "Hello."

"Hi."

"I'm Costas . . ."

"Wendy . . ."

"Would you mind grabbing me some cigarettes," Aristos says, thrusting his wallet at his girlfriend, "please? While I sort this out, for a minute?"

Wendy eyes him, coolly, before sauntering off towards their nearest *períptero*.

Aristos turns back to their building, shielding his eyes even as he closes them.

"Looks bad, doesn't it?" Costas says. "One of your neighbours was having a new bed lifted in. Apparently, they didn't attach it very well to the crane . . ."

"Fuck," Aristos repeats, reopening his eyes to the same crater, the same country.

His taxi pulls away, and he wants to run after it, right back to the airport. But then where? Beneath every tree in Athens, he saw an unmarked grave. Behind every smile in London, the threat of its discovery. Exhaust fumes trail into Aristos's nostrils, and he lowers his hands.

"You know, I could have someone fix that railing for you. I'd be happy to," Costas says, "if you indulged me in a coffee, sometime."

His trainers look well-loved, their laces tied in a double-bow knot that tugs at Aristos's heart. Agathi used to tie hers the same way. Slowly, Aristos nods at them.

"Yeah," he says, before Wendy comes back across the road. "Okay."

The investigator's smile is so sincere, it is all he can do not to break out in tears.

NINE

THE FIRST THING ARISTOS must note is that the Committee on Missing Persons is not a police force. It has investigators, yes, and it collects blood samples from relatives of the missing to aid its future identification processes. But when it starts digging – hopefully, not too much longer from now – any areas that it cordons off will not be crime scenes. They will be wells and ditches and pits of bones, whose flesh will have shrivelled away in three months under the Cypriot sun, caked in dirt and reeking, faintly, of horror. Perhaps forensic anthropologists could prove who buried the bodies, between anonymous tip-offs and technological advancements, but they will not. The CMP has no interest in serving justice or agitating politics. It seeks only to return what remains of those lost – to the inter-communal violence of the 1960s, and the all-out conflict of 1974 – to their families. To bring closure and dignified burials to both Greek and Turkish-speaking Cypriots.

Some of the mothers and fathers whose children disappeared – stepping off buses and out of shops, never to return – are ageing now, and afraid to die without answers. This troubles

Costas, and others at the CMP, he says. But the killers and their parents are growing older, too, with more than one deathbed confession having exposed an unmarked grave.

Costas explains this on the car ride from Larnaca to Tochni, a forty-minute drive between mountains and sea. August has burned the winter's fields to brown plains. There is a haze of dust, making Aristos squint through the windscreen of Costas's car. A beaten-up Toyota Starlet, rattling past old men in vests trailing cigarette smoke out their windows, and pickup trucks piled high with watermelons. Aristos doesn't say much, just leans his head on the door and listens.

It is extraordinary that you can live in such a small place as to presume you know it all, when in fact you have scarcely seen anything. Tochni is an elusive corner of Cyprus, set over a hill from the Limassol highway. A mound of houses like sand grains, held in the hand of a shallow valley, ready to scatter. Many of its residents did scatter, on the hot wind of the conflict. Aristos knows this. He has known it since he read up on this village, late into the night and his teenage years. Yet it is something else to stand at the scene, in broad daylight, as a man.

Costas's car-door slam resounds, and Aristos follows him down the hill. He stumbles on the uneven street, between hous- es rough with Tochni Stone.

"Beautiful stuff. They quarry it just up there," Costas ges- tures, slowing his pace.

Aristos stops beside him, in the flat of the village's palm. A church tower cranes overhead, the blue sky framing its cross in a picture that Aristos has seen countless times, between his forced visits to Saint Lucas and other Orthodox sites. But not this one, which his parents likely frequented before. Unless they didn't, he realises, with a pulse of alarm. Marios and Nausicaa might have come to their faith as they did their new-build – entirely after the conflict – and done no more than get married here. Even that Aristos cannot say that they did for certain.

"You know a lot about this place," he mumbles, to Costas.

"I've picked up bits and pieces. Of course, that's not the same as having history somewhere," the investigator adds.

He is smiling, gently, when Aristos looks up. Like some uncle at an extended gathering, bemused by quite how they are related. A wind casts dust into Aristos's eyes, and he narrows them.

"You said I might find this interesting," he says, shrugging at the village that he regrets, with a sudden violence, agreeing to visit. "What about it? What are we doing here?"

"I'm glad you're with me today, Ariste," Costas responds, calmly. "Speaking for myself, the journey to Tochni began much longer than an hour ago. I can tell you about it, if you'd like."

He leaves this offer to hang in the air, with the sound of bees and the scent of pine, until Aristos concedes a nod.

"Can we walk?" he manages, through tight lips.

"Certainly."

As they start up a hill facing the one that they climbed down, Costas talks of his childhood. He grew up in a village not unlike this one, he says, tangled with prickly pears and pomegranate trees, only high up in the Troodos Mountains. Its views were of Morphou Bay, glittering in the sunlight. Costas begged his mother to take him there, not understanding that since the conflict, a border had severed their home village from the town of Morphou, where Costas's father had once worked. His friends' fathers had worked there, too. With their only commutable town gone – within sight and yet out of reach – the local villages would die. They were in a stranglehold, with families like Costas's unable to sustain themselves at an altitude which, overnight, had become remote. It was only a matter of time until they surrendered to Nicosia, and Costas gazed from the plain of that other city at the Kyrenia Mountains, their peaks as inaccessible to him as Morphou had been.

"So, you see. I was always disturbed by the divide and intrigued by what lie beyond it," he says, stepping over a snapped Adenia vine. "I met my first Turkish Cypriots at university in London, and found that many of them shared my desire to see Cyprus heal from its wound . . ."

Stepping after him, Aristos imagines the border as a gash across the belly of an animal, bleeding its time and attention and a terrible number of its young people. Was he one of those, who had left unable to conceive of a bright future in the shadow of the conflict? His foot lands hard beyond the Adenia vine, sending a lizard scuttling. For years, Aristos has guarded his suspicions about his mother and father, growing more alone and tightly wound. Yet here is this man, assuring him that his history is not just his parents', and their history is not just theirs, either.

It is Cyprus's, merely one panel in a tapestry of the nation's suffering.

"That's why the CMP doesn't look to punish killers," Costas says, as they come to a plateau overlooking the village. "It doesn't want to discourage anyone from coming forward with new information. We must heal together, all of us Cypriots."

His words sound distant, and yet they are beginning to make sense, washing over Aristos in waves as the sand of his old beliefs slides out from under his feet. He thinks, he could swim now. Or he could drown.

With his lips pressed firm, he follows Costas down an alleyway between houses, overhung with bougainvillea vines and littered with pink bracts. It opens out into a broader street, on which half the properties appear abandoned. Many lack windows. Some have caved in, revealing the palms – unnatural to Cyprus – that have sprouted inside.

There wasn't so much of this on the other hill of the village. Perhaps this side housed more Turkish-speaking Cypriots before the conflict. Tochni had served as a refuge for those displaced from Kalavasos and Maroni. Then came EOKA B. On the fourteenth of August, 1974, its members rounded up more than eighty Turkish-speaking men. They wrestled those men onto two buses and drove them towards Limassol, then saw them off in a blaze of automatic gunfire. Only one boy survived, having played dead. He ran into the arms of the British to tell his story, at one of the two military bases that their 'administration' had left in its wake. And so the carousel of allies and oppressors went around.

At the end of the street, Aristos stops. He feels heavy with the history of his life and this land, all of it on his shoulders, all the time. He cannot conceive of carrying it a step further. He is sinking towards the ground, towards the fallen carobs and sun-crisped leaves, when he looks up. Before him, another house stands hollow. It has the same sideways tilt and unhinged doors as the others, with bees hovering around a hole in its roof. Except that it is ringing like a tapped glass, reverberating at a pitch that Aristos feels certain only he can hear. Costas crunches to a stop at his side. His silence is watchful, ever patient. But Aristos cannot keep him waiting here. Even if he believed that his parents' old house was calling to him, across time and all logic, he couldn't say whether his father had been one of those EOKA B killers – or just a resident who had aided them on the day of the Massacre – or not. That is what Costas wants, Aristos knows, some personal insight that might point him towards any bodies that remain missing.

"I'm sorry," he says, hanging his head.

The investigator puts a hand on his shoulder. A stifling gesture, in this heat, and yet Aristos allows it to rest there. Before him, a house stands decomposing. Soon, the worms will come for his father's body, too, and then it will be too late for closure. Aristos blinks. Is that what he wants? The answer arrives clear as the day in his mind, as though it has been there all along. Yes, he wants closure. An admission from his father to assure him, at last, that he hasn't spent ten years torturing himself over nothing. He wants the catharsis of laying his suspicions to rest, not letting them fester between himself and his loved ones any longer. He wants to feel able to stay in Cyprus. This shocks him, until he understands that it was never Cyprus he wanted to leave.

"I wasn't planning it," he told Petros, the night of his return.

And it was true. Aristos had never wanted anything more than to live next door to his friends, with the love of his life. He just hadn't wanted to live with himself.

Costas withdraws his hand, and Aristos stands taller. Whatever horrors his father takes to his grave, Aristos will not let them haunt him any longer. He might not feel ready to come out from behind Wendy's foreignness just yet. But the will is there, he thinks. Slowly, he is going to find his way back to a self and a Cyprus that he can bear. To the woman he still loves, if she will have him. He just needs some time to figure out how.

Accident Investigation Report

Date: 27 August 2004

Time: 16:00 AKDT

Aircraft Type: de Havilland DHC-3

Operator: Mavrik Aire, on behalf of Exousia Inc.

Registration: N197TT

Occupants: 3

Fatalities: 1

Aircraft Damage: Destroyed

Synopsis:

At 15:26 h on Friday 27 August, a cargo-carrying de Havilland DHC-3 aircraft, N197TT, departed McGrath Airport, Alaska for Unalakleet, Alaska. No flight plan was filed.

The pilot obtained weather briefing from the FAA, which included AIRMETs for mountain obscuration, and IFR conditions due to low ceilings and visibility in smoke, light rain and mist. At take-off, visibility was 1 to 3 miles. Upon entering lower visibility, the pilot attempted a 180 degree turn but collided with trees and crashed to the ground. The aircraft came to rest upright with extensive fuselage damage, about 1 400 ft msl. One wing was torn off the airframe and a post-crash fire consumed the wreckage.

On 29 August, search personnel located the 2 survivors and transported them to Anchorage Hospital. The aircraft was destroyed.

TEN

ON THE DAY OF her first solo meetup with Wendy, Melina wakes before dawn. Petros lies sleeping with his back to her, his breaths washing up and away from the shores of her ears in waves. Their steadiness doesn't soothe her as it would have years earlier, when she was a girl picking her way over the rocks at Cessac Beach. Rather, it drives her from bed with the madness of someone repeating a word so many times that it ceases to make sense, or stroking a patch of her skin raw with the gentlest arcs of their thumb. Breath held, Melina creeps from the room.

She is slow to swallow her yoghurt, its sheep's-milk sweetness eluding her. The bin calls out across the kitchen that she designed and Petros saw built, and yet Melina perseveres. Neither she nor her fiancé has left a meal unfinished since primary school, for them – as for all the refugees of Dasaki Achnas – a prefabricated building with no fence to stop its yard from spilling out into the forest. On rainy days, their teachers told them off for whining about the short distance that they had to walk to the toilets. Unlike children in the first three years after the invasion, Petros and Melina had more than a tent for their school, as well as squat bungalows to go home to. Setting her bowl on the draining board, clean, Melina pads back up to her bedroom. She has lived in her own, custom-built house for six months, and still the stairs feel novel.

As she surveys herself in her brown mules and yet another shapeless dress, Melina regrets her aversion to food waste and then scorns her regret. She seldom wears makeup or looks for long at her reflection. But she does look at other women. Sliding the clasp of her crucifix to the back of her neck, she turns from the mirror. She knows what the Bible says about self-comparison, and the rest.

"Have a good time this morning, moráki mou, my baby," Petros mumbles, into his pillow.

Her hardworking man, dead on his feet by every weekend. Melina gives him a peck on the cheek, scratching hers on his beard, before she sets out.

"Thank you, moráki mou. I love you . . ."

It is a ten-minute drive from their house in Livadia to Larnaca City Centre, where Wendy has suggested that they should meet. She found the address of a wedding planner and told Melina that it would be fun, like in that film. With Jennifer Lopez and Matthew McConaughey? Melina went along as she does with every idea that assured tones tell her she ought to.

Parking her car in an unpaved lot, she approaches a períptero selling canned coffee and suncream to tourists already swarming the seafront. It unnerves her, this season of low necklines and bare legs. Every summer, hundreds of thousands of people come clamouring for it. Melina watches their planes fly in over Larnaca Bay, where she and Petros built their home especially. And yet she averts her eyes from those foreign girls, whose reddened shoulders she fears could infect her with burning if their owners were to catch her looking.

Down a side passage from the períptero, Melina comes to a door with a diamond-ring sticker – peeling, slightly – on its Flat Five buzzer. She is smoothing it down when Wendy appears, stark white despite her three months here. In that time, Melina has seen this girl – her kouméra, her maid of honor – infrequently, and always in the company of others. The word 'hello' sticks on her tongue.

"Hi," Wendy says, coolly. Then, "You look nervous."

Melina blushes. "Well . . ."

Following her gesture towards the sticker, Wendy nods. "Big day. Shall we ring up?"

Her ankles flash up the stairs, slender and tattooed with wings. Melina stares, wondering if there is any significance to the designs, until they stop still in front of her. She looks up.

"Flat Five," Wendy says.

The door hangs open, inviting them into an apartment fragrant with rosewater. Wedding-day photos adorn the walls, each one of a different couple. Some of them stand before mountain views, others at the edge of the sea. All wear smiles of impossible sizes. Melina pictures herself putting one on, ill-fitting, and she wants to flee from the building.

"Geiá sas," a woman calls, coming out with a tray of water glasses.

She lowers it, tinkling, to a coffee table and stands upright to reveal bright eyes.

"Welcome, girls. You're Wendy?"

"Yeah. Hi," Wendy says.

"I'm Chloe," the woman responds, spreading her arms wide. "We spoke on the phone, nai?"

"Oh. Yeah."

"Nice to meet you."

She sweeps Wendy into her embrace, then turns towards Melina.

"And you," she says, with her first signs of ageing in smile lines, "are the bride-to-be?"

The tiled floor echoes her question.

"Nai," Melina admits.

There is a squeal and then she is in Chloe's arms, rocking from side to side. A strand of hair tickles her nostrils. She pulls back, and Chloe catches her hand.

"Let me see . . . ómorfi," she says, angling Melina's engagement ring under the ceiling light, "beautiful."

It is the only piece of jewelry that Melina wears, beyond her crucifix. Despite its compact stone, the ring feels heavy on her finger.

"Your boyfriend has good taste, huh?"

"Thank you."

Wendy nods.

"So," Chloe says, indicating a pleather sofa. She takes an adjacent armchair. "Tell me, what kind of wedding do you have in mind?"

Melina bumps to a seat, lower than she expected.

"Have you thought about location, or colour scheme? Do you know how many guests you're going to have?"

"Erm . . ."

"You won't overwhelm me, don't worry," Chloe smiles, uncapping a pen. "Even in Cyprus, the girls these days come with crazy ideas. They still have church ceremonies. But afterwards, they want cupcake towers and disposable cameras. Tropical flowers, some of them. And keeping those fresh, in this climate, is . . ." She waves a hand.

The air conditioner drones lower, like an aeroplane spooling down. Melina clasps her elbows in opposite palms and feels her sweat drying to goosebumps.

"Girls, sorry. Can I offer you some coffee?" Chloe asks, starting to her feet. "Tell me what you want, and I'll pick it up from the períptero while you get your thoughts together. Okay, Melina mou?"

Melina nods, releasing her arms. Chloe steps out the door, giving her the space to breathe, while Wendy wonders, aloud, what kind of wedding she would have. An urban one, most likely, with an open bar and no children allowed. Also a bold dress, perhaps that she had painted herself.

A key rattles in the door.

"Okay, girls," Chloe says, setting down their iced coffees.

Wendy takes hers – plain black – at once, while Melina watches her own sweat its milk and sugar onto the cardboard holder. Across the table, Chloe resumes her seat with a notepad and pen.

"Why don't you start by telling us how you met your fiancé?" she suggests.

As though it is apparent that Melina feels blank. That even Wendy – her dearest friend, as far as this wedding planner knows – might have questions as to what she is doing here.

"We met as twelve-year-olds, on the beach. I was alone," Melina starts. "He came over to me, and—"

"What's his name?" Chloe asks.

"Petros," Melina says, and breathes. Her fiancé's name like a sigh of relief.

In moments like this, speaking it is as comforting to her as he was, that first day on Cessac Beach. There was a shelf of rock overlooking the sand. Beyond it, the sea that imprisoned Melina in Cyprus. Above, the sky that had stolen her most beloved friend, Alison, away. Melina had scrambled up there to sit with her tragedy, beneath the planes making their approaches to Larnaca Airport. They lowered their wheels just as they turned across the bay. Why wasn't Alison on board, flying into Cyprus and not out of it, never to return? Melina craned her head back until her neck ached, searching the underbelly of every aircraft for an answer.

She would more likely have received one on the ground, from the British Army whose territory she was encroaching on. Or were they encroaching on hers? It was murky to Melina, the history of who had invaded whom in the years preceding her birth, and exactly when and what for. There was her parents' story of running to escape the Turkish tanks that had rolled into their home village, Achna, in 1974. Her grandparents talked of the fifties and their struggle to oust the British. By the time of her parents' flight, the Dhekelia Army Base had been one of two left over from Britain's colonial rule, and its soldiers had let them in to take shelter. The conflict had ended. The island had cleaved. Achna had been lost, and so its residents had resigned themselves to their forest settlement just up from the base, calling it Dasaki Achnas.

Petros, too, had been born a refugee in his own homeland. Like Melina's parents, his mother had fled from Achna. And like Melina herself, he had waved a loved one off to the Gulf War of that August, 1990. When they met, Melina was beside herself with the suddenness of so many soldiers' redeployment, Alison's father among them. Petros revealed that his father had flown out, too.

Melina turned and saw that Petros was, indeed, a shade paler than she was. She saw that, like her, he had spent considerable time on the Dhekelia Base, and not gritting his teeth the way that her mother did as she cleaned the houses. For Petros, Cessac Beach held meaning. And so he came to mean something to Melina, in their many returns for plane-watching.

Chloe lowers her pen. "I'm sorry."

Melina nods.

"So, Petros's father was British?"

"Yes."

"And his mother?"

"Cypriot."

Chloe opens her mouth, glances at Wendy, and closes it. Melina, too, decides to stay quiet rather than admitting that Petros's mother was not only on the run from Turkish troops the night that she conceived him, but sixteen years old. She decides not to say that she and Petros have agreed to keep both their mothers at a distance from their wedding planning, for fear of reminding his of the cake she never cut, and the photos she never framed, and the siblings she never gave him, because Cyprus remained a stoutly traditional place despite – or perhaps in resistance to – its many invasions and overhauls, and so no one would marry a displaced and disused child-mother. Petros grew up in his grandparents' house, to be fiercely loyal. Hardworking. Protective.

"We comforted each other. We were best friends," Melina says.

"Just friends, at that time?" Chloe asks, with a smile.

Blinking, Melina finds that her eyes are wet with tears. "Yes, well. He told me he was planning to get on a plane one day himself . . ." She stops short of saying 'to find his father', before going on, "I was afraid he would break my heart. But he was persistent. And when I finally agreed to go out with him in high school, he said he would stay."

"How romantic!" Chloe cries, clasping her palms to her chest. "Brávo, Melina mou. You have a beautiful story . . ."

Even as Melina thanks her, she feels troubled by this tale. By the fact that Petros never fulfilled his dream of going to London, and by the chair at their top table that will sit empty as a result. Over the years, Petros has become more outspoken against Britain. His hatred has grown with every person that has left him for that Promised Land. First his father, then Aristos. Melina feels acutely aware of Wendy, the walking reminder of Aristos's betrayal, sitting beside her. She feels acutely aware of her ancient love for Alison, which Wendy's arrival has stirred up inside her.

"We still watch the planes, sometimes," she says, stupidly.

Chloe picks up her pen. "You know, I think that could make a lovely theme for your wedding. To show how you're overcoming borders, bringing your loved ones together from wherever they are."

"You could make your invites look like plane tickets," Wendy offers.

"Yes!" Chloe shrills. "And for your first dance, you can choose that song . . . Pós légetai, how is it called? Erm . . ."

"'Fly Me to the Moon'?" Wendy suggests.

"Yes! From Frank Sinatra."

"That's the one."

They share a laugh, Melina holding her hands tight in her lap.

"Okay. Maybe we're taking it too far for you now," Chloe concedes, "but you see the idea."

"I do," Melina says. "It's nice."

She remembers her coffee only once its ice cubes have melted to pebbles.

"That was fun," Wendy says, when they emerge from their meeting.

Just as she had said it would be, before the sun was so high in the sky and the café-bars were blaring their music. Melina looks at the girl, swaggering towards the seafront, three years her junior and yet so assured. It is as though Wendy arrived fully formed to the country, perhaps to the world. And yet she must have known some origin.

"Yes," Melina says. Then, "I haven't asked you. How did you and Aristos meet?"

Apparently, Wendy can't disclose the details. "Let's just say there was some crossover between Arty and my ex," she says.

"Ah," Melina responds, straining to keep her tone neutral. "And was it bad, between them?"

Wendy tosses her head. "Not between them," she says, "but it was awful between her and I."

Melina misses a step. The word 'her' shrinks in her ears – as though she is on a plane after all, with the air pressure impounding her.

Eleven

"Kyría Christodoulou," the children call Melina, "Kyría Christodoulou, Kyría Christodoulou!" raising their voices and flapping their hands.

Melina blinks, and her vision clears. She is standing at the head of her class, shepherd to its seven-year-old sheep, in the school playground. Teachers stand to either side of her, steering their own flocks through the storm of home time.

"That's my mum over there, Kyría Georgiou . . ."

"Okay, Pano," Miss Georgiou says, releasing one child.

"Kýrie Iannou, that's my aunt . . ."

"Okay, Anna," Mister Ioannou says, releasing another.

Melina watches, amazed by their competence. These are her colleagues. This fact occurs to her as though for the first time, and she looks down in disbelief. On her feet, the flat brown mules of a woman firmly beyond her youth. And yet the ground appears so much further away than Melina feels it should, it makes her dizzy. All day she has gazed at these children, unable to believe that she is not another one coming back from a long summer break. Except that there is no one to tell her how to think or what to do, no sense of September – both a bore and a relief – restoring structure to her life. All the order she had known fired off last week, from the trigger of Wendy's tongue.

"Kyría Christodoulou," a scruffy-haired boy whines.

Melina musters a smile. "Yes, paidí mou?"

"My giagiá is here." He points.

At the sight of an elderly woman, hunched waiting by the school gate, Melina nods.

"Go on, then. See you tomorrow . . ."

Panic descends on her as she watches him walk away, satchel bouncing against his side. He hangs it on his grand-mother's shoulder, and Melina mourns the days when she could so freely hand off her responsibilities and go skipping down the street. What is the boy's name? She should know that. It has never taken her more than a day to get acquainted with a new class, until this year. She fans herself, overcome with the heat. It has dropped since August, and still she is struggling. The fear that everyone knows – they can see her unravelling – makes her pull her students closer.

"Are you okay, Kyría Christodoulou?" Mister Ioannou asks her.

"Yes, sorry. Fine," Melina smiles, hastily.

"She doesn't respond to 'Christodoulou' anymore," Miss Georgiou calls, over the heads of her children. She wiggles the fingers of her left hand. "She's getting used to her fiancé's name!"

Melina laughs, a beat later than her colleagues. This is as close as she comes to befriending them, making small talk about her engagement. But the first time these people meet Petros will likely be on her wedding day, when they hand him an envelope of cash in thanks for inviting them and proceed to the buffet. Being self-employed, Petros doesn't have any real colleagues, yet Melina has met the builders and plumbers with whom he partners many times. She knows the boys that he barracked with in the army – Kyriakos is going to be his best man – and the men who frequented the souvláki bar he ran in the years after that, while he was training to become an electrician. They have the odd dinner together, and Melina smiles at all their stories without sharing a line of her own. She avoids getting caught up with their girlfriends and wives, particularly.

"Geiá sas," Miss Georgiou bids her, when they have seen off the last of their charges.

Melina gives her a wave and Mister Ioannou a more lingering smile – they get along well – but even him she cannot draw closer to. It is tough luck, if you prefer the company of men and are engaged to one. You cannot spend time alone with any others or people will talk, and so you end up without a friend in the world.

Melina beckons to two children on a corner bench, and they come scampering over. Her niece Sofia and nephew Andreas, ages six and eight, look more like her older brother every year with their curly hair and wide-set eyes. Herding them into her car, Melina starts the drive back to her house.

"So, how was your day?" she says, to both and neither of the children at once.

"Kalí," they chorus, "good," before Andreas recalls, "No, actually, my day was rubbish! Kyría Georgiou told me off for talking, when it wasn't even just me. I told her Christos K and Christos N were doing it as well, and then at breaktime they said I wasn't allowed to sit with them! So I got in trouble with my teacher and my friends!"

"You can't win, huh?" Melina says, giving her nephew a sideways smile.

"Sostá," he agrees, with a shrug of outrage all his father's.

It is on the surface with men, Melina thinks, the violence of every upset and the brilliance of every triumph. Since he was Andreas's age, her brother, Theodoros, has had the air of doing everything right. Building a house, marrying his high-school sweetheart and raising two children with her. Melina's parents are so proud. She sees it in the looks of love they give their grandchildren and in the looks of expectation they give her. Time now, isn't it?

This thought has mortified Melina since Petros's proposal. She isn't lacking in instincts with children – she teaches a classful every morning and looks after her brother's each afternoon – but when she pictures birthing her own, there is a sense of disconnect. By nature, Melina is a carer. A nurturer. But 'mother' is a term that makes her recoil, inwardly, even as she nods along with Petros's talk of names and age gaps. In the same way, much as she is happy to be his fiancée, the thought of becoming his 'wife' makes a part of her shrivel. This must be cold feet. Nothing more, she tells herself. Because who else could she imagine committing her life to?

An answer comes to Melina unbidden, and she swerves to avoid an oncoming car.

"Sorry," she breathes, as the children cry out. She hadn't noticed that she was drifting. "How about you, Sofia mou? How was your day?" she asks, slowing the car to a cruise.

Another jolt as she finds her niece watching her, intently, in the rear-view mirror. As though she saw the thought that flashed through Melina's head, before her life flashed before her eyes with that other car. Its beeping rings in Melina's ears. This is why she is fearful of women. From girlhood, they look at the world with a penetrative gaze. They are capable of things that, in her experience, their male counterparts are not. Boys lack the subtlety to harbor secrets. They might create them – with their slashing, indiscriminately harmful actions – but they move on, oblivious. It is girls that remember, that regret and resent.

For all the likeness to Theodoros that she sees in her nephew, Melina cannot decide who her niece reminds her of. Her eyes flick again to the rear-view mirror as she wonders. Is it herself or is it Alison? The British girl whom she called 'friend' as a child, but who meant something much more to her. Are Sofia's the secrets of tormenting other girls, or of being tormented by them? And does she understand yet that this torment can only be the result of a fierce and forbidden love?

"My day was good," Sofia says, in her babyish voice. "We drew pictures of our favorite animals." She turns her gaze out the window.

Melina throws the car around a corner – again, later than she should have – and speeds towards her house. There is the metal gate that Petros painted sky blue, and beyond it the rose bush that Melina waters after sundown. Contained in these details, in these habits as much as this home, is her present life. How outrageous that she should put her historical one on these children – as if there is not enough of that in Cyprus, people pushing their hardships down generations – and imagine that every little girl is engaging in the ill-informed, illicit 'games' that she was at their age. How indulgent, too, that she should think of those games as amounting to a history. Parking up, Melina pulls her keys from the engine. A woman like Wendy, who implies a lifetime of varying and experimental relationships, would surely laugh or roll her eyes at Melina's claims of any past. After all, Melina has been with her fiancé since she was a teenager. Yet she has this sense of something unfinished, a word on the tip of her tongue or a dream she cannot quite recall.

The children unbuckle their seatbelts and go frolicking towards the house, while Melina shuts their doors and locks the car.

"Theía Melina," they clamour, as she follows them up the concrete path. "Can we have a snack?"

"Of course," she smiles. "What would you like?"

The children sit in the air conditioning, squabbling over which video to watch – *Teenage Mutant Ninja Turtles* or *Pocahontas* – while Melina makes them halloumi and tomato pitas without the tomato. As usual, she resolves their dispute by suggesting the *Pink Panther* cartoon that she first watched as a teenager at Petros's house. His was the only one in Dasaki Achnas – or any village, at that time – to have a video player. A gift from his father, by which they were both quite enchanted before words like 'payoff' and 'appeasement' entered their understanding.

The cartoon works its same magic on Melina's niece and nephew, making them giggle. There are the sounds of tenor saxophone and canned laughter, the children crunching into their toasted pitas and squeaking through their halloumi, until Andreas lowers his plate.

"Do you think Christos K and Christos N will still be angry with me tomorrow?" he asks.

"For telling Miss Georgiou that they were talking in class?"

He nods.

"No, I don't think so," Melina responds. "Why, are you worried?"

Looking down at his pita with its missing bite, Andreas shrugs.

"They're your best friends," Melina soothes him. "I don't think they'll hold something like that against you."

Sofia squeals as the Pink Panther, draped in leopard skin, chases down a caveman with a bone. As though struck by his whereabouts, Andreas nods.

Then, "Theía Melina?"

"Yes, Andrea mou?"

Melina turns her head towards him without taking her eyes off the screen, where a small dinosaur has in turn made off with the bone.

"Who are your best friends?"

The caveman catches the small dinosaur by the neck, only to find himself at the feet of a larger one. Melina stiffens. There is the tinkling of piano keys as the large dinosaur steals the bone away, but no more crunching or squeaking. The children have lowered their halloumi pitas and fixed their eyes hot upon her cheek.

"Well," she starts. "How about your mamá and papá?"

Sofia gurgles. "You're not Mamá's best friend!"

"No, but that doesn't count anyway," Andreas rules, "because Papá is your brother."

"Is that right?" Melina says. "Well, then . . ."

Her heart is thudding with their revelation, that her sister-in-law has spoken ill of her. Not that Melina can blame the women she sees often, but never by choice, for taking her reticence personally.

"How about you two?" she asks, leaning towards her niece and nephew.

"No!" Andreas cries.

"No?" Melina echoes.

"You can't say us because we're your family as well," he insists.

Melina sits back. But family is where she has focused, to distract from her aloneness, for years. Family and Petros who, once they are married and making babies, will turn from her partner into a quasi-relative, too. This strikes her as an injustice, a loss of him at odds with the intention of those acts. Before they started dating, he was her best friend. And afterwards?

"There is someone who was a dear friend of mine, at school," Melina admits.

"When you were our age?" Andreas asks.

"A bit older," Melina says. "His name was Aristos."

"A boy?" her nephew shrieks. "But boys and girls can't be friends."

"Yes, they can," Sofia says.

"No, they can't."

"They can!"

"Only if they're erotevménoi," Andreas says, in a singsong voice, "in love."

"But Theía Melina, aren't you in love with Petros?" Sofia asks, wide-eyed.

"Of course I am," Melina says, more sharply than she means to. "But I missed Aristos very much when he moved away, and I hope we can find a way of fitting him and his girlfriend into our lives now that he's back."

Apparently satisfied, Sofia returns her gaze to the television. Andreas is opening his mouth to say something more when the

Pink Panther charges smack into a boulder, losing the bone that he had just regained to the caveman a second time.

The children fall back into laughing, and Melina does her best to join them. Despite Andreas's questions and Sofia's piercing stare, they don't suspect Melina's loneliness any more than her work-focused brother or grandchild-focused parents do. Naive curiosity can be cutting. That is all, she assures herself. Onscreen, the caveman runs into the large dinosaur's jaws. The only person who worries about Melina's lack of friends is Petros, or so he says. How silly, then, that he should stand against her rekindling with Aristos and Wendy. How devastating, that he should sacrifice Melina as a friend once again, by making her his wife instead.

Twelve

Adjusting her apron, Melina looks out the kitchen window. It is the last week of September, and already the sun is hanging lower in the sky as she makes dinner. Tonight, gemistá, with more red peppers than green because Petros prefers their sweetness. Melina has hollowed out each vegetable from the top, keeping its 'hat' on a plate for later. The insides of the tomatoes she has scooped into a large steel mixing bowl. She pictures her niece and nephew wrinkling their noses and cannot help but smile at their youthful aversion to health food – a privilege of their generation – still intact. It is a good thing that her brother picked them up on time tonight, or there would have been a terrible fuss.

Melina bends to take her mechanical scale from its cupboard and watches the pointer settle into stillness. She has asked Petros to come home at a decent hour this evening, not just so that she can serve him his favourite meal. It is time, she has decided, to admit that she is not ready to get married.

"I mean, not yet," she catches herself, aloud. "I'm not saying I don't want to do it at all, I just . . . It's not you, it's . . ."

The cupboard gapes at her.

Kneeing the door shut, Melina addresses it, "Petro? Se agapó, I love you. I'm just saying, maybe we could postpone the wedding until . . ."

When? The room rings with her silence.

"This is stupid," she mutters, and clamps her mouth shut.

Returning to her scale, Melina weighs out a good amount of pork mince and drops it, heavily, into her mixing bowl. The tomato juice seeps through it, a bloody-looking mess. She hastens to add the other ingredients – parsley, lemon juice, and glazed rice that rains down like pellets – for she has always been squeamish about raw meat, despite her culinary skills. To season the mixture, salt, pepper and dried mint. A dash of olive oil. A cube of vegetable stock. And what else?

Melina is reaching for the missing components before their name has formed in her head. Onions. Their weight comes as naturally to her palms as this recipe does to her mind, without her so much as glancing at a cookbook. She knows what Petros likes on his plate. Evidently, that is enough to make her wife material, never mind what he might like beyond that.

Melina tears the skin off her first onion. When they were teenagers, Petros held her hands during sex and insisted that she lie still for hours afterwards while he kissed and stroked and asked, intermittently, whether she was enjoying herself. And then, when he was grimacing through wrist or neck ache, whether she had finished enjoying herself. It seemed so important to him that, after those first few disappointments, she started pretending that she had. That in turn seemed so gratifying to him that she never stopped pretending. Eleven years have passed, and Melina hasn't once enjoyed the rush that Petros does every time they sleep together. Naturally, they have done so less and less over time, Melina having no reason to initiate. She goes along with it when Petros does – to keep him happy and appearances up – but her mind goes elsewhere.

Perhaps sensing this, Petros had ceased to make so many advances. Their love had found its home in other areas of their relationship – a broad and spectacular landscape, after their years spent building it up – until his proposal. Since sliding his ring onto her finger, that suggestive manoeuvre, Petros has come pawing at the drawstring of Melina's pyjama bottoms as often as twice a week again. At first, she was flattered – almost aroused – by the surprise of this. It felt like the reignition of something between them, and she enjoyed the effect that it had on their wider relationship. It was like they laughed more, if only with their eyes. They touched and kissed in passing. It was nice. Except that it made Melina feel like a fraud and a failure, like something was wrong with her because, try as he might, Petros still could not give her the rush of joy that she went on pretending. Only one person had ever done that, and Melina had been too young to comprehend what it meant.

She plunges her knife into the first onion, and its gas draws tears to her eyes. There is so much beauty in what she has with Petros, she reminds herself, blinking them back. An inevitability that she sensed from the moment she met him, at twelve years old. She saw her future washing up on Cessac Beach, in Petros's readiness to put an arm around her before he knew why she was crying, and in the precise angle at which he cocked his head to listen. He was kind and steady, everything that Melina or anyone else could ever need.

Yet there is something so gruelling about the assured. Even in the case of celebration, some annual cheer like Easter coming around again. Year after year, the same old soup and pastries – avgolémoni with its egg-lemon sauce, and flaoúnes with their goat's cheese and raisins – until they lose their taste. Melina wants to enjoy the festivities as wholly as her cousins appear to, because what kind of person can't appreciate predetermined joy? Shared tables and neighbourhood walks, calling kaló pásha to other families, with a belly full of their grandmother's food. What kind of person could feel that all that goodness wasn't enough? What more could they be looking for?

Sniffling, Melina peels the skin off the second onion. She brings her knife down, and pain blooms from her left thumb. With a cry, she rubs her eyes clear of tears and sees her blood spilling onto the chopping board.

"Panagía mou," she breathes, running her cut under cold water.

It stings, keenly, before settling down into an ache she can bear.

Just as she is wiping off the chopping board, her thumb wrapped in a paper towel, Melina's phone rings.

"Geiá sou, moráki mou," she answers, balancing it in the crook of her neck. "Hi, my baby."

"Moráki mou," her fiancé responds, in the same cooing tone. "My baby . . ."

Tipping the onion into her mixing bowl, Melina puts down the board with a hollow thud. Something is wrong. She can hear it in Petros's voice – even as he sweetens it – as surely as she could her own lifeforce through a seashell. She takes her phone into her right hand.

"What's going on?"

"I don't think I can be home for dinner tonight," he says.

She stares at her hollowed-out peppers and tomatoes.

"Agathi called. She said Aristos had shown up at her bakery, wanting to talk. She sounded really shaken up. I don't think she should be on her own with this," Petros goes on, in a tone both decided and cautious.

"Aristos went there looking for her?"

"Apparently."

"Wow. I wasn't expecting that."

"I know. If he thinks he can hurt her again," Petros starts.

Melina leans back against the counter. "Well. You'll miss out on the gemistá I've made you."

"I know, I'm sorry. You'll save me some, won't you?"

"Of course. But . . ." She trails off into a silence.

To fill it, she could say that she missed him today. That she had been looking forward to their evening together. But the only truthful thing would be to admit that with no friends of her own to call, she is terrified of being without him.

"It's okay, I understand," she relents.

For she cannot say that she doesn't want to get married now, with this feeling like looking out of an aeroplane window to find it banking over icy seas.

"Thank you, agápi mou, my love. She needs this," Petros says. "I'll come home later, and we can . . ."

Melina lowers her phone, just to check that it is still in call. She doesn't envy her fiancé the task of filling this silence. He will come home later, and they can what? Make recycled conversation and unfulfilling love, before disagreeing, inwardly, about what to watch on TV? He must feel it, too, the undercurrent of dissatisfaction beneath their unrippled life.

"Yes, my love. I'll see you later," she says, to spare him the indignity of floundering in it.

Petros is a good man, a good partner and a good friend, as evidenced by his attending to Agathi. He shouldn't be made to feel bad.

"I love you, moráki mou," he reminds her, in his baby voice.

Melina softens. "I love you, moráki mou . . ."

Ending their call, she rips the paper towel from around her thumb and plunges both hands into her mixing bowl. The lemon juice sears her cut as she kneads the meat which, just moments ago, she weighed out with the sparest touch. The pain and revulsion of it all is cleansing. It brings her mind to a fine point, and she is marching upstairs to Petros's office no sooner than she has put her filled and 'hatted' vegetable skins in the oven.

The office door falls open without a creak, so new are its hinges. It unnerves Melina. She turns on the light and the darkness scatters, into the corners and out of her sight. The air, too, flinches like a skittish cat from her touch. With light footsteps, she crosses the room. It is empty but for a filing cabinet and the desktop computer upon which Petros prepares his clients' invoices. Other than to check her email, on occasion, Melina leaves him to it.

She stands back as the computer taxis – as though up a runway – towards powering on, not wanting to miss the sound of Petros's key in the door. One by one, icons appear on the screen. The Internet Explorer icon blinks in and out before settling in the top left corner. The noise of the fan subsides. Cruising altitude, Melina thinks.

She lowers herself onto the desk chair. Clicks on the Internet Explorer icon, waits, then double clicks it and holds her breath as the screen lurches into whiteness. A search bar appears, her cursor already inside it. Again, Melina looks over her shoulder. But Petros is not coming home, she reminds herself, not for hours yet. Her chest sags, perhaps with forlornness. And something not unlike relief.

The screen glares with Alison's name, sending a jolt through Melina's stomach. She takes her hands from the keyboard, trembling, only to click 'search'. The results pile in. An esteemed epidemiologist's biography page. A university newsletter. A handful of personal websites by soft-armed, brunette women – many of them American – nothing like the wiry, fair-haired girl whom Melina recalls from the British Army Base. She returns to the top of the page and, knowing nothing about where that girl's life took her later, adds the word 'Cyprus' to her search.

The first link to come up is to a Myspace post, with the preview, 'when we lived in Cyprus . . .'

As the website loads, the fan starts up again. Melina feels its breath hot on her shins and shifts them. Then stills. Staring at her, with the pale eyes of a ghost, is Alison. In her late twenties now, but unmistakeable as the child that Melina grew up with. The child that grew Melina up. In place of her knobbly knees, Alison displays her ankles beneath a long denim skirt. Rather than a boxy short-sleeve, she wears a cropped top that cuts low to reveal round breasts.

'The happiest I ever saw Mum was when we lived in Cyprus', her post reads. 'She said the sun set her free, and now that she's free forever, I want to be too . . . Catch you in Oz!' It is dated eight months ago.

Melina touches the screen. Eight months ago, Alison thought these words, and typed them out, and shared them with the world. Since then, she has posted a range of photos from Australia's outback and beaches, and a series of others from sunny climes closer to home. Spain. Italy. Malta.

'I go where the wind takes me', she claims, 'as long as it's warm'.

Melina is halfway to smiling when the fan quietens down again, and she becomes aware of her nausea like a background noise that she hadn't quite managed to discern. The girl on-screen has been all over the world, and yet she has never left Melina. No prayers to God could rid her from Melina's head, nor could any love for Petros – even in the early days – replace her in Melina's heart. The memory of what had gone on between her and Alison, when they were two little girls who knew no better, lives on in Melina's body. Treasure or trauma, fantasy or regret. Whatever it was, her thoughts of it have grown bigger – and more rapidly, since Wendy's arrival – and she is bursting to talk about them. In fifteen years, Melina hasn't confessed those childhood 'games' to anyone but their choreographer, Alison. Her eyes slide to the 'Add to Friends' button, and yet she holds herself back from it.

Because she and Alison were never just friends, were they?

THIRTEEN

IT IS ONE OF those October days, with no clouds and enough warmth still for short sleeves, but not so much as to render a walk outside unpleasant. Perfect for Dasaki Achnas.

Melina slows her car to a crawl along the Larnaca seafront, and Wendy saunters over just in time to climb inside. She appears to have gone on dressing for August, in the fashion of the many foreigners who cannot separate the idea of Cyprus from 'hot', in one of her graphic tees and a plaid miniskirt. The footwell is shockingly full of her legs. At the blare of a horn, Melina drives onwards.

"How are you?" she asks, following the road around to the right. "It's been a while, huh?"

"Yeah. Well," Wendy says, with something like a scoff.

Glancing sideways, Melina sees the old bungalows converted to gýros joints. Ice cream parlours. Shops selling magnets and postcards.

"Have you been painting much?" she asks, at the sight of so many tiny prints.

"Painting," Wendy echoes.

"Painting, yes," Melina says, in carefully enunciated English.

When Wendy maintains her blank expression, she gestures to the gardens on either side of them. Bright with cyclamen and burgeoning with pomegranates, they are alive with the second spring that comes to Cyprus after the dry season. A plane soars overhead, the sun glinting off its back.

"Just that sky," Melina smiles. "I think I'd paint it every day, if I had the talent."

Again, that catch in Wendy's throat.

"Here?" she says. "You'd get bored quick."

Melina looks at her and away again, at the road opening out into a dual carriageway. No turning back now, from this trip that she had thought they were both looking forward to. She grips the steering wheel tighter, at a loss for what she has done to offend Wendy. And Petros wonders why she doesn't make plans like this more often.

It is a long thirty minutes to Dasaki Achnas. Wendy is an uncomfortable person to be silent with – her thoughts are loud, filling the car – yet Melina dares not attempt to engage her again. Only when they have disembarked in the village centre does she face her friend.

"What?"

"I said, sorry," Wendy repeats, from across the bonnet. "I didn't mean to be, like, shitty."

"You weren't . . ." Melina starts.

"Yeah, I was," Wendy says. "I have been the last few days, since . . . I had kind of an incident."

"An incident?"

She nods, her eyes downcast and smeared with liner.

Across the street, commotion erupts around a távli board. Six white-haired men sit with cigarettes wagging between their lips, outside a tavérna that is just starting to emit the smell of slow-cooking meat.

"Shall we walk and talk?" Melina suggests, turning away before they can see her.

This is a place where people will look, and not in the mountain-dwellers' way of being unused to strangers. The residents of Dasaki Achnas have, conversely, had all too many unknowns showing up at their doors. They are ever on their guard – even those who, like Melina, were born after the invasion, have inherited their elders' wariness – and so the village has a prickly air. It squats on British territory, with its back up to the wall of the buffer zone between the island's north and south.

"So, what are you doing here?" imply its stares, at anyone unfamiliar.

For someone like Melina to appear, however, is a delight. For every stern look that they fix upon a stranger, the locals shower each other in affection. This is a community that, since laying its foundations in tent poles, has relied upon its members pulling together and taking care of one another. Families arrived full of holes, mothers missing children and wives missing husbands. It was up to them to fill those in, as best they could, with what they had. What better place for Petros and Melina to cement their union?

Reaching into her bag, Wendy nods.

"I'll take you to Saint Marina's Church in a minute," Melina says.

"The one where you want to get married?"

"Yes. But first, let's see Ágios Dimitrianos."

"Ágios," Wendy says, taking out her tobacco.

"Sorry. Saint," Melina translates, as they fall into step.

"Ágios. Saint," Wendy repeats.

Melina glances sideways at her. "Are you trying to learn Greek?"

"I don't know," Wendy sighs, pulling up short.

She sets about rolling a cigarette, while Melina looks over her shoulder. They are halfway across the village square, in the full light of the sun. The community has cut back the pine trees that once were its shelter, so they provide no more than a woody fragrance. Wendy's first plume of smoke goes straight up to cloud the sky.

"What's been going on?" Melina asks her, softly.

"I told you, there was an incident . . ."

She nods.

"At work." Wendy takes another drag on her cigarette. "So, there was this festival in town. I think on the first of October or something?"

"Independence Day," Melina confirms, recalling the military parade to which Petros had marched her, as always.

The drums banging, feet stamping, arms swinging by uniformed sides. This year's had marked forty-four since the end of British rule.

"Right," Wendy says, tapping off her cigarette. "So, yeah. These three guys came into the bar afterwards, already quite pissed. I served them each a beer, and when I asked if they wanted another round, one of them started muttering at me. I didn't know what, it was like he was speaking in fucking tongues," she says, gesturing.

Melina blinks the smoke from her eyes.

"I told him I didn't speak Greek, and he made this face, like, pretending to spit at me, and then he wouldn't let me serve him the rest of the night. He just kept giving me these aggressive looks."

"Spit at you?" Melina looks back at her friend, open-mouthed. "What did you do?"

"Well, nothing. Another customer came up, so I just served them and then ignored the guy." Wendy shrugs.

In this jerk of her bony shoulders, Melina sees a lack of assurance that she never has before. Was it always there, beneath the smirking and the smoking? There is a crack in Wendy's voice as she describes the Greek-speaking colleague who told her, later, it was her addressing the man in English that had angered him. He had just come from the parade, celebrating Cyprus's ousting of the British.

"So he was all hyped up on that adrenaline, I guess," Wendy says. "But I don't get it. Just because I happen to be British . .

. I wasn't even born when Britain had control of Cyprus. Why would he take that out on me?"

In the smoke of her exhalation, Petros appears to Melina. He is mid-flow, lambasting the colonial legacy of British immigrants – or 'expats', as they call themselves – not even trying to learn Greek. Their comfortability not adapting to new environments, their presumption that those environments – and the people in them – will, instead, adapt to them. What is it if not a form of ethnic cleansing? Even to one-week holidaymakers, Petros refuses to give English directions.

His image dissipates with the smoke, and Melina recalls her British-born cousins whose parents, as though having caught scent of the coming war, joined the tens of thousands of Cypriots emigrating in the 1960s. Apparently, Melina's aunt has never spoken much English. All of London at large, and enough Cypriot neighbours that she has seldom ventured outside her small pocket of it.

Melina offers her friend a smile. "You can't help where you're from, any more than anyone else can. It sounds horrible, what that man did to you. I'm sorry."

"It's fine," Wendy says, stamping out her cigarette. "It's just, Arty never wants to talk about, like, any of the politics around it, and . . . I don't know."

She looks restless, like a horse raring to bolt with no sense of direction. Melina points, and they resume their walk across the square.

The church they come to is no ordinary one, inspiring a feeling unlike the calm of any other. Melina stops before it, crunching something underfoot – dust, a twig – with the sun on her back. Then, a wash of awe. Of horror, of gratitude and, finally, of anger. For the marvel of the structure, the atrocity that it commemorates, the acknowledgement that it stands in, and the fact that it isn't enough. A concrete tent, roped to the ground, with three others pitched over it and forming steps up to a belltower. Though topped with a cross and dome, the tower is textured to suggest more tents overlapping. Because that is all there was here, once, and for all the houses that have come up since, in certain heart wells it is what remains. A proud scar. A scaled beast, lying dormant with the village rising and falling on its every breath.

"Wow," Wendy says.

Melina follows her gaze inside the mouth of the thing. There, a statue of women spliced in two and slipping out of height with their other halves. The foremost of them holds an incomplete photograph in each hand, one showing half of a man's face and the other half of a woman's.

"Creepy," Wendy says, as they step closer.

The sun disappears from Melina's back.

"Ágios Dimitrianos is the protector of refugees," she explains. "This church is a monument for the people of Achna, who lost their homes in 1974. When Turkey invaded," she adds.

"Oh," Wendy breaks out, from under the surface of her blank face, "right." She takes a breath. Then, "I should probably know this stuff, shouldn't I? If I'm going to be here."

Her voice is so quiet, the walls almost swallow it up.

"Should," Melina starts, tilting her head from side to side, "is a strong word, maybe. But . . ."

"I'm not sure your husband would agree."

"Fiancé."

Wendy raises her eyebrows. Melina opens her mouth, but there is no cramming the correction back in. She had meant to apologise for Petros, not renounce him. Respectfully, Wendy turns her gaze back towards the statue.

"You're right," Melina concedes. "A lot of people do blame the British for Turkey's invasion. Including Petros, although he has his own reasons."

"And you?" Wendy asks.

Her eyes look their palest blue, the whites around them as large as a child's.

"My experiences with British people haven't been all bad," Melina says.

They exchange timid smiles.

After a round of the church, past statues of refugees curled up on the ground and a crucifixion scene, lit by the single window in the main chamber, they come back to its entrance. Wendy is a pace ahead, about to step out into the sunlight, when Melina grabs her arm.

"What was it like?"

Wendy turns back, her face rippled with confusion. Melina's grip is too tight, her tone too urgent, but she cannot help herself. It was from this village, twenty years ago, that her mother used to drive her to Dhekelia, where she worked cleaning British soldiers' houses and ironing their clothes. She let Melina out to play there, not knowing the girl Melina would meet. The obsession she would develop. The accent she would affect, until her mother fretted that their forced move onto British territory had stripped Melina of her Greek identity. As long as she didn't get mixed up with any Turkish identities, her father said, that was fine. Dasaki Achnas swims before Melina's eyes. Today, it is the village from which she will return to gazing at photos online, of the woman that girl has become. To what end? Until Wendy's arrival, with the revelation that alternative paths might have been available to Melina after all, she couldn't have said.

"What was it like," she asks now, unable to suppress it any longer, "to be with a woman?"

Not just to love or touch her, but to live with her. Hold her hand walking down the street. Come home to a meal with her after work. These are things Melina will never get to know for herself, now that she is set to marry the only person with whom she has ever shared a proper, adult relationship.

"Arty doesn't think I should talk about that here," Wendy reminds her.

"But it's part of you," Melina insists. "You weren't kids when you met. You have a history."

"Yeah, well." Again, that scoff. "History can make things complicated."

"Can't it clarify them, too?"

The women meet and drop each other's eyes, just as Melina drops Wendy's arm.

"Sorry, I shouldn't pry," she says. Then, restoring her smile, "Let's go to Saint Marina's and see about this ceremony, shall we?"

"Sure," Wendy nods.

They step out into the sunlight, and the confidence between them burns off.

FOURTEEN

"Where are we going?"

"I told you, it's a surprise."

Melina laughs. "Moráki mou . . ."

"Are your eyes still closed?"

"Nai."

"Good," Petros's voice sounds, from her right. "Don't open them, okay?"

Melina laughs again, and the car lurching over a bump makes her catch her breath. It twists around a corner and down a slope, and her lips stretch upwards. She knows this route. She has travelled it many times, since she was a child. The sun comes warm through the windshield, even as they trundle towards winter. They pause, roll back, and shudder at last into stillness.

"Okay," Petros says. "You stay there, and I'll come and help you out. Entáxei?"

"Entáxei," Melina agrees.

Despite having guessed their whereabouts, she feels vulnerable in this state. Wary, as well as renewed, as the car rocks in the wake of its slammed door. Outside, footsteps sound. Then the cold comes in with a pair of thick arms, to guide Melina to her feet.

"This way," her fiancé says.

So deep, his voice. Authoritative. And yet with a gravelly edge, that makes his words sound like whispers just for her. Indeed, as Petros leads her across the gravel – stopping at intervals to let other cars drag past – his murmurs brush her ear.

"Almost there . . . Keep them closed . . . We're going to take a step up here . . ."

With her knee lifted, Melina paws at the air until her foot finds a surface. Rock, followed by clumps of coarse and tangled shrubbery beneath her palms. A short clamber and then she is standing upright, wind grazing her nostrils with the salt from so many ancient wounds. The heartbreaks and horrors that have washed away from each generation only to break upon the next – the same seas, the same sorrows – forming new waves. Melina is unsheltered upon this ledge, from the sounds of planes flying overhead and children playing below. Open to the world.

"Okay," Petros says.

She hears his boots crunch closer and feels his warmth a breath away from her.

"Ready?"

"Yes," she smiles.

"Here we are."

She opens her eyes, and the world comes to her in more colour than she had remembered it. Vivid blue, the sea and the sky and the eyes looking down, into hers. Her stomach thrills.

Perhaps it is just the crescendo of the surprise settling, the wind whipping and the waves crashing onto Cessac Beach, where she has spent so many wonderful days. But it feels like a rush of love for the man who has brought her.

Melina tilts her face up, and Petros leans to meet it. A lingering kiss, unlike any that they have shared for some time. She savours the scratch of his stubble and the smell of sawdust clinging to his collar. Then draws back.

"Surprised?" he asks.

"Well."

She casts around, at the view they have come for countless times, and they share a laugh.

"Okay," he concedes. "Maybe it wasn't the best surprise."

"Well, no. Actually, it was a surprise," she says, "for you to come home and suggest something like this. Especially on a Thursday. I thought you'd be out with Agathi."

"No." He drops her hands. "Agathi? Not today, no. No," he says.

One too many times, Melina thinks.

"I just wanted to be with you." Petros smiles.

Melina smiles back, a little less naturally than before. "Well, I'm glad," she says, then looks to their old perch over the water. "Shall we sit down?"

"Yeah. Ah, I brought some stuff," Petros recalls, aloud. "Let me run back to the car."

He returns with broad towels and a plastic bag. Melina shakes the former items out for them to sit on, and raises her eyebrows at the latter.

"What do we have in here?"

With a flourish, Petros lifts two plastic cups from the bag.

"Xynistéri," he says, following them up with a bottle of white wine. "Galaktoboúreko," he goes on, producing a bakery box.

Melina coos with delight, first at his knowledge of her favourite treats, and then at the appearance of his. A can of beer to dispel the romance, the brashness of its red-and-yellow tin a familiar joke. No one else would understand why this was so funny, without the context of the many romantic settings in which Petros has made an event of looking over his shoulder before filling his wine glass with lager. This is the beauty of long-term partnership, Melina recalls, with a thud of her heart. Knowing someone's ins and outs. Speaking a language that no one outside your nation of two could hope to translate without intimate tutelage.

"Moráki mou, this is lovely. You're so thoughtful," she says, counting their spoils across the rocks.

Her chest feels full, with gratitude for the love they share, and guilt for her having questioned it.

With a pop, Petros uncorks the wine.

"Not too much," Melina reminds him. "I've got school tomorrow."

"Yes, Kyría Christodoulou," he jibes, passing her a cupful.

The green plastic makes it look a funny, off-yellow colour. The liquid slips down Melina's throat, too warm, yet charming for it.

"Not the standard pairing for galaktoboúreko," she admits, "but . . ."

"It's your favourite," Petros says, opening the bakery box.

He saws at the filo pastry until one plastic knife cracks, before dividing it into successful quarters with another. Custard oozes from between the layers, making Melina's mouth water. She takes a forkful.

"Thank you, for doing all this."

As though it were nothing, he thrusts out his chin. Then asks, "How is it?"

The syrup enlivens her tongue, sowing cinnamon in its wake.

"Panagía mou. Nóstimo," she responds. "Delicious."

He smiles, reaching for his beer.

"Try some," she starts, proffering another forkful, before a cry rings out across the beach.

They turn as one to see a large, middle-aged woman at the edge of the sand.

"Jack. Jack! Get back here," she is calling, after a child just past toddling.

In English, Melina observes, with a smile. Hearing voices like this is part of what she loves about Cessac Beach, or what she loved about it as a child. At the cracking open of a can, she looks back at Petros and sees, in his grudging look, that she is alone in this. They shared similar experiences as children, of loving and losing people who spoke in this flat tongue. And yet, while the sound of it now takes Melina back to the loving, it seems to remind Petros only of the losing.

It is like with the Annan Plan, Melina thinks, as she watches Petros pour his beer. They had agreed that the so-called 'Cyprus Problem' needed solving, but in April, when it came to the referendum on establishing a United Republic, they diverged. Of course, Petros doesn't know this. He thinks that his say – on the Plan's unforgiveable disregard of the Geneva Convention article that prohibited colonisation by an occupying power – was final, in their house. But Melina had other concerns. All year she had read, with quiet urgency, of organisations cropping up in the north to demand equal rights for minority groups. Women. The disabled. Gay people. Her heart shrank when she saw news of the latter, suffering hate crimes and unjust jail time. The world watched, hoping that a month after the referendum, when Cyprus joined the European Union, it would do so as a unified country. The Europeanisation of its northern territory would stop women who happened to love women, and men who could not help but love men, from being classed as criminals.

And so, feeling a private affinity to them, Melina voted for it. She told no one, even after seventy-five per cent of Greek-speaking Cypriots had voted against and it no longer mattered. She pulled away from Petros, feeling that she had been disloyal. Then Wendy arrived and sent her thoughts even further astray.

Petros takes a swig of his beer, lowers the cup and lifts it again. Melina puts down her fork and watches a square of galaktoboúreko roll off it.

"How is Agathi, anyway? What's she up to?" she asks.

"She's agreed to meet up with Aristos," Petros admits, after a third swig of beer, "to see what he has to say."

He smacks his lips, affecting nonchalance, but Melina knows better. The thought of Agathi with another man – especially Aristos – is painful to her fiancé. Her first instinct is not to feel threatened, but to feel for him. Petros. The man she has spent her life with, watching a woman he loves, deeply, teeter on the verge of slipping away. Not that he and Agathi have been dating – a man and a woman can be just friends, Melina knows that better than anyone – but there is a specialness between them. She would have to be blind to miss that. Perhaps so long as Agathi has remained single, Petros has been able to indulge an idea of the two of them together. Of what it would be like if he, too, were unattached. Melina understands this urge. It was the reason why she chose, years ago, to distance herself from friendships with women, including Agathi. She couldn't bear the longing that tugged at her after Aristos left, when Agathi came over almost nightly and gave her lingering hugs goodbye. Their faces brushed, Agathi's neck exhaled orange blossom, and Melina suffered a ripping open of the greatest wound of her life. Was Agathi feeling what she was? What would happen if Melina kissed her? She thinks Petros is braver than she could ever be, for exposing himself to such agony, continuously. She admires his self-restraint. Though, clearly, circumstances are testing it.

Chasing the galaktoboúreko back onto her fork, Melina notices the name on its box lid.

"You went to her bakery," she realises, aloud.

"Yeah. I mean, I was passing by," Petros says. "And they do have the best glyká." He shrugs.

"Sostá," Melina agrees, as her fork reaches her mouth.

The plastic comes cold to her tongue. So, Petros did go looking for Agathi today, only to find that she had plans with her ex-boyfriend. It was then that he bought Melina these things, to save face or console himself. Melina looks sideways at him. Just how caught up has he become in his fantasy? Does he have any doubt that he would be with Agathi, if Melina were not around? She follows his gaze, to another plane making its turn over the bay, as though to see through his eyes. She is on that plane, flying away. He is alone, with his future as unclear as the sky is cloudless. How long does he wait, before calling Agathi? Running up to her house, without stopping to turn off his engine. She opens the door. They stare at each other. Their lips part, and no words emerge.

As their bodies go crashing down on top of one another, their scents mingling, breaths fogging all the windows whose shutters they have found no time to close, Melina watches through the glass. A throbbing between her legs. A thudding inside her chest. A wave breaks upon Cessac Beach, and she thrusts a kiss upon her fiancé. Heat between them, like August again, exciting

Melina as much as Petros as it turns from clumsy to clasping. She senses his shock in the seize of his lungs, before his hands find her back. She pulls her lips from his.

He scoffs. "What . . . ?"

"Surprise," she smiles.

Even as she sits back, blushing, he laughs as though in awe. They guess the airlines of a few more planes flying in. They eat and drink the remains of their incompatible picnic. They revert to the baby voices in which they cannot be serious about any issue, however adult. And later, when they get into bed and Melina paws at Petros's pyjama bottoms – for the first time in years, if not in her life – it is not the fear of him sleeping with another woman that drives her, but the thought of that other woman herself.

FIFTEEN

IT SMELLS OVERSWEET IN the wedding dress shop, like flowers are unfolding into Melina's face. She feels withered and falls back a step, letting the door tinkle shut before her.

"Sorry," she starts, as her heel meets a toe.

Its owner catches her shoulder.

"Are you okay?"

"Fine. Sorry," Melina repeats, turning around. "I didn't mean to step on you."

"Don't worry," Wendy says.

Behind her, an old man sits smoking while the house next door to his crumbles. Melina sees the grandeur of times past in an arch protruding, like a fractured rib, from the roof that has caved in around it. A car trundles past, trailing exhaust fumes, and the old man calls out a greeting.

Wendy glances over her shoulder. "Are we going in . . . ?"

"Ah. Yes," Melina responds.

Her laughter sounds strained beneath the jingling of the doorbell.

"Geiá sas," the shopkeeper says.

She appears to be around Melina's age, with perfect makeup and glossy hair. A ring on every finger but her fourth one, and her smile thin-looking for it.

"You're getting married?" she addresses Wendy, in English.

"She is," Wendy answers.

Their heads turn towards Melina, and she feels herself still wearing her spluttering laughter. The shopkeeper looks her up and down.

"Is this your first time wedding dress shopping?"

"Nai," Melina confirms.

"Okay. Well . . ." The shopkeeper gestures towards a wall of gowns before adding, "Na zísete, congratulations."

"Efcharistó," Melina thanks her.

They exchange nods, a little of the discomfort between them thawing.

"My name's Kiki, by the way."

"I'm Melina. And this is my kouméra, Wendy."

"Hi."

"Nice to meet you both," the shopkeeper says. Then, to Melina, "You brought photos?"

"Photos," Melina repeats.

"Of the dresses you like."

"No." Her smile fades. "Sorry, I didn't think of that."

"Okay," Kiki responds, lowering her eyelids to reveal nude sparkles. "But you know the style you want," she presumes, flicking them back.

"Erm. I guess I haven't thought about that, either," Melina realises, aloud.

With another slow nod from Kiki, the discomfort creeps back.

"We were thinking she could look around and get some ideas," Wendy suggests.

She sounds bored with this exchange. Still, Melina feels a rush of appreciation as the shopkeeper comes around.

"Yes," Kiki says. "We have many different designs, you will see. And I will see also, with your body type . . ." Giving Melina a second look up and down, she smiles. "Entáxei?"

"Entáxei. Thank you," Melina says, ducking back behind Wendy.

The shopkeeper retreats, and Melina exhales. Despite her proficient English, there is always a lag before she speaks it, the second it takes her to work out the equation – like a mathematical sum – of one word to another. She has had a good amount of practice since Wendy's arrival, and still she questions, sometimes, whether there are things she has not accounted for in her translations. The limits of functional language are freeing, compared to the in-depth questions with which native Greek speakers can push her into revealing the messy and unchecked parts of herself that no textbook would ever teach her to. As a barrier to this, Wendy is a blessing.

Only as Melina steps forward does she notice the absence of any language at all, the echo of her shoes upon the laminate wood floor. She creeps towards the wall, where dresses hang. In her ears, the beating of her heart as she faces the first gown. Then the whirring of a CD player, followed by the pattering piano keys of Franz Liszt's 'Liebesträum'. Melina sends a grateful look to Kiki before she sees that the shopkeeper is appraising her again. Her coat feels at once too slim fitting.

"See anything you like?" Wendy asks, sauntering over.

Melina turns back to the dresses. "Erm . . ."

The hibiscus and rose smell wafts again, from the petals of their skirts. Wendy pulls at one, absently, and it makes a rushing sound like the wind tousling through leaves.

"These colourful ones are cool. Or are you thinking of going more traditional?"

"Traditional," Melina says, automatically.

She watches the pink taffeta sag from her friend's fingertips.

"Something white? Ivory?"

"Yes."

"Okay. So that narrows it down by, like, three," Wendy laughs.

Melina echoes her, hollowly.

"Oríste," Kiki's voice sounds. "Here you are . . ."

Melina turns to see her sweeping across the floor, two dresses trailing behind her. They flutter to a stop.

"I think, for you, something like these will be very nice," Kiki says, raising her hands.

From them hang two garments, one a pearly satin and the other a powdery tulle.

"Both have an A-line shape."

She attempts to mime this when Melina looks blank, then jerks the dresses up off the floor.

"Shall I put them in the fitting room for you?"

"Okay," Melina says, if only to lighten the shopkeeper's load. "Thank you."

"If you see any others you want to try, we can bring those also," Kiki calls back, as she crosses the shop.

Melina casts a final look over the rack of crystal sashes and flowing skirts. She hears them hissing again, contemptuously.

"Are you okay?" Wendy asks.

"Yeah," Melina says. Then, turning after Kiki, "Would it be okay if I just tried on those two, for now?"

"Of course," Kiki says, sliding a tray out from under the counter. "Do you have anyone else coming to join you? Your mother?"

"No," Melina says, with a faltering smile. "She wasn't able to make it."

A half-truth. Melina's mother would have cancelled anything to be here, but Petros's made that unthinkable. With her history, Panayiota can neither be included nor singularly excluded from anything wedding-related. The day itself will be hard enough on her.

Melina understands this, and yet she has felt her own mother's absence more keenly than she expected to in the last few months. Something turned cold between them the day that Alison left Cyprus, when Melina's mother found her sobbing over a stash of papers that she had brought home from their 'games'.

Letters and poems that described – with eerily innocent use of such adult language – the acts that those games had entailed, and that Alison had encouraged Melina to write about wanting certain boys on the base to perform on her. Melina's mother turned as white as the pages. When she learned that it was a girl who had instructed Melina's hand, though, she stopped demanding their address. This could stay between the two of them, she said, as long as Melina agreed to steer clear of any other girls who tried to talk to or touch her like that. Did she understand?

Melina knew then that she had been hiding more than just her friend's Britishness. She ceased talking to her mother about much, besides the facts of her relationship with Petros. They were dating. A couple. Renting an apartment. Building a house. Engaged.

"So, you are two?" Kiki says, running her eyes over Melina and Wendy.

"Yes," Melina confirms.

She watches the shopkeeper walk away with her tray, between the tapestries of happily-ever-after looks. Costumes, Melina fears. Yet her mother has rejoiced at every milestone moment, reassuring as much as disturbing Melina that she has done well to end up in the kind of relationship she has, and not in the kind that they, clearly, both feared she might. Her mother, the average woman. The good example. The dutybound housewife, who wears her boredom like a badge of honour. Melina craves her presence more than ever.

When Kiki returns, it is with champagne.

"Stin agápi," she proposes. "To love."

Recalling this toast from the night she met Wendy, Melina smiles at her friend. They touch glasses with a faint, bell-like sound, before the bubbles fizz up Melina's nose and behind her eyes. She puts her glass back on the tray.

"Ready?" Wendy asks her, with a cool smile.

"We'll be waiting for you," Kiki says.

With a nod, Melina slips into the fitting room. It is dark, with no mirror to reflect the ceiling light. She will have to survey herself in view of the others, she realises, unhappily. The smell, apart from the floral perfume of the dresses, is of the heavy velvet curtain. There is room enough in the rectangular space, and still Melina steps clumsily out of her trousers and flat boots. Shivering, she takes down the dress that looks least fiddly to get into and gasps at the drag of it over her skin like cold bedsheets. When she has zipped up the back as far as she can, she turns towards the light.

"Okay . . ."

Overhead, the curtain rips across its rail. Before Melina, faces appear – and fall. This is not her dress. She wants to retreat into the fitting room, but Kiki is already behind her, zipping it up the rest of the way.

"Now, turn." She tucks Melina's bra straps off her shoulders and under her armpits.

"Sorry," Melina mumbles.

"It's okay," Kiki says, fussing further along her neckline.

Melina warms at the brush of the shopkeeper's fingers and blushes when she stands back.

"There . . ."

"Wow," Wendy says, unconvincingly.

At Kiki's instruction, Melina waddles, skirt in hand, to the mirror. A tall, thin pane in which she appears short. Wide, with the fabric of her dress clinging in all the worst places – to the bulge of her lower stomach and the sag of her behind – before falling shapeless. It sits too low, flattening her breasts and overhanging her feet. The sight of it makes her insides curdle.

"What do you think?" Wendy asks.

"I don't know," Melina starts, crossing her arms over her chest. "I don't think the strapless thing is for me . . ."

"This dress, maybe, is for someone taller," Kiki admits, ushering her back towards the fitting room. "The other one is also strapless, but it's a different material. Softer. Try it and see . . ."

Before Melina can argue, she is back behind the curtain. Unsheathing her hips from the satin, losing her limbs in tulle. In a break between songs, she hears a champagne glass hitting the tray. The shopkeeper attempting small talk, before Wendy shuts it down and there is the sound of Kiki refilling her glass to fill the silence. Then, just as Melina is stepping out of the fitting room, Johann Pachelbel's 'Canon in D' swelling from the CD player.

Gasps of awe accompany the violins as Melina makes her way to the mirror. She knows, by the swishing of it about her calves, that this dress is different. Then she sees it, crossover bodice shaping her bosom, sash belt slimming her waist, skirt stretching away from her with all the splendour of a snowy mountainside.

"You look beautiful," her companions coo.

And yet, tears well in Melina's eyes. No one warned her that the ugly dress wasn't the one that would make her cry. In this dress, she looks as unspoiled as a blank page, even as new fears write their way across her face. How ill this all suits her. How unworthy she is.

She turns side-on to the mirror and her first teardrop catches the light, a diamond on her cheek glinting at the one on her finger. She is crying. Because it is December and she is dressed for August, with the cold pinching her arms. She is crying because August will come and there is nothing she can do to stop it, just as she is crying for her mother and the terrible history that she could not undo to bring her here. She is crying because, more acutely than ever, the seasons of her future – far beyond next summer – feel as inevitable as those past. Because she has known, since the day she agreed to marry Petros, that it was the biggest mistake of her life, just as she had known from the moment they met that he was the man with whom she would spend it.

Another person – one who felt that they were living aligned and not a lie – might call this fate. A star-crossed love, meant to be. But the certainty of their partnership has felt, to Melina, like the answer to a closed question, leaving more and more to be desired. The looping script in which she once expressed those desires leaks out, from the inkwell that darkens her heart, across the page of her dress. All the purity that its white should suggest is laughable. Gone. Was never there to begin with.

What, then – black? Melina presses a sob back into her mouth. She is crying uncontrollably now. Because she exists in a cycle of feeling already dead, recalling her luck and rebuking herself when Petros does something nice for her, resolving to appreciate her life with him anew, forgetting again as time goes on, and then suffering a fresh rush of guilt. Because she has never deserved him, has she? With her private, ungrateful misgivings, when he has shown her utter devotion. Closing her eyes, Melina vows. She will do better. She will remember. Petros is her person, she is blessed to have him, and God preserve her if she should lose sight of that again. Silly girl. It is time she gets a grip and accepts her role as a woman, no matter how much harder this feels for her than it appears to for others. It is the done thing, so just do it. Open your eyes, tears webbing your lashes, and say that you do. You will. With honour and respect, forsaking all others, until the blessed, final death when you may cease to without remorse.

"Are you okay?" Wendy asks.

"You don't like the dress?" Kiki frets.

Melina turns to see their eyes wide, and feels the heat of her tears afresh.

"Óchi, no. The dress is stunning," she assures the shopkeeper. Then sobs, "I just love him so much . . ."

Because this remains true, and she cannot reconcile it with her unhappiness.

"Aww . . ." Kiki puts a palm to her heart.

Wendy drains a third glass of champagne. Melina changes back into her trousers and flat boots, and she buys the dress.

Sixteen

Christmastime, as always, is a blur of children and church and chowing down on all manner of treats. Melina gets off for the holidays the same day that her niece and nephew do, and so she takes full custody of them in the week before Christmas Day.

"You're a lifesaver," her brother says.

As though this is the first time that Melina has acted as a defibrillator, restoring the rhythm to his days. She smiles, waving his children into her house. She will get no real, heartfelt acknowledgement for this – Theodoros is already turning away – for her relatives expect that she will help out whenever they ask. And why not? The way they see it, especially now that she is engaged, Melina is merely wiling away the months until she becomes a wife and mother in her own right. She shuts the door on her brother's heel.

"Get your practice in now," her sister-in-law has said.

"Enjoy your quiet nights while you can," her mother has warned.

Both women have cackled as though Melina herself is a child who knows no better, while relying on her to meet their needs. She has smiled, weakly.

On the sideboard, a photo of Petros in his army uniform. He seems better equipped for the elbow-jostling and eye-rolling that the associated fathers do, keen as he is to join their ranks.

"How do you know we'll be good at it, with our own?" Melina asks him, that evening, as the children dose off in front of *Mickey's Once Upon a Christmas*.

"I know you'll be good at it because you're you," Petros says, kissing her forehead. "And I know I'll be good at it because my parents weren't, and I want to do better."

This quietens Melina.

The following afternoon, they drive over to Dasaki Achnas with a pine tree strapped to the back of their Isuzu pickup. Petros hefts it into his childhood home and frees it from its binding, only for its branches to fall, sparse-needled, to its sides. Still, his relatives coo with pleasure as he gifts his grandmother a pot of poinsettias, and his weedy-armed grandfather the illusion that he is helping to balance the tree on its base. Panayiota, Petros's mother, lurks scarecrow-like in the corner, until Petros invites her to hang the decorations.

This happens fast enough to break Melina's heart, so few baubles do the family own. And yet, stringing them up is an activity that restores Panayiota to her stolen youth. She appears absorbed, her smile almost eerie amid her straggly tendrils of hair, both very young and very old. Watching her, Melina thinks

– there was a woman who had motherhood thrust upon her. A family utterly unprepared, and they turned out a wonderful son. With Petros by her side, why couldn't Melina, too, make a go of it?

Snow falls overnight, softening the jagged peaks of the Troodos Mountains. When the children arrive, pink-cheeked with excitement, Petros lowers his toolbox. With one call to each of his expectant clients, citing an emergency with the other, he takes the day off.

"Poiós eísai?" Melina chortles, climbing into his truck. "Who are you?"

Petros overacts a look around before laying a palm on his chest, and Melina laughs. With Andreas and Sofia in the back, they drive up – first through common pine and olive trees, then past riverside plane and laurel trees – until the pines turn black. By the time they park up in Troodos, they are above the clouds, Melina feeling so far beyond the reach of her life that she cannot miss the view. There is no phone signal, and even her fingers are losing touch. It is as freeing as flying.

"Hey!" Petros calls out, after a thud.

He turns around, snow crumbling off his back. Andreas giggles, naughtily, before Petros gives chase and they all descend into shrieking and hurling snowballs. Sofia's are unformed, scatterings of snow like confetti, while Melina shapes and throws her own with equal amounts of caution.

"Careful," she warns, before lying back to form a snow angel beside her niece's.

There, beneath the swirling sky, she finds calm.

They walk into the village, hand in hand, where the smells of hot chocolate and roasted chestnuts pervade the air. Strangers nod greetings, their coats bead-bright against the snow. All along the roadside, men heat cobs of corn over open flames. As she bites into the charred flesh of one, Melina realises that she and Petros must look like parents already. Complete in their unit of four, with nothing left to prove. She could view starting a family the way that he does, couldn't she? As an opportunity to right the wrongs of her own childhood. She could protect her children from having the kind of private life that corrupted her. Hide behind motherhood, folding herself deeper and deeper into the tapestry of family life until she became so much daughter, sister, aunt, wife and mother that she barely remained an individual at all. She could think no more of Wendy in London or Alison on Myspace, but of snow angels and corn on the cob, exclusively.

In the days that follow, Melina romanticises it all. Petros's talk of names – Panos for a boy, Stella for a girl – and her niece and nephew's fussy eating. She does some baking with them on Christmas Eve, of classic festive cookies. They begin with kourabiédes, all chopped almonds and powdered sugar, and move on to spiced and honey-soaked melomakárona. The first come out hard and send explosions of sugar up from every bite, so that Melina has to go around dusting off the children's faces and the floor. The second are cakier, inviting her teeth to sink in until she has to put them away. Then Petros comes home with two boxes of the same cookies.

"From Agathi," he says.

Melina looks through the plastic window in each box at the cookies, perfectly uniform, and the giggles of the children turn distant in her ears. Soon they will be the giggles of her children, she reminds herself, and for all the cookies in the world, Agathi will be able to give Petros nothing so sweet as that.

"How kind of her," Melina smiles, and pecks her fiancé on the cheek. "Moráki mou . . ."

He her baby and she his baby with a baby of their own, all crawling around in the baby-proof world that they build for themselves. What could go wrong?

They take Andreas and Sofia back to her brother's house, wrapped up ready to go Christmas carolling before the Divine Liturgy of Saint Basil.

"Kalispéra," Melina greets her sister-in-law, with a kiss on each cheek.

"Kalispéra," her sister-in-law returns, jovially.

And for all the world, it is as though they are true friends.

In church that night, as her mouth moves in unison with all the others in the congregation, Melina prays. That she may never wake up from this dream in which she is just like everyone else. That she may be content with the kind of life her friends and neighbours are, and not slide back into wanting something more. Something different. Something wrong.

On Christmas morning, Melina wakes up with a feeling not unlike a hangover, though she barely drank. Her hands tremble. Her head aches. She feels unnerved by the ringing of church bells outside, as though she might have committed some terrible sin and forgotten about it. Slowly, she pulls the blind away from her bedroom window. For once, there are no aeroplanes in sight. Everyone in the western world has woken up where they should be today. Who would think of travelling now, away from their home or family? The church bells ring louder, and Melina releases her blind. It is time to get dressed. The Divine Liturgy, and another day of rounding up children and roasting potatoes and entertaining her in-laws, awaits.

Seventeen

Melina parks her car at Cessac Beach and stumbles away feeling as though she is still inside it, with the world rushing past her ears at high speed. It is the final day of 2004. And what? Another year will commence at midnight, just as it did last year and the one before that. She has visions of smashing a clock against the rocks where she has sat with her fiancé so many times. The planes overhead blur into one. They touch down and turn around and take off again, while bells toll to mark the passing of time and the changing of nothing. In her mind's eye, Melina drives the clock down harder. She walks faster across the bay, her shoulders tense, until the last and most crucial mechanism splinters between her palms.

She pulls up short, catching her breath. The wind twists around her, damp with sea salt and devoid of voices. A dramatic choice, to spend this last and most desolate afternoon here. And what for? When, again, Melina knows that next year will pass just the same way this one has. Unless it does not.

At the end of the bay, Melina climbs the bank to a playground. Shiny, unlike the tattered swing set upon which she and Alison used to burn their palms and scuff their shoes. They giggled and goaded each other, pushing so high off the ground that Melina's stomach soared. She felt herself smiling, maniacally, even as she screamed, convinced that she could go flying as high as the planes if she let go. She went home with her hands calloused from gripping the ropes. And yet she leapt in the car to come back, every day that her mother had cleaning to do.

The new swing set stirs in the wind, eerie with no children in sight. Melina winces at the cold of its chains. Her hip catches, sending the seat spinning out from under her. Years wider, as well as older. With a grimace, she pulls it back. There is a creaking in her left ear before the swing settles under her weight. She digs her hands into her pockets.

Against her knuckles, a brush of paper. Melina draws out a receipt from the petrol station. That was as far as she was supposed to go before bringing the car home ready to drive to Kyriakos's New Year's Eve party. Before failing with makeup and wiping it off, fretting over who else would be there and protesting no problems with anyone, floundering beside her fiancé and faking beat-late laughter. Then, as ever, forcing her eyes from the many wonderful women to whom she could not hold a candle. Not in her shapeless dress, and certainly not across the table in a romantic restaurant.

Melina turns over her receipt and stares at the sheen on its back. It was on this bank, as well as in Alison's bedroom, that she used to squat and write letters – addressed but never delivered – to select boys on the base. Alison told her just what to say.

What had that girl seen at home? It didn't occur to Melina, until much later, to wonder. She had been too caught up in the swelling of her heart and the singing between her legs, too young to comprehend the seriousness of the 'games' they played together, even as she wrote their descriptions in scientific detail.

Now, as she uncaps a tooth-marked pen from the depths of her handbag, Melina asks herself. What is it about Petros? What depraved things does she want him to do to her? The receipt blows up from her lap, and she smooths it back with a trembling hand. She doesn't feel the sparking low in her abdomen that she did when Alison asked similar questions, but high in her chest. A deep breath. Melina loves her fiancé. Why does she love him? Her pen comes shakily to the page.

Ergatikós. Pistós. Storgikós. The words look as flat as a shopping list – items stripped of sentiment – and Melina crosses them out. It is shocking how you can go blind to a person, both their beauty and their blemishes, by looking for a long time at them. You go on knowing the facts, just enough that when people ask, you can answer with what your partner does and where they are from. But step back, ask yourself. Can you say what their day entails, from the time they leave the house to the time they arrive back? Do you know where they have felt 'from' in their bones, since leaving the village where they grew up for the town in which they live with you? If not then you have become complacent, with the presumption that you already know everything there is to know about them. You have stopped asking questions, forgetting, in your naive comfortability, that people are always changing. The closer you stand, the more gradually each shift will appear. You may not even notice it, until someone new points your partner out to be something unrecognisable. Meanwhile, what have you become? This question, always answered with a jolt.

Melina starts a new line, with the first word from her crossing out. Ergatikós, hardworking. This has applied to Petros since she has known him. After school, he studied for hours each day and even tutored his mother, when she was in the mood to let him. He ran a souvláki bar while training to become an electrician and has worked dogged hours since qualifying.

Pistós, loyal, is a word more fitting still. Petros has been loyal to the idea of Melina since before they were a couple. He remains loyal to his mother no matter how many outbursts she has. He is even loyal to Aristos, in a way, holding him to the promises that he broke seven years ago.

Petros was storgikós, affectionate, from that first day on Cessac Beach. Offering his sympathies for Melina's loss – without even knowing the extent of it – and his shoulder for her tears. He is always holding her hand and stroking her hair, making her coffee with all the milk and sugar she likes. He is attentive by instinct. Attuned to her every whim. He is her baby, and she is his baby. Yes, that's what they are, Melina thinks. A couple of tots who have been cooing at each other for so long they haven't noticed themselves shooting up and failing to talk like adults.

Melina ceases to write and finds her fingers frozen stiff. Her pen, too, has dried up at the nib. She puts on the lid, gives it a shake and then doesn't know why. She has finished writing.

The words stare at her, no longer flat but as full of memory as evidence. Accusatory. They are words of love, and yet they do not reassure Melina. Instead, they read like reasons why she doesn't deserve her fiancé. Reasons why she should let him go.

Melina lowers her receipt and sees the truth washing up upon the shore. Its break is violent and leaves her shivering. She was, probably, never in love with Petros. Happy with him, yes. Lucky to have him, certainly. After what she had been through as a child – loving and losing Alison, then learning from church and her mother's response to suppress all feelings around it – she had needed to feel safe. Shielded from the nature of her true self and sure that another partner would not abandon her to it. But, again without noticing the change, Melina has grown clearer-eyed. She sees reflected in the sea, a blaze of blue tossing about on the wind, that the solution Petros offered was for a difficult time. She shouldn't have kept him past his army conscription, when they began saving up for their first apartment. Their commitment had turned material, then. And now, they are bound by common furniture and a decade of photo albums.

How to divide two people, when they have built one life to share? How can one be sure they will get out with all of themselves and not find that the thoughtfulness was never theirs – all those nice gifts for friends, their partner had organised – or that their 'health enthusiasm' had relied on their partner's cooking them wholesome meals? Melina pictures the home she has built with Petros and knows it is not just the CDs or the saucepans that they would have to carve up. There are the sentimental things, too, framed pictures and cards from their many birthdays and name days, anniversaries and Christmases, the pieces of her heart she can never claim back now that she has made them a part of his history.

Peeling her heels up from the ground, Melina pictures leaving Petros. After the panic will come a rush of freedom and then, she predicts, regret. Guilt, too, for Petros has built his life around her. He wouldn't know what to do with himself, any more than she would. Is it right to stay with him, though, just for fear of leaving? Again, Melina looks to her list. She wants to feel the devotion that her fiancé shows her. She should, by every measure accounted for here. And yet she has a sense of him like a hot stone in the hands of her heart, that she goes on holding even as it blisters. Since their engagement, every kindness he's shown her has singed hotter. She deserves this pain, she has chided herself, for failing to pay him the love he has earned.

The wind pushes the swing beside hers and, despite herself, Melina smiles. She is thinking of who else could sit there, tasting salt on her lips as an eleven-year-old question reoccurs to her. Could she be okay forever, in a relationship with someone she did not love as they loved her? From the balls of her feet, she rocks her swing in time with its neighbour. Apparently, no. It is not enough for her just to like and trust a person, after all, with the knowledge that she could be capable of cherishing another. Every day, the void inside Melina echoes louder. She feels it pushing outwards, a ribcage making room for a pregnancy. And what will she deliver, from this period of gestation? She stands up, and the swing hits her thighs. Perhaps nothing so insubstantial, nor so significant, as the notion that she cannot go on just feeling safe. She needs to feel alive.

Melina runs, streaming tears and laughter, along the beach. She gets in her car. She drives to her house. And before she can think for a moment longer about it, she sends Alison a message on Myspace.

Accident Investigation Report

Date: 1 January 2005

Time: 11:20 CST

Aircraft Type: Cessna 551

Operator: Jet Services

Registration: N35403

Occupants: 5

Fatalities: 0

Aircraft Damage: Substantial

Synopsis:

At 08:08 h on 1 January 2005, Cessna 551 N35403 departed Reading Regional Airport, Pennsylvania. At 11:13 h, the aircraft was cleared to approach Runway 17 at Ainsworth Municipal Airport, Nebraska.

The pilot stated that the aircraft began to accumulate ice at approximately 4 000 ft msl. He had "all of the anti-ice and de-icing equipment working", but "at some point the icing conditions became more than the equipment could handle". He had difficulty seeing the runway due to the accumulation of ice on the windscreen and decided to land the aircraft rather than executing the Missed Approach procedure.

The first point of impact was approximately 439 ft north of the approach to Runway 17. The aircraft travelled approximately 18 ft south before contacting an airport access road. It bounced and came down a second time 54 ft south, then slid approximately 700 ft and stopped parallel to a Runway 17 taxiway.

2 of the 5 occupants received minor injuries. The aircraft was substantially damaged.

EIGHTEEN

Wendy's sleeve drags through spilled beer, and she grits her teeth. January was always a grim month in England, with the comedown from Christmas and the many friends and family members at whom she had to smile and nod, knowing that their self-improvement drives would not see the spring. But at least the summer was never much brighter. In Cyprus – working at a seafront bar – Wendy knows what she is missing. Every night that her sweatshirt clings damp to her wrists she feels cheated. This is not what it was supposed to be like here. These are not the conditions that she came for.

The door swings shut after the only customers for an hour, and Wendy saunters out from behind the bar. The music – a Britney Spears song, last year's and too upbeat for the weather – plays through overhead speakers, showing up the room's stillness. Red-and-green paperchains hang from the walls where the manager – a stubby, balding man with a froglike voice and a cigar-fried cackle – insists they must until the sixth of January. Wendy pulls at one as she walks past, and it sags from her touch with a sigh. The couple just gone were only here forty minutes, him nursing a pint and her stirring the plastic straw around her gin and tonic. She didn't finish it. Wendy lifts the drink onto a tray. The glass is too cold, its contents too warm, to have made for anything but the kind of joyless drinking experience that is true to this time of year, when you have overdone it and run out of excuses.

Dumping her tray by the kitchen sink – Tang will deal with it, after her cigarette – Wendy resumes her place behind the bar. Her heart sinks. This shift may not end as soon as she had hoped. The door is swinging shut again, this time after the entry of a man who could be aged anywhere between forty and seventy-five. He is a slab of a person, with a sheen over his ruddy cheeks. He takes a seat at the end of the bar, and Wendy's mind winces back to the boys who sat there on Independence Day. Unnerved, she edges closer.

"*Geiá sas* . . ."

The man fixes her with bloodshot eyes.

"*Píneis?*" she musters, still not convinced that her colleagues aren't having her on with this Greek word for 'you drink'.

He raises an eyebrow. "*Vy ne dolzhny.*"

She falters.

"It's okay," he translates, from a more lilting language. "You don't have to."

"Oh," she starts. "I thought . . ."

"*Vy ne Russky?* You're not Russian?"

"No," she says. Then, since 'English' and 'British' have become dirty words, "I'm from London."

"London," the man repeats, with a detached fondness. He looks at her, beady-eyed. "You tricked me."

Wendy gives him a coy smile. There are two kinds of Russian in Cyprus, she has learned. The kind that will come bounding towards her from behind a makeup counter, before slumping to discover that her soft-hued features are from elsewhere and she just wants a new eyeliner. And the kind with money – slower moving, always male – that seems equal parts entitled and loathe to address her at all.

"Sorry," she says, taking this man for the latter, "to disappoint."

"London cannot disappoint," he declares, with an assurance that could be profound or simply the outcome of limited English. "Too many galleries."

Laughter bubbles from Wendy's lips.

"I'm an artist," she says.

"You?" The Russian flicks his eyes, from the shelves of spirits at her back to the logo stamped on her sweatshirt. "So, I should not order drink from you. You do not work in bar."

Her hand turns stiff on her heart, and he lets out a bark of amusement.

"Well. Larnaca isn't exactly London," her ego protests, through a taut smile. "I don't know how long you've been here, but . . ."

"Thirteen years," the Russian says. "Since end of USSR."

Wendy nods, no longer able to think past the sketchbook that has been collecting dust on her bedside table, or the fact that all the ink on her arms has been tattooed there, for months. She feels the flat-chestedness under her sweatshirt, acutely, as the Russian turns his gaze.

"So, *pineis*?" she repeats, with a sniff.

"What?"

She gestures towards the taps, silver and fogged with the cold.

"*Pineis*? Do you want a drink?" She rolls her eyes. "My Greek . . ."

"I told you, don't do this," the Russian says. "I will have vodka."

"Wow. That bad, am I?" Wendy returns, reaching up for the Absolut.

"You don't have chilled?"

"No."

He grimaces, and she uncaps the bottle. She is feeling vindictive now, with the spiking that comes to her chest when she thinks she has already failed and might as well do so spectacularly. Go home with a story, if not a success. Eyeing the Russian, she reaches under the bar for a glass.

"I don't speak," he says.

It hits the wood and resounds.

"Greek? After thirteen years? You must speak some," Wendy says.

He extends two fingers. "Smaller glass."

At his instruction, she exchanges the tall, thin vessel that her old countrymen would have topped up with ice and Coke, for one the size of a thimble.

Then insists, "You're being modest."

"No, I don't speak. I don't need. You don't either, with English." He makes a small, circular motion, his hand as flat as a paddle, before taking his drink.

Wendy watches him knock it back, the smell of vodka grazing her nostrils. It is not uniquely English, then, to live in Cyprus and never learn Greek. Not impossible to get by.

As the Russian purses his lips, Wendy recalls the boy who made to spit at her on Independence Day. She had wanted to shout, then. To ask, didn't he think that she'd like to pick up a second language? Effortlessly, like a book whose pages she could strum on a sun-soaked blanket? To be a young woman about Europe, slotting into Venetian *piazzas* and French *boulangeries*, and leaving each city with her tongue seasoned in that much more than just the food? Of course. Who wouldn't want to live in such a romantic image? But having English – the world's lingua franca – for her first language means that Wendy will never face a true sink-or-swim encounter with a second. Whenever she runs out of the Greek that she has learned in the last few weeks – shortly after 'hello, I'm well' – whoever she is talking to switches, without blinking, to English. They prevent her from persevering, by relieving her of any need to.

"I guess there are other ways to engage with a culture," she says, feeling as warm to this idea as though she is the one necking vodka. Ways that are easier and more interesting to her, personally. "Like exploring its art." She smiles.

The Russian scrunches his nose. "Here? Not much to explore."

The door swings open for Alex, one of Wendy's only Cypriot colleagues, and she flushes hot.

"I've seen some decent stuff," she says. Then, as he goes into the kitchen, "Just not very much of it. I mean, Cyprus is a small place, so . . ." She glances over her shoulder.

When she turns back, the Russian is pushing his shot glass at her.

"I am from Saint Petersburg. I have connections with collectors in the Ukraine and Czechoslovakia. Or Czech Republic," he corrects himself, with a smirk, "okay."

Wendy refills his glass, just as a t.A.T.u. song starts overhead.

"They have one painter here, not trained but quite famous," the Russian concedes, reaching into his pocket. "I bought this . . ."

He flips open his phone to show her a photo of a painting. The screen is small and the image dark, so she must lean close to inspect it. Her heart trembles. A precious sensation, and one that she hasn't felt moved to for months.

"Ten thousand pound," the Russian reveals.

"Wow," Wendy murmurs.

"Mmn. It is unskilled, for this," he says.

And yet she gazes on, transfixed by the painting. With so many pockets of action, it is like a tapestry bundled up. The scenes of a play showing all at once, without competing for centre stage. Watching them, Wendy feels privy to something more like a backstage rehearsal, an intimate display unlike any that she could see in a crowded theatre.

The Russian withdraws his phone.

"Who's the artist?" Wendy asks.

"Michael Kashalos," he says, pocketing the device. Then sneers, "Too much money. I will wait and sell for more."

"I'd like to see it, sometime. In the flesh," Wendy adds, with brighter eyes than she would ever have flashed at this man without knowledge of his cultural worldliness and the flurry it has caused in her chest.

He gives a grim smile, before pushing his glass at her once more. "And for you."

She takes another from under the bar and joins him in downing a shot, the vodka a pleasant burn. Not so hopeless an encounter, after all. Alex re-emerges from the kitchen no sooner than Wendy has finished congratulating herself, and she stashes her glass in her back pocket. Damp sleeves again. No matter. For the first time in months – certainly since she has worked mixing cocktails and not her paints – Wendy feels stirred.

Nineteen

It is only when she is standing in Marios's penthouse, days later, that Wendy realises she doesn't know the Russian's name.

"Well, he never asked for mine."

Her boyfriend is smiling, amusedly, his father looking perplexed.

"But it was a long conversation you had with him."

"Yeah," Wendy says.

Marios's frown deepens, and Aristos waves it off.

"You see, Papá. Wendy doesn't bother herself with silly details," he says.

"A good match for you, then."

She laughs, but Aristos's scoff is incredulous.

"Me?"

The men exchange dark looks. Or is it the light? Straining again, through thick clouds and dust on the balcony doors, to cast the bookshelves in a dreary grey. They run floor-to-ceiling along every wall, leaving no plaster in sight. Marios steps towards one as though into a mirror, its tomes of history and culture – all very important – covering up what lies peeling beneath.

"So, you want something on Kashalos," he says.

"If you've got it."

He has grown older-looking in the months that Wendy has known him, slower to reach out and trace his fingers along the spines. She catches Aristos with his teeth clenched.

"I believe I do, but . . . are you sure?" Marios asks, turning back. "You don't want an artist more . . ." He motions. "Classical? I have books about many others, better educated and more eloquent. From Greece."

Wendy shifts her stance, conscious of Aristos's stillness.

"Yeah? I mean, I'd take a look at those, too. But I'm really interested in Kalashoss."

"Kashalos," he corrects her, quietly.

"Kashalos." She shakes her head. "I keep doing that."

With a nod of 'suit yourself', Marios leaves the room. There is the smell of books – like his age, only woodier – carrying from as far down the hallway as his footsteps. Then of tobacco, as Aristos pulls out a cigarette and Wendy sets to rolling one.

"I don't know how you have the patience," he says, lighting up.

"It's part of the experience, that buildup of anticipation. Of really wanting something," she adds, watching the smoke curl from his lips.

"Is it?"

"Mmn . . ."

They are standing face to face, Aristos wearing the same gratified smirk that he might have last summer, in response to such an allusion, but with less glee in his eyes. Wendy can hardly blame him. She is still walking the walk – taking him in her mouth or between her legs most days – but she, too, has felt less enthused by it, of late. They are losing their novelty to nuance, something she has done well to run from before.

"Anyway," she says, standing back. "I can't see the point in anything I haven't put together myself."

"Ah, yes. Artist's integrity," Aristos grins.

Wendy seals her cigarette. Is this true? Well, why not. She was an art student – at University College London – long enough to learn that you could claim anything had been a part of your creative process, after the fact. Like her classmate Hulda, whose mangled and lopsided hourglass sculpture purported to demonstrate 'the fleeting nature of life'. Hulda said she had made it in a short space of time to reflect this meaning, rather than in her rush to meet the deadline after too many nights spent with a rolled banknote up her nose.

Wendy sat in that class seething, and yet its lesson sank in. The story that accompanied a sculpture – or any art piece – was as important as the piece itself. Wendy announced that she had worked on her own sculpture only at night, in hours as lonely as the isolation that it was meant to represent. Who was to say that her concurrent bout of insomnia had been a coincidence? It struck her as fitting to the point of divine, and so she came to believe that she had not worked on her sculpture because she couldn't sleep, but that she had forgone sleep in order to work on her sculpture.

Lighting her cigarette, she smiles smoke at the ceiling. "You see? Worth the wait."

Her boyfriend is leaning to kiss her when Marios comes blustering back.

"Ariste. What have I told you about smoking in here? Doors open," he says, shunting one wide.

The cold tears inside.

"Papá, it's January–"

"And we keep first editions year-round. Open," Marios repeats, pointing his finger.

Wendy saunters out onto the balcony, a broad rectangular ledge overlooking a park and several other apartments, holding her cigarette down by her side.

"Well, but you don't have to stand out there," Marios starts, after her.

"That's okay," she answers. "It's actually warmer than inside."

Stepping out, he casts a dubious look towards the sun – just breaking through the clouds – before turning to shield what is in his arms.

"What do we have here, then?" Wendy asks, from her pose at the railing.

"Three books," Marios says. He raises the first two in turn. "This one is about Nikos Hadjikyriakos-Ghikas, and this one Yannis Tsarouchis. Both were Greek painters working around the same period as Kashalos, but very well-trained. In Paris and Athens."

Wendy affects a beat of interest in their covers. Then asks, "And that one?"

Resignedly, Marios lifts the third volume. "An encyclopedia of twentieth-century Cypriot artists. Only two or three years old, I believe."

"And it's got stuff on Kalashoss?"

"A biography, some quotes. And pictures of his works."

Tucking the other books under his arm, Marios flips open the encyclopedia. It smells as glossy as it looks, like he has never been through it before.

"Here," he says, presenting a double-page spread of the artist's paintings.

Wendy stops mid-drag on her cigarette. The images daze her with same the wonder that she has been adrift in since her encounter with the Russian. His phone screen, the smallest and most unlikely square of promise, delivered upon in the light of day.

"Papá," Aristos's voice sounds, from inside.

"*Nai?*" With a glance over his shoulder, Marios straightens. "Here. Do you want to . . . ?"

"Oh. Yeah . . ."

He frowns at Wendy's dropping her cigarette, but she is already making a frame of her forearms for the book. A baby, in need of holding just so.

"Thanks," she murmurs, as Marios hands it off.

His words turn obscure, leaving Wendy alone with Kashalos's landscapes. If it weren't for the sun warming her back and the air cooling her cheeks, she is sure she could lose herself. In the gathering of men around his oxen-drawn cart, hefting sacks of wheat. Air of farmyard and sweat. Or in his coffee shop, with one table playing cards and another smoking hookah. Fumes of ground beans and wood. Or in his forest, among people planting lime sticks and plucking feathers from the songbirds caught in their traps. Shocks of twigs snapping and birds ceasing to chirp. Or in his kitchen, with two women frying *loukoumádes* for a third to toss up to some rooftop goblins. Sounds of the former spitting oil and the latter cackling, devilishly.

"The *kallikántzaroi*," Wendy sounds their name out, from the description.

Her tongue does not mould to the word, does not turn liquid and take the shape of its container, and yet her eyes do. They pore over the pictures' corners, as though into the riverbeds of rainy seasons past. Instantly flowing, innately familiar.

And so, the word 'naive' is startling. It strikes Wendy as an unjustly diminishing term for Kashalos as a painter, until she has read enough to see the compliment it pays him. His style is one that cannot be taught. It is born of the absence of tutelage, from the artist's intuition like a single-celled organism. It is immune to falling out of fashion, having arisen from within one person and not from the fads of their surroundings.

'It takes place on an emotional level', Wendy reads, 'rather than an intellectual one'.

She traces her fingertips over this sentence. Barbed, perhaps, coming from an academic. Yet it whispers to Wendy in the way that every one of her favourite artworks does, as though it is meant for her alone. She leans in, for another whiff of the ink-heavy paper and the smoke on her sleeve, and listens. It is just as well that she has struggled with Greek. Like her, these works lack language – the language of further study – and yet they transcend it, too. They meet her in a place where meaning passes without words and sentiment without ceremony, where only the rarest of creations do.

"This is great," Wendy says, carrying the book back inside. "Thanks."

As ever, her sincerity comes out sounding pinched – it draws a sharp look from Aristos – and she stashes it away without meeting his eye.

"You're welcome," Marios responds, apparently no keener to dwell.

The men are bending over a file. Back to speaking their native tongue, which Wendy felt unmoved towards in her first months here, hyperaware of when that boy in the bar turned aggressive, and aggrieved by as she tried and failed to learn it. Now, she feels restored to a sort of acceptance, knowing that she has found her own path into the local landscape.

Wendy looks down at the book in her arms, heavy and vivid with colour. It is astounding to her that its owner has so little interest in what she might want with it. Her boyfriend, too, remains incurious as to what she is painting, if he cares that she is painting at all. She stares at his head and cannot help but see her ex, Yvonne's, ever bent over her sketchbook or between her legs. Curtained with sensible hair and crammed with knowledge of art history, as well as firm ideas about how everything else 'should' be. Yvonne was ten years Wendy's senior.

Wendy feels a pang as she recalls their first meeting, at an art auction in Saint James's. She had gone merely to spectate, being twenty-two and unemployed. She was living in an overcrowded apartment at the time, drinking and smoking away her money only to stoop for the notices that slid in under the door and think oh, so this was how it felt to miss rent. Aside from her parents' divorce – which had been far more amicable than she let on – Wendy had known none of the hardships that had rendered her fellow undergraduates' works so 'probing' and impressive to their professors. She was accumulating the experiences that she needed to be a good artist, she told herself, along with lots of tattoos and piercings. But by the time of the auction, the novelty had worn off this phase of her life – as it had so many others, from her mother's house to her father's and back, time and again – and she was painting less and less.

Drunk on cheap wine, she confessed to a woman at the drinks table.

"Well, maybe you're the canvas right now," the woman suggested, with a wry smile. "You're your own masterpiece."

"Finally," Wendy snorted, "someone gets me."

She went home with Yvonne that night.

The sun slips back behind the clouds, casting Wendy into the shade of something not unlike wistfulness. Yvonne was only an amateur potter, but she worked as a museum curator, too. She knew what artists needed – time and space – and could supply those things to Wendy, free of charge. Or so she said.

That excessive support hadn't helped things, either, Wendy reminds herself, as her boyfriend talks on without her. It is only in contrast to his behaviour that she is glorifying Yvonne's. In reality, her creative resurgence didn't last a year of living in Hampstead, with the constant questions about her projects and her progress while there was no real pressure on her to complete any of them. Yvonne was too smitten to push her for rent or risk disturbing her hallowed 'process', and now she is a part of Wendy's history. A point to which Wendy will compare all future partners, inevitably.

With a sigh, Wendy turns the page to Kashalos's biography. She curses the past – not just her own but the past as an entity, life's cruel insistence on chronology – and its tempting her to look back in longing. A lie. She tries to focus on reading, 'emphasis on detail', 'meticulous narration', 'multiplicity of plot', until her eyes catch on the phrase, 'absence of perspective'. She looks back at the double-page spread of Kashalos's paintings, the people in them above rather than behind one another, and sees. He removes the perspective of distance. What if she did the same thing with time? Stripped the past of its power to overshadow her present, by painting scenes from her life out of order? Struck by the thought of Aristos and Yvonne alongside each other – for the first time since they all met – she snaps the book shut.

"Everything okay?" Aristos asks, looking up.

"Yeah, good. Fine. I'll leave you guys to work," Wendy says, with a parting nod to Marios.

And she steals from the penthouse, breathless with the beginnings of an idea and the book that has inspired it in hand.

TWENTY

An hour past closing time, Wendy has had more to drink than any of her colleagues and remains the most sober among them. A badge of honour, and a bore. She rubs at the fog on her vodka-martini glass. Behind the bar, Evangelia – twenty years old, cute-looking, in Cyprus to study forestry – stands with a knife and a maniacal grin.

"What?" Alex asks her.

"I said, for my next experiment . . ." Evangelia descends into laughter again.

"Crazy girl," Tang chuckles, from her seat in the corner.

Craning around in his, Alex asks the same question – Wendy presumes – in Greek.

Evangelia recovers herself. She answers him in the higher-pitched, more nasal-sounding Greek that is, allegedly, particular to Thessalonians. Wendy can't hear much distinction, only the bright notes in her colleagues' voices as they talk to one another. She averts her gaze. She has never liked girls like Evangelia, who splash around so loudly at the surface-end of conversation that there is no getting to the depths. Somehow, they make Wendy feel both superior and drab, with her impatience for all but a few, profound things.

"Okay, look. *Paidiá*, guys," Evangelia perseveres. "I am saying, for my next experiment, I will do ouzo, rum and Cointreau."

"No mixers?" Alex asks.

"No mixers," Evangelia declares, bringing her knife down on an orange.

Alex shakes his head.

"She's crazy!" Tang chortles, again.

Wendy shoots a smile at the woman, four thousand miles from her native Beijing, who seldom comes out of the kitchen even when there are no glasses to wash. She is easily pleased and overly grateful. Inoffensive, Wendy decides, and just as uninteresting.

While her colleagues go on indulging the performance behind the bar, Wendy looks at the tables, wiped down ready for another day. The room is dim-lit and threaded through with some plucky Greek folk music that Evangelia calls '*laikó*'. Even as she raises her arms and jolts around full circle with her feet pressed together, there is a taut atmosphere. A disquiet to being here after shutters down, like setting up camp in an abandoned house.

Wendy looks over her shoulder, to see a figure standing outside. Grisha, for the third time tonight. How does she keep missing her colleague leave? Slipping past Alex, who has joined Evangelia in clicking his fingers and tapping his toes, she retrieves some vodka from the freezer where she has been keeping it for her art-collecting acquaintance. Nikita, as she now knows him. And, just as she does when he stops by, Wendy fills two shot glasses.

"Cheers," she says, carrying them out to her colleague.

Grisha startles, mid-drag on his cigarette, before exhaling and accepting a drink. "Thanks."

They clink glasses, and Wendy drains hers in a rush for its warmth.

"Nice," Grisha says.

"Mmn, I'm starting to like it," she responds, pulling her hands deeper inside her sleeves. "But you know that smoking ban hasn't come in yet?"

"Here?" He pulls a face. "It will never."

"Well, no. Maybe not," she concedes, recalling her whereabouts.

Coalsmoke on the air. City lights on the sea.

"And yet you're standing outside."

Grisha snickers. "I know. It just doesn't feel the same to me," he gestures, cigarette dangerously low to his fingertips, "the burn without the cold."

"Contrast," Wendy says, her thoughts thrown back to her project – they are never far off, in the early stages – of disarming time. Doing away with comparisons, of the past to the present. Fire to ice.

"Exactly," Grisha says. "That, or I miss *Rossiya*."

"Yeah, right," Wendy scoffs, for his constant complaints of corruption and jingoism. She puts her glass on the kerb and says in jest, as only one foreigner can to another, "Go back, then."

"That, I will never do."

She looks at him, backlit by the bar. They are both twenty-four, and yet his pale eyes are deep-set with having seen enough of the world, his cheeks as hollow as if desperate hands had scrabbled and dug them out.

"I told you, it's a terrible place."

"Nikita doesn't think so."

"Nikita," Grisha sneers, tossing his cigarette end.

It barely misses Wendy's glass.

"Nikita is not from the *Rossiya* I am," Grisha says, all trace of his amusement gone. "What does he tell you about, the magnificent galleries? Do you think he goes by foot to any of them, and sees the street crime? Or by *metro*, and sees the dirt?" He shakes his head. "I don't know why you like him so much."

"Like is a strong word," Wendy says. She takes a cigarette – rolled during Evangelia's performance – from behind her ear. "He's someone I can talk to about art, and I haven't found a massive scene here. Nothing like where I was, in London . . ."

"Then why did you leave?"

A flame blooms from her lighter, then gives way to the darkness.

"What?"

"Forgive me," Grisha says, placing his glass beside hers. "I don't know your life. But I think, what's the point in moving forwards if you're just going to look back?"

"No, I agree," Wendy says, exhaling smoke.

She holds still as it dissipates, overcome again with a sense of magnetism between his words and her work. A conviction that if she just waits, she will get something stimulative out of him.

Indeed, Grisha takes a breath of the cool air – sea salt and pine trees and car exhaust and barbeque fumes – and tells her. As a child, his mother had been a ballet dancer. A promising one, *en pointe* by age seven and prancing around in them day and night. Then, eleven years old and set to start at Saint Petersburg's prestigious Vaganova Academy, she had lost her place over the findings of their medical exam. Her ankles were too big for the frames of her feet. Determined, she had gone to an unspecialised school and carried on dancing around the problem. Until age fifteen, when she had suffered excruciating pain and received a diagnosis of secondary arthritis in her left big toe.

"Age fifteen?" Wendy repeats.

"Early onset, from the pointes," Grisha confirms.

"Oh my god."

"Yeah, it was pretty awful. She had to have an operation that meant she could never dance again."

Smoke drifts from between Wendy's fingers.

"Wait. Why do I think . . . Have you talked about doing ballet before?"

"Yep." Grisha raises his eyebrows. "And now you know why."

"Oh."

"Mmn."

"Your mum was living vicariously."

"Big time."

Grisha didn't want to dance, he says, especially once he reached secondary school and other boys started sneering, calling him gay and a girl. Little did they know that because of his close relations to the girls at ballet, he was getting more action than any of them. This makes Wendy laugh. Unfortunately, it was also because of those close relations that Grisha picked up an eating disorder. So much pressure on ballerinas to be thin, and fierce competition behind the scenes of their rehearsal days over who could go the longest eating the least. It was in the air of every mirrored studio and decorated theatre, a poison impossible not to succumb to.

"So, that's why I never see you eat."

Wendy sighs, relieved to know that it is not judgement but jealousy with which her colleague has eyed her when she has accepted a meal from the kitchen, and he has not. She is conscious that people assume a food issue from her knobbly elbows and knees, and feels a strange sense of letting them down when she reveals her healthy appetite. Resents people like Grisha for showing it up.

He is better now, he assures her. He just needs to do his eating at home, where he feels best equipped to. And stay away from Russia, the ballet and his maddened mother, who would have gone on pushing him – long after his second hospital stint – to pursue her dream. She had put her heart into dance and left not a piece of it for him.

"I'm sorry," Wendy says, dropping her cigarette.

Meanwhile, its ash has caught alight in her chest. In sharing his sadness, Grisha has granted her passage to a new plain of the human experience. A feeling like lust, hot and heady. And yet, free of her cigarette, Wendy finds that it isn't him she wants to wrap her hand around so much as a paintbrush.

There is a crash inside the bar, followed by hoots and squeals. Wendy exchanges looks with her colleague. It isn't that she wants to paint him, exactly – though she can imagine sweeping her brush in arcs like a ballerina's arms overhead and twisting it into knots at the roots of a piece – but she wants to paint something. Just as she wants to throw herself open to sex after a good day's painting. They feed one another, infatuation and inspiration. They come with the same expansive feeling that is, at its best, enlivening. And at its worst – in the hours that Wendy must spend away from her person or her painting – a death.

Wendy feels dangerous with it, like she is cheating on Aristos just by having this conversation. Low-voiced and in darkness, about the wounds of so long ago and faraway that they are enshrined in their own lore. She had forgotten how much she needed connection like this, creatively. She had left her sketchbook to lie alone. She feels a great upswelling of love for Grisha as she decides, no longer.

"So, okay. No, I don't miss *Rossiya*," Grisha concludes, as their colleagues quieten down. "Just the cold, sometimes."

Wendy affects a shiver, and he shrugs.

"We want what we know."

"Speak for yourself," she snorts. "I don't want what I know."

"The rain?"

"Yeah. Fuck that," she says.

Grisha smiles, and Wendy delights in her discovery of his dimples. New people allow her to be innovative. Merely by meeting her, they restore her to a blank-canvas state, unspattered by history. Wendy has tried to preserve this in her relationship with Aristos by not getting to know him too well – perhaps an overcorrection, after Yvonne – but still. Aristos has nothing on the unknown of Grisha. Grisha who is stooping for their shot glasses, as elegantly as though in arabesque. Grisha whose touch sends shockwaves through Wendy as he passes hers back. Grisha who Wendy will not paint in so many brushstrokes, because she doesn't paint anyone that way. She paints about how it feels to know them. To know herself all over again.

"We should probably get back inside," Grisha says.

"Yeah, to thaw out."

He rolls his eyes, pulling open the door. The *laikó* music has given way to hip hop, and their colleagues are lining up shots.

"Hey!" Evangelia calls out, in greeting.

As she follows Grisha inside, Wendy glimpses a decades-younger Nikita and feels a pulse between her legs. She blinks and her colleague is himself again, though it is all coalescing in Wendy's head. She is romanticising Russianness, in her newfound inspiration, as though it is art itself. Wondering whether she shouldn't say that she, too, is from Saint Petersburg, the next time someone asks.

"Cheers," Grisha says, this time passing her a shot.

"Cheers."

They touch glasses, and Wendy knocks hers back in one motion.

TWENTY-ONE

ART IS A PETTY friend, not content to 'pick up where they left off' when Wendy calls for the first time in months. It demands her attention, constantly. She opens her sketchbook to a double-page spread of past works, and it leaves her to wonder. When was she capable of such brilliance, and how can she achieve it again?

With no messages to respond to, Wendy slides the keyboard back behind her phone screen. Through her living-room window, she watches a plane descending from the blue sky towards Larnaca Airport, and casts back to the day that hers touched down. Nine months ago. She can't recall thinking, then, that she would stay here so long. Only that she needed to come.

Wendy forces herself on through her sketchbook, a gift from Yvonne towards the end of their time together. On the early pages are long, laboured lines. Then the short, breathless kind that came of her meeting Aristos. The radiance of Cyprus, in the corridors of light through her shading.

These drawings are good – they smell as woody as the pine trees outside – and yet Wendy can see less of her heart in each one. For her, novelty left Cyprus with the spring. August rendered her world as small as the distance she could stand to walk in its forty-degree heat. And it changed Aristos. After Athens, their game of emotional hide and seek turned from teasing to sinister. Wendy sensed that he was no longer playing with her but against her, no longer the parent looking, indulgently, under the table before addressing the bulge of their child behind the curtains, but the one leaving them there. Counting to one hundred with no intention of coming to look.

Wendy turns the page from her last surreal picture to a series of literal renditions – of Finikoudes Beach and Larnaca's Medieval Castle – unlike her usual style. They aren't bad. They just don't say anything of their own. They repeat after their subjects in the straightforward terms that even unartistic people could understand. People like Aristos, Wendy thinks. And she wonders whether she hadn't wanted him to know her better, after all.

She takes a breath. Slides the keyboard out from her phone. Toys with the thought of texting Grisha before sitting back in her butterfly chair. Arriving at a blank page, she watches it settle like a fresh bedsheet.

'TIME, UNCHRONICLED', she scrawls.

The words stare at her.

Wendy's phone rings, scattering the silence.

"Mum," she breathes, snatching it up. "Hi."

"Hello, darling," her mother's voice drawls, into her ear. "How are you?"

"Fine, thanks. You?"

"I'm well, thank you, yes. It's been a while."

"Yeah," Wendy realises, aloud. She lowers her pencil. "Sorry, I have been meaning to call. I've just been busy."

"So your father tells me."

"You talked to Dad?"

"Only briefly," her mother says. "When he called to wish Granny a happy birthday . . ."

"Oh, shit . . ."

"She would have liked to hear from you."

"Yeah," Wendy says, through a grimace. "I'll call her."

"Will you?"

"I will." She fingers a corner of her page. "I'll do it tonight."

"Make sure you apologise," her mother instructs her.

As gratingly as ever, Wendy thinks. Suddenly, she is holding her phone not with relief but regret, and the art that she couldn't wait to get away from, a moment ago, is all she wants to focus on. She picks up her pencil.

"We had a nice time celebrating, anyway . . ."

With her mother droning on in her ear – distracting her from her work just enough that she can face it – Wendy sketches. A suitcase falling upon a child, from inside the heart that a man and woman have torn in half overhead. In truth, their divorce was painless. A seatbelt coming unclicked before Wendy noticed that the car had stopped moving. By then, her mother was lifting her out into a Dulwich townhouse, and her father was booking her tickets to whichever film or theme park she wanted every other weekend.

On the next page, Wendy outlines her university experience. Solitary, while her fellow fine art students thronged together. All those more talented than her, she resented. Anyone less so, she ridiculed. She draws knives in the backs of her more sociable classmates, certain that London had rendered them just as competitive, really, with its vibrant and oversaturated 'scene'.

Of course, Wendy had other friends – her old roommates and a handful of secondary-school pals – but she hasn't called them since she left England. She looks back at her depiction of the divorce which, despite her teenaged efforts to discover otherwise, had been entirely peaceful. Her parents had spent years saying, simply, that 'life was in chapters', setting her up to form no lasting attachments. People drift in and out of Wendy's life as is convenient. Sometimes, they drift back after months or years, and their greetings come to her as though through the fog of a dreamscape.

"Oh, yes. You," she feels like smiling, vaguely.

Though she has rarely missed them. It is only art that comes with her through every chapter, the narrative voice that defines her whole story.

"It sounds like you've made nice friends out there," her mother goes on.

Grisha's high cheekbones flash through Wendy's head.

"I've got some nice colleagues, yeah," she says. "And I think I told you, I'm the maid of honour at this girl Melina's wedding? So, we're doing a lot of stuff around that."

"You mentioned, yes. That's amazing. I can't believe how believe how quickly you've settled in."

"Yeah," Wendy murmurs. "I mean, I don't think she had a lot of friends before. Apart from Arty, it seems like they were close . . ."

"How is Arty?"

"He's good," Wendy says.

She is onto another outline, of the time she spent sub-letting. Sleeping with two of her – too many – roommates, drinking and smoking to excess, all parts of her drive to gain life experience. She draws as many piercing and tattoo guns sticking into her as though they are acupuncture needles, and the paintbrush in her hand turned onto herself.

"Maybe you're the canvas right now . . ."

Yvonne's words, spoken truer than she knew. Wendy does become the canvas, in periods of disconnect from her painting. Without the creative outlet that turns her brooding, she is restless. She picks fights with her friends. She cheats on her partners. She swings from joy to despair, wildly enough that she could jump off a bridge in either state. An introvert turned outwards, she suffers disastrous consequences. She needs to stand back and observe the world, or she will exist too much within it.

Wendy draws, in sharp lines, Yvonne's stifling of her creativity. She draws herself, wild-eyed, in her search elsewhere for inspiration.

"Like I said, I don't date many bi girls." Part confession, part warning. Yvonne had a knack for being vulnerable and threatening at the same time.

Wendy sketches the cogs that she felt turning behind her eyes as she supposed that was what she was. A bi girl. Huh. She goes back and illustrates her first night with Yvonne, the bursts of elation she had felt as she had moved her body in so many new ways.

Then, another sex scene. Their final one together. They had been fighting for weeks, Wendy too far untethered from her painting to care how savagely. Desperate and drunk on red wine, Yvonne brought into their bedroom a third party from the pottery class that she taught on Monday nights. Wendy can still taste the crimson on her lips. She sits back from her sketchbook, overcome with the desire that both Yvonne and Aristos – before Wendy knew his name – had shown for her. She had desired only the experience and found an ecstasy in her detachment. In the moment, she saw none of Yvonne's last-ditch effort or Aristos's stroke of luck. Only legs, tangled together. Hands, everywhere. Then her new boyfriend flying her away, to Cyprus.

Wendy roughs out the three boys who cornered her on Independence Day, making her eyes unshaded and wide, and theirs dark and narrowed at her. Not a popular choice, perhaps, to say that she has experienced racial abuse as a white person. But it is the most shocking thing that has ever happened to her. A tangle of tongues to show her struggle with Greek, and an extension of the eloquent ballerinas' arms that have invited her – far more graciously – towards the Russian influence.

"Good," her mother says, with a sigh. "Well, I'm glad it's all going so well for you."

"Thanks, yeah."

Wendy sits back from her sketchbook, and her heart thuds.

"I should probably go," she says.

"Okay, darling," her mother responds. "Just make sure you call Granny, won't you?"

"Yeah . . ."

"Take care . . ."

Wendy gets off the phone to find the sun lower in the sky. A good sign for her work, she thinks, until she comes back from turning on the light and sees. The work is terrible. She has tried to put her own, surreal spin on scenes that look like Michael Kashalos's – exaggerated objects in human hands – and the effect is cartoonish. Will the pictures look better painted, in bold colours? She cocks her head and, finding no comfort in reminding herself that these were only meant to be rough drafts, cocks it back.

At once, all the inspiration that she had derived – from discovering Kashalos and connecting with Grisha – makes Wendy feel foolish. For weeks, she has nursed not just the idea of stripping time's perspective from her work, but the idea that this idea was ingenious. It is ingenious – Wendy still believes that – despite her poor execution. She can hear the speech with which she would introduce *Time, Unchronicled*, about her desire to stop the past from hanging over her relationship with Aristos and her experience as a British immigrant to a former colony. It is the most profound concept she has ever come up with.

As she pours over her drawings, Wendy sways from thinking that they are not good enough to fearing that they are too good. Unlike Kashalos, she studied art for years. She cannot affect the 'naivety' for which he is renowned.

With a thud, Wendy drops her sketchbook facedown on the coffee table. She huffs and paces, becoming more agitated with every aeroplane that flies past her window, as though she has someplace to be and no means of getting there. She fills the kettle and stops it halfway to boiling when its roaring, against the drone of an engine, becomes too much. She thinks of calling Melina but can't face saying that she is well, thanks, or admitting that she is not. Like a shot, she throws back her tepid coffee, and turns off the light to watch the sun sink.

By the time Aristos arrives home, it is dark. Approaching planes have been reduced to their strobe lights, and Wendy to a gargoyle in her butterfly chair. Her boyfriend restores the ceiling light, and she blinks.

"Ah. Hey," he says.

"You're late."

"Not very, am I?"

She watches him lower his briefcase and look everywhere but at her.

"No, not very." She crosses her legs. "Long day?"

"Yeah. We had a nightmare with one of our Islington properties over the weekend. The management company sent someone out to fix a leak, but the tenants say the problem is still there. They're worried the ceiling is going to collapse. And Papá, these days . . ." Aristos shakes his head. "He just can't handle what he used to."

"And then?" Wendy says.

Stepping out of his dress shoes, her boyfriend looks up at her.

"I stopped by to see Agathi," he admits. "Just briefly, on my way home . . ."

Wendy turns her head, a whipcrack motion that leaves him red-faced.

"You haven't had enough closure, yet?" she asks him, quietly.

"I . . ." He falters, visibly, before his panic falls away. "No, actually. I haven't."

She scoffs.

"Agathi and I were together for four years."

"Right. And then you broke up."

"But that time still matters," Aristos insists. "It was almost half a decade of my life. I don't expect you to understand, but—"

"Oh, because I've never had a past relationship. Or not one that I'm allowed to talk about," Wendy sneers, with her sketchbook glaring up at her. "For some reason, I just have to sit back while you rekindle yours."

"I am not rekindling anything. Wendy," Aristos says, running his hands through his hair. He lowers them. "Maybe that's your problem, too much sitting back. You're winding yourself up with these ideas that aren't even based on anything. I ended a long relationship with Agathi overnight, and I'm in the process of setting that straight with her. I advised you to think carefully about sharing, you know, your history—"

"You can use her name, Arty. It didn't bother you when you were fucking her."

"Fine. Yvonne," he says, through gritted teeth. "I advised you—"

"Told me."

"– to think carefully about sharing your history with Yvonne here, because it's not like London. You've seen how religious my parents are. I wanted to protect you," Aristos says. "The fact that you'd think otherwise . . ."

Wendy stands to face him.

"Maybe you need more friends here than just Melina. And more to do than working in that bar."

"I do have more friends here than just Melina," Wendy says, the wind of her late-night talks with Grisha in her sails. "And I've spent all afternoon sketching."

"You have?"

"Yes."

For the first time, Aristos's eyes go to her sketchbook. Wendy considers showing him her work as a means to stepping closer, making up. Then she recalls how awful it is, and their fight recovers its succulence.

"Obviously, I'd have been able to concentrate better if I wasn't worried that my boyfriend was out cheating on me."

This is cheap, and she knows it. Good as it feels to blame Aristos for her failure today, Wendy cannot accuse him of being more distant now than he ever was. They hadn't bared their souls to each other, even before his reconnecting with Agathi. It just hadn't bothered Wendy in the early days, when all their lust and late-night whispers had still been inspiring to her. She'd had her art to focus on.

"That's a big accusation," Aristos says.

But he doesn't deny it. He turns on his heel, and she watches him walk away.

TWENTY-TWO

Then, because she feels she is losing her hold and this renders him sort of new again – a figure in the shadowland between hers and not hers that precedes both the beginning and end of a relationship – Wendy finds herself obsessed with Aristos.

"Does he know you're doing this?" Melina asks, as they come to a halt outside a tattoo shop.

"No. It's a surprise," Wendy grins.

Melina gives a head-shaking chuckle like a bakery door tinkling open, and Wendy urges her forwards.

Of course, there is no such sound as they enter the shop. Just the mosquito-like buzzing of a tattoo artist at work, which gives way to the drone of heavy metal as he lowers his gun. He saunters over – long hair, Slipknot tee – and a thick forearm falls limp in his wake.

"Hi," Wendy says, before she recalls that the needle trays and body-jewellery cases, however familiar, do not mean home turf.

She looks sideways to find Melina taken up with the butterfly-and-flower designs displayed on boards overhead.

"Hi," she repeats. "*Eímai apó* . . . Erm . . ."

"*Nai*," the tattoo artist says. He nods a second later, as though she has said something more. "I speak English. Tell me."

"Oh. Thanks." Wendy shoots him a smile. "I'd like to get a tattoo."

"Just you?"

"Yeah."

Another glance confirms it. Melina is uneasy, biting her lip and wrinkling her nose at the disinfectant-wipe smell of the place, as though it belongs to a morgue. It is cold enough, with the air conditioning on full blast.

Wendy draws a scrap of paper from her pocket. "This is what I was thinking."

The tattoo artist takes it.

"You drew this?" he asks, looking up with wide eyes.

"Yeah."

"It's good."

"*Eínai kallitéchnis*," Melina chips in.

"*Nai*?" the tattoo artist says. Then, to Wendy, "You're an artist?"

"Well." She shrugs.

"A modest one," Melina says.

The tattoo artist laughs, and Wendy re-examines her friend. She hasn't seen Melina so relaxed around any of the women who have cooed over her engagement ring or pitched her wedding-flower arrangements. She might appear out of place in this monochrome shop, with her soft lashes and unblemished skin. But she is settling in by the minute.

"Let me see," she says, as the tattoo artist returns to his other customer.

"Ten minutes," he calls, resuming his work.

With the static of the gun sounding, Melina leans close enough that Wendy can smell her shampoo – sweet as honey – for the first time, and marvel at the fact that they are planning a wedding together. How involved two people can get, before they have been intimate at all.

"It's a bold statement," Melina says, looking up from Wendy's drawing. "Are you sure . . . ?"

"I mean, yeah. It is a statement, but only as long as I want it to be," Wendy reminds her. "'Arty' isn't just his name. The word applies to me as well, so if we break up . . ."

"You'll say it's because you're an artist."

"Exactly."

They share a laugh, Wendy struck by Melina's expansiveness. With no time spent sketching since her last attempt, Wendy has found outlets for her own creative energy in her experiments with new eyeliner techniques, her designing of this next tattoo – the word 'Arty', in licks of paint from a brush at the 'y' – and an alarming number of masturbation sessions. She feels yet another buzz between her legs as the tattoo gun falls silent, its vibration echoing through her body. The drive of the needle to come, irrefutably erotic.

At a hoot of approval from his other customer, the tattoo artist dabs clean and bandages the man's forearm. They approach the till, talking payment and aftercare, while Wendy and Melina stand aside.

"It's warmer out there," Melina says, shivering in her thin jumper.

Wendy, too, is wearing fewer layers than she has all winter. It is March, and she had so wanted to believe in the promise of the sun on her balcony this morning.

With his other customer gone, the tattoo artist says something in Greek.

"Ah," Melina responds, unclasping her arms.

She asks a follow-up question and starts to translate his answer, but Wendy stops her.

"He said it stops the tattoos from bleeding so much, right? The cold," she says.

Melina looks awed. "Yes. Hey, your Greek – *ta Elliniká sou* – are getting good!"

"No," Wendy scoffs. "I just know some stuff about tattoos, believe it or not."

She lifts her sleeve to show the thorny black roses blooming up her left arm, and Melina laughs.

"Of course . . ."

Her hair falls around her face. With a new looseness, Wendy thinks. Or perhaps she is projecting her own.

"I should be painting," she admits, as she gives the tattoo artist her passport and signs his paperwork.

There is only the faintest trace of guilt in her voice, for she knows. This is part of the process. She cannot manage the works of *Time, Unchronicled* yet, any better than she could their first outlines. She needs more inspiration from out in the world – where half of every great painting happens – to compel her back towards the canvas. A scar in the name of Aristos, to inspirit her the way that bonding with Grisha had.

"But," she starts.

And stops, mid-shrug. Melina isn't listening. She is standing over a book, with a page pinched between her finger and thumb.

"Okay," the tattoo artist says, taking Wendy's design. "I'll take this to make a stencil. If you want to sit down over there—"

"*Perímene*," Melina says. She almost drops the book, rushing it over to him. "Will you do this one, too? For me?"

"Are you sure?" Wendy asks her.

The tattoo artist looks up, from Wendy to Melina.

"Yes," Melina insists.

Even as she pushes the book at him, Wendy cannot help but think that Melina is too gentle to be pierced by a needle. Too soon to be wed – to her conservative fiancé in her pure white dress – for the stain of black ink.

"What about Petros?"

"This isn't about Petros," Melina says, looking back at her. "This is for me."

"Great," Wendy drawls, in the hollow beat between songs. "More reason for him to love me."

Melina laughs, her seriousness scattered by the drums of a System Of A Down intro. The tattoo artist swaggers off to ready their stencils, and they sit in chairs opposite the till.

"Oh. I didn't see what you asked for," Wendy realises, aloud.

Melina smiles. "Maybe I'll make mine a surprise, too."

"Fair enough," Wendy says.

And yet, her eyes crawl the design book open before them. Lots of dolphins and stars, along with a Greek word. It might say the same thing that Wendy's design does, for all she understands. Aristos's name, in his first language. Would that mean something more to him than seeing it in his second? Does he hear home in a rolled 'r' and a docked 's', despite his seven years spent as 'Arty' in England? Wendy thinks of the many moments, since their move to Cyprus, that her boyfriend has laughed at a joke she could not comprehend, though they were standing side by side with the same sun on their faces. She wonders if he is the same person, when he answers to Arty, that he is when he answers to Aristos, or if he is a version altered in translation. A book that can never be read more closely than in its original language.

"What's she like?"

"Who?"

"Agathi."

The name is out of Wendy's mouth before she can stop it, tainting the antibacterial air.

"I mean, Arty's told me bits but he's my boyfriend, so. Not everything, I'm sure." She attempts a smile.

"Well," Melina starts, her eyes on a box of disposable gloves. "She's . . . erm . . ."

"Seriously, it's okay. You can tell me she's hot if she is," Wendy says.

Good-humouredly, she thinks. But Melina looks mortified.

"Forget it, I shouldn't have asked," Wendy says, shaking her head. "She's your friend . . ."

"No."

Melina catches her wrist, and they are outside the church in her village again. Behind her, the statue of women slipping out of synch with themselves. Melina appears afraid and yet more aligned than ever, staring Wendy in the eye.

"You're my friend," she says. "So, if you want to know, I'll tell you. Yes, Agathi is beautiful. And faithful and kind, and a lot of things that would drive another woman mad." She lets out a breath. "But she's not creative, like you. She's not adventurous. She never made Aristos laugh the way you do. And," she goes on, with tears in her eyes, "I'm talking selfishly now, but she hasn't changed my life."

Wendy stares at her.

"Wendy *mou*, since I met you I've been on such a journey. That's why I'm getting this aeroplane tattooed today," Melina says, pointing back at the design book. "Maybe it's not obvious yet. I can still feel myself changing, so I don't expect you to understand . . ."

A second tear rolls down her cheek no sooner than she has wiped away the first. Wendy sits back and then forward again.

"Right, can I ask. Why do people keep saying that to me? 'I don't expect you to understand'. Is it because I'm foreign?" she asks, affecting a frown.

Melina laughs. "You're paranoid."

"Wouldn't you be?"

She wipes away another tear. "I don't want to be, by the end of this year. I've promised myself. Somehow, my life is going to look different. And better. And that's thanks to you."

Wendy's smile fades. Recalling the many times her attention has wandered from wedding planning, and the clear discomfort that her involvement causes in Melina's relationship, she drops her gaze.

"I'm glad you feel that way," she mutters. "But I'm not sure what I've done to help."

Melina looks to the ceiling, and her dark eyes reflect the light.

"You've just," she says, with a breath in, "been."

"*Étoimoi*," the tattoo artist says, reappearing with their stencils. "Ready."

"Are we?" Wendy asks, recovering her smile to flash at Melina.

"Yes," Melina says.

She pulls Wendy to her feet, and they walk, hand in hand, to the back of the shop.

Twenty-Three

"Teach me."

"Fuck you."

"What?" Wendy laughs.

Grisha's smile is a jet of ink, blooming, slowly and spectacularly, through a pool in her chest. He looks out of place on her sofa before the tall, blank wall. And yet warmer, in the lamplight, than she has seen him at work.

"One move," she persists, from her butterfly chair.

"I told you," he says, "I don't want to do ballet."

"But I do. Come on." She gets unsteadily to her feet. "Or I'll just keep doing these bad impressions . . ."

With her arms arched overhead, Wendy kicks out one leg and almost topples. Grisha cackles into his vodka.

"You can't laugh. I warned you."

"I'm not laughing."

She points, and his smirk stretches into a grin.

"You just look so . . ." He gestures. "Twiggy."

"Twiggy?"

"Yeah. Your legs, like matchsticks. You'd fit into ballet, actually."

Grisha puts down his glass, and Wendy smiles. To know she is something he once desired to be – so terribly that he almost destroyed himself – is intoxicating. It makes her feel gorgeous and twisted, like she should parade and obscure herself all at once.

Wendy turns to the CD shelves, conscious that she is swaying, slightly, as she scans through. Lots of Aristos's classic rock albums, and fewer of her emo ones. She slots Dashboard Confessional's *A Mark, A Mission, A Brand, A Scar* into the disc tray and luxuriates in its opening riff, the plucking of an electric guitar, before she turns back to Grisha, mime-beating the drums. He joins in on air guitar.

No Aristos, tonight, to turn down the volume. His father went into hospital an hour before Wendy was due at work. She was shrugging on her T-shirt when Aristos broke the news. Marios's health had taken a turn for the worse. Nausicaa needed Aristos, most likely overnight. He said this so accusingly Wendy wasn't sure why or what to do. She didn't have a job that existed on her own terms, with hours that she could defer – or write off, entirely – at such short notice. Instead, she had a late shift at the bar. A late close, due to overstayers. And a late departure, for Grisha was working.

The two of them stayed on to drink after locking up. At first, they slagged off their colleagues – Evangelia with her attention-seeking, and Alex with his hopeless crush on her – and then they talked of their own troubles. Less eye contact, lower voices. Wendy's ears pricked up. She could have idled for hours in that state of ignition. She wanted to. And so, with vodka burning in her belly, she invited Grisha back to her apartment.

Would she have done this, if Aristos were home? Would she have made a ceremony of introducing them – her boyfriend to her friend, and her friend to her boyfriend – and sat with them both for a longer, more civilised drink? Of course, Wendy would like to think so. But looking at Grisha, she thrills. She sees his brilliance and his brokenness. She sees the distance he is from everything that he grew up with – just like she is – and the impunity that this third country, this impartial rock, offers them both. It is a detour they have taken from life's obligations, of lunches with pushy parents and coffees with outgrown friends. An open plane, with the winds of disbelief streaming through its grasses. Wendy feels she can run across it, windmilling her arms, with only a few other people. Not Aristos, who has grown stiffer and more watchful since their move – for him, a return – to Cyprus.

"Do you ever feel like you've cheated?"

"Cheated?" Grisha says.

"Yeah." Wendy lowers her imagined drumsticks. "Just, like, generally. In life."

Slowly, he unfurls, and the table between them melts.

"Here . . ."

She reaches towards his hands before realising that she is supposed to mirror them at the ends of oval-shaped arms.

"Closer together, your fingertips."

"Yours aren't that close together."

"Because I'm a man," Grisha says.

He smells like cigarettes and white-carnation spice. With her arms bent at the elbows, Wendy does as he says.

He nods. "Preparatory Position."

Following his lead, she takes a step back.

"That's not a move. I was just making space . . ."

"Oh . . ."

The music breaks down for a mawkish, American-accented bridge, and they laugh.

"First Position," Grisha demonstrates, sweeping his arms out in front of him. "Second Position," he says, stretching them out past his shoulders. "Yours, hold lower down."

"Why?"

"Because you're a woman."

Even as she rolls her eyes, Wendy lets her shoulders drop. She watches Grisha's strong, slender arms as he lifts them overhead into the crowning glory of ballet.

"Fourth Position . . ."

Holding his gaze, she brings her hands up. Air between her fingers and on her tongue, full of his scent.

"What position next?" she asks him.

Taking her hand, he spins her around, and then his chest is at her back, laughter hot on her neck. She leans into it. Fire sparks in her belly. A buzzing rattles the coffee table, and her father's name lights up her phone.

Wendy jolts away from Grisha, her ringtone echoing through her.

"Hi, Dad," she breathes, trying to recover her cool and, instead, recalling her drunkenness. "How are you?" she asks, too loudly.

"Good, thanks. You sound like you're having a nice time," her father says, into her ear.

Wendy turns towards the stereo to find Grisha pushing his hair back, flustered. Not knowing what Nikita has told her could happen, art-wise, if she gathers a little funding. Why she had to pick up the phone.

"Oh, I was just dancing," she says, turning back. "Ballet. I was . . ."

"Dancing?" her father repeats. "I thought Arty's dad was in hospital?"

"He is."

"Aren't you two with him? When you texted me earlier, I thought . . ."

"Yeah, no. Arty is," Wendy says. "I couldn't go, though. I was working."

"Right," her father says.

"*Gavno!*" Grisha curses, knocking over the vodka bottle.

Wendy turns to see its contents surging towards the edge of the coffee table.

"The rug," she starts.

"*Da*, I've got it . . ."

"Who's that?" her father asks.

Wendy slides open the balcony door, and cool air slices inside.

"My colleague, Grisha. I just invited him back for a drink, which he seems to be spilling all over my apartment," she laughs, stepping outside.

"Right," her father says, again. Then, "Don't you mean your father-in-law's apartment?"

"Marios isn't my father-in-law."

"No."

Wendy slides the door shut behind her.

"He's your boyfriend's father. In hospital, presumably quite unwell, and you're out drinking with some other bloke?"

The sea breeze comes as a slap to Wendy's face. Below her, cars rush and waves break. She stares out at a cargo ship's light until she feels it is staring back at her, and the balcony is crumbling beneath her feet. Her fingertips find Aristos's name on her lower back. The night she revealed her tattoo, he was silent. Sombre when she turned to face him, and then insatiable for hours. They fucked like new. At four a.m., they came out here to smoke, Wendy pleasantly achy and asking herself, how had she done it? How had she managed to find a friend who called her life-changing, and an exotic boyfriend to fuck all night, and a balcony – her own balcony – to bask on afterwards, watching the sunrise reflect on the sea? And all this while fostering a buzz of assurance – along with anxiety – that she had within her the most groundbreaking art project of the new century. This was it, she felt. She had taken a chance at a fork in the road and found herself on the right path.

Except, Wendy realises, with her phone's weight in her hand, her father is right. This apartment belongs to her boyfriend and his parents. Aristos ceased to be 'exotic' the moment they stepped off the plane at Larnaca Airport, and she became the foreign one. The stranger in a faraway land, detached from her friends and family. Through the sliding door, she watches Grisha struggling to mop up his spillage with paper towels, all oversaturated within seconds. Down-and-out immigrant might be an interesting experience to draw on, artistically, but it would not be an easy position in which to draw. That project Wendy has within her might be groundbreaking, but it has not yet broken ground. How foolish of her, to jeopardise its chances. And for what? Inspiration, she told herself, when wasn't it, really, infatuation all along? She thinks of the many artists with messy love lives – all the great ones, actually – and feels a pang of empathy. Slides back into wondering whether a chaotic life isn't a necessary part of the creative state, after all, and then catches herself.

"Wendy?" her father says. "Are you there?"

"Yeah, I'm here," Wendy murmurs.

She is looking beyond her colleague now, at the door to the bedroom. The one in which she and her boyfriend awoke from their wild night with her tattoo, Aristos sullen. He didn't like what she had done, she saw, and her renewed obsession with him soured. In the weeks since, she has watched the clock every night until he has come home, and stared with a dark satisfaction at the creases in his shirt each morning. She has hated herself for wanting him. She has pulled closer to Grisha – pretty, novel Grisha – with no regard for any consequences.

Reopening the door, Wendy inhales the scent of the washing powder that she shares with Aristos. She sees everything around her – the now stained coffee table and the tangled blankets, all Aristos's – as the fabric underpinning her ability to make art.

"I know you think your mum and I are paranoid," her father goes on, "but you've run off with a virtual stranger, to live in a foreign country. You're reliant on him out there, aren't you? For the language and the roof over your head. So, if you keep behaving like this, I just worry . . ."

"You're right," Wendy says.

Grisha looks up, his hands full of wet paper towels.

"Pardon?" Wendy's father says.

"I'll call you back, okay?"

Lowering her phone, Wendy slides the balcony door shut again.

"I think I got most of it," Grisha says, standing up.

"Thanks," she says. Then, "I can deal with the rest, if you want to go."

Another acoustic guitar riff starts from the stereo, at odds with the thrashing drums that ended the last song.

"No more ballet? We still have some positions . . ." Grisha's frown becomes a grin.

"Yeah," Wendy smiles, cursing the flare between her legs. "But it's late. And I should probably see how Arty's doing, so . . ." She shrugs.

With a slow nod, Grisha drops his paper towels to the coffee table. Watching him drag on his jacket, Wendy knows. She must begin work on *Time, Unchronicled*. Forget her image as an artist, her piercings and her Myspace presence. She must do what she suspects many failed artists never manage to, with their stormy relationships, and learn to distinguish inspiration from infatuation. Stop getting consumed by other people and forgetting herself. Forsaking her art, when that – though she takes it for granted, sometimes – is the only true love of her life.

TWENTY-FOUR

ONLY WHEN SHE GETS out of his car does Wendy see that Nikita hasn't dressed up for their 'special viewing'. Still, his tracksuits probably cost more than all the coreset dresses she owns.

Smoothing her skirt down, Wendy looks to the gallery. Glass-fronted at street level, with no windows on its first floor. In the fading daylight, the paintings shine out of their fishtank – depicting seascapes and flower-filled vases – while their concrete lid glares down. Warily, Wendy follows Nikita up the front steps.

"Aren't we going inside . . . ?"

He is lifting his phone to his ear, looking away as though she hasn't spoken.

She follows his gaze, to the cars tearing past with sounds like they are stripping paper off the wall of the evening. Facing the gallery is a broad road, before a law firm and a flat-roofed apartment building. No cobbled square. No queue of tourists. No London. This gallery is in Limassol, a city which – despite being coastal, like Larnaca – doesn't smell of sea salt or lavender, but of car exhaust and construction-site fumes. Apparently, it has grown rapidly since the Turkish invasion of 1974, when the Greek-speaking Cypriots fleeing south needed new homes, as well as a shipping and commerce centre to replace Famagusta.

"But we brought the money," Nikita said, on the journey from Larnaca.

An hour-long drive, in which Wendy felt acutely aware of his meaty thigh beside her bare one. Of the April air – warm at midday, but cool once the sun set – and the curious, within-and-without life that Nikita led here.

Looking at the apartment buildings around the gallery, all greyed walls and inset balconies, Wendy sees that Grisha was right. Nikita is from a different *Rossiya*, one that can sink its money into whatever premises it likes, however ill-placed. It will not matter. Nikita will never come far enough on foot to see how out of the way it is, or take a bus that shows him how unfit for their surge of purpose these old roads are. He will simply keep driving his BMW 5 Series from place to place, with the air conditioned to just the right temperature, and enjoying his time inside each.

A key turns in the gallery door, no sooner than Nikita has lowered his phone.

"*Privet*, Nikitka," a man says, pulling the door open.

"Filipka," Nikita greets him.

The men shake hands, about as middle-aged and overlarge as each other, though Filipp – as Nikita introduces him, formally – appears sharper-eyed. Better dressed, too, in a shirt and chinos.

He gives Wendy a nod, before garbling something incomprehensible at her.

"*Ona ne govorit po-russky,*" Nikita says. "She is from England."

"England," Filipp echoes, withdrawing his hand. "The only country they hate more than ours, here."

"I don't know about that," Wendy laughs. "Some people really hate you guys . . ."

In her mind's eye, Grisha sneering at Nikita, and Aristos disparaging Grisha. Russians with money swanning around poor Cyprus, and Russians without it stealing – jobs and women – from poor Cyprus.

With his finger pointing at Wendy, Filipp looks back at Nikita. "Nice girl."

Nikita gives a bark of amusement.

"*Zachodite,*" Filipp bids them, pulling the door open wider. "Come in."

"Thanks," Wendy says, slipping past him.

Inside, it smells like oil on canvas and the marble staircase that stretches up and away from the entrance. Paintings hang on the walls to each side, inviting Wendy to venture deeper.

"Go and look," Filipp instructs her.

She turns to see him relocking the gallery doors, and a twig snaps inside her.

"From six o'clock, we are closed," he explains, pocketing his keys. "Tonight, I open only for you."

Nikita raises a hand.

"And for my friend, Nikitka," Filipp adds, "okay."

Nikita says something teasing in Russian, and the men push at each other, affectionately.

"You go around," Nikita says, to Wendy. "Don't worry."

With their voices echoing after her, Wendy walks around the staircase. She feels childlike, with her arms swinging loose and the adults' conversation going over her head. Like she could do with something to hold. Instead, she picks at the skin around her right thumbnail and thinks so hard about what she looks like, looking at the paintings – all generic, of fruit bowls and beachy sunsets – that she spends a stupid amount of time at each one. Too much at the most basic, and not enough at the one or two that might be of interest, if she could focus. Then she circles back to the men, and they cease to smile.

"Finished? Shall we go up?" Filipp asks her.

"Yeah?" Wendy says, glancing over her shoulder.

Nikita waves her towards the staircase.

"So, are the paintings downstairs for sale? I noticed some signs," Wendy says, holding her dress to her thighs as Nikita trails behind her.

"Downstairs is for sale, yes. Upstairs, I have exhibition," Filipp answers.

He slows his pace, and they surface in the centre of a room.

"Wow," Wendy says, taking the final stair up.

Nikita stops beside her. On the walls around them hang columns of paintings no larger than textbooks, softly lit from below. Their lines are blurred, their colours bold, their frames thick and bronzed. From a side table, Wendy takes an introduction to the artist by some Academy of Athens art historian, with Russian and English translations. Her eyes skim the text, taking in only a few stock phrases about his collection 'defying categorisation' and 'blurring the boundary between art and the human experience'. So this artist is just like every other one asked to describe their work. Wendy stifles a snicker. And yet, she cannot help but long to see her paintings on these walls, and to read such testaments to their profundity.

After gazing a moment longer towards the nearest wall, Wendy turns back to Filipp.

"So, is this guy local?"

"Yes, from Pegeia."

Nikita utters something that sounds like a curse.

Wendy frowns. "Pegeia?"

"Pegeia, yes. It is in Paphos," Filipp assures her.

But the men look too grave to be talking merely of that expats' town.

At Wendy's questioning look, Nikita explains, "This time last year, three people were killed there. Police found them in villa, bagged up in bathtub."

"Shit." Wendy lowers the academic's paper. "Paphos is on the other side of the island, though. Right? So, we should be safe . . ."

No one joins her in chortling, and she sounds ugly doing it.

"They were *Russkimi*, the three killed. Russian," Nikita says.

"Vyacheslav Shevchenko, Valentina Tretyakova and Yuri Zorin," Filipp recites, with his eyes on the floor.

Wendy is opening her mouth to ask whether Filipp knew the victims, when she understands that it doesn't matter. If three English people were to turn up dead here, she would feel every bit as unnerved as her host looks. She would wonder who had targeted them, and whether that person would come for her next. She would walk the streets faster, and not so late at night if she could help it.

With this thought, Wendy's mind jumps to the swift departures that Grisha has made from his bar shifts of late. For a moment, it comforts her to think that he might be feeling perturbed by the resurgence of this news story, rather than avoiding her. But the moment passes. Of course he is avoiding her, just as she is avoiding him – and most everyone else – in the name of her art. Staying up past dawn to sketch her outlines, and painting over her mistakes until they are perfect. Saying no to after-work drinks and daytime outings with anyone but Melina. Apparently, at some point in the next few weeks, Melina wants to arrange a wedding-dress fitting with her mother, her future mother-in-law, and Wendy. Fine. As maid of honour, Wendy will attend that. But any event that she doesn't have to, she will not. Not until *Time, Unchronicled* – her masterwork – is complete.

"Anyway. This artist is Cypriot," Filipp says, gesturing back at the paintings.

"He's good," Wendy says. "Do you show a lot of local artists' work?"

"Some, yes. And I am doing exchanges with my friends, my colleagues, in other places. Some I bring from *Rossiya*. Some from the Ukraine. Some from Czechoslovakia . . ." He waves a hand, as though to imply so many more countries.

"Wow."

"Yes. And Nikitka tells me you have some paintings for us?"

"Oh," Wendy starts. "Yeah. Well, I mean . . . if you're interested, then . . ."

She curls her fingers around the hem of her dress, wanting to tear its lace and all the skin underneath it to shreds. She has never felt so anxious meeting anyone. But it is not just 'anyone' that has a gallery space to offer her – for her own exhibition, at twenty-four years old – and so this impression matters.

"I am interested, yes. Why do you think you are here?" Filipp asks. Then, pushing at Nikita again, "To watch me talk with my friend?"

Nikita responds with another of his barks, and Wendy does her best to laugh along.

"Tell me about your collection," Filipp says.

"Well." She takes a breath.

Then exhales *Time, Unchronicled*. Where it came from. How much it means. As jitters overcome her, she fears she is scrambling her words and clenches her fists. This pitch could change her life.

"Interesting concept," Filipp responds.

"Really? Do you think so?"

"Yes, especially with your experience in post-colonial environment. I think my friends in Prague may be interested also, living in old USSR."

"Right," Wendy nods, overeagerly. "That makes sense."

"So, after we exhibit your paintings here, we could send to his gallery there."

"Are you serious?" She stares at him. "I mean, just like that?"

"Why not?"

His cartoonish shrug sends her laughing, deliriously, recalling the question that first occurred to her when he locked the doors. She is going to have to take off her clothes for this, isn't she? Surely.

"Nikitka tells me he has seen your work," Filipp goes on. "I trust him. And which artist inspired your style, you said? Kalashoss?"

"Kashalos," Wendy corrects him, gently. "Michael Kashalos."

Nikita says something in Russian, and Filipp nods.

"Yes, I know his work. He is famous Cypriot painter, yes? So, that is also interesting for people here."

"Yeah," Wendy says. "Hopefully."

Her heart is racing as though she has just climbed the stairs again, ten times over.

"You know," Filipp recalls, aloud. "My next artist, Russian girl, just asked me to postpone her exhibition. I was going to move up artist after her. But, if you can finish your collection in next few weeks . . ."

"I can do that," Wendy says. "Definitely."

"Perfect. Done," Nikita declares.

Wendy could kiss him. She could jump up and down with her arms around his neck, sending her dress up to expose her underwear, and perhaps that would be only right. Perhaps a part of her wants to, in light of the opportunity he has granted her. Instead, she shakes Filipp's hand. For it is not by indulging men, or indulging herself in men – she still cannot work out where her weakness lies with them, exactly – that Wendy has achieved what she has tonight. It is by putting in the time at her easel. By remembering, her work is her love. Her work is her life. The only thing that she owes herself to.

"Time to paint," Nikita says.

"*Time, Unchronicled*," Filipp jibes.

They share a laugh, and Wendy follows them down the stairs glowing.

TWENTY-FIVE

"You know," Wendy murmurs, into Aristos's ear. "When I moved across the continent with a stranger, I didn't think I'd be spending my Saturday nights in church."

Aristos smirks. "Sorry to disappoint."

A car sweeps past, illuminating the suede jacket that she first saw him in last March, outside Yvonne's house.

"I don't know." Wendy shrugs. "You've surprised me. Ironically, by being less shocking, in some ways. But there's no such thing as a disappointing surprise."

"Isn't there?"

"Nope. Not in my world."

"Your world sounds nice," Aristos smiles, through a sigh.

They are standing outside his parents' house, in the final hour of April. The late-night air is fragrant with lemon, and Wendy's stomach whiny from fasting all day. With shaky hands she lights a cigarette.

"*Éla, agápi mou,*" Nausicaa's voice sounds. "Come on, my love . . ."

Wendy turns to see her holding open the front door, Marios's coat draped over her forearm.

"I'm fine," he snaps, at her touch to his back.

Nausicaa withdraws and restores her hand to him again, as she has been doing all day. Marios leans on his cane, and Wendy cannot believe he is the man whose sternness turned Aristos so glowering and reticent just last year. Now, Marios is unsteady on his feet. He has lost enough weight for several Lent periods and, apparently – after a series of low-voiced conversations with Aristos – the will to resist further meetings with the man from the Committee on Missing Persons who, last summer, saw Wendy and Aristos's balcony fixed.

Marios lands, heavily, over the doorstep.

"Okay, *paidiá*," Nausicaa smiles, wet-eyed. "Shall we go?"

They start down the hill towards Saint Lucas's Church, Wendy for only the second time. And yet, as she trails along behind Aristos's parents, she gets the sense that she is treading a well-worn path. Like one of the lanes between sheep fields that her mother and stepfather – or her father and stepmother – used to take her down every couple of months, when they felt that self-conscious, urbanite's urge to expose their child to some country air. Those walks always ended in quarrels, when one parent misread or thought they knew better than the map, and the other knew better than that. At the sound of raised voices, Wendy looks up. Tonight, the quarrel is over whether they shouldn't be travelling by car.

"It's too cold for you, Marie . . ."

"It's fine. We're ten minutes up the road."

"But your cane, on this hill . . ."

"I told you, it's fine."

They keep walking. Because this isn't just Wendy's second time on the family's old route, but likely one of Marios's last. That's what no one is saying, isn't it? Wendy wants to ask Aristos, to tug at his sleeve like the child she was on those country lanes, but she knows it is wrong. If Aristos wanted to talk about his father's decline, then he would. As would Nausicaa, as would Marios himself. For Mediterranean islanders, always on about the stiff-upper-lip mentality of the British, Wendy thinks, Cypriots can be very repressed. She follows them on through the darkness.

At the base of the hill, other families appear. They come from all corners of Aradippou, to converge on the lamplit square. Grandparents are hunched to the same height as their grandchildren, all shepherded by men and women of middle-age. Wendy startles at the tenderness these women stir in her, with their tired faces and darkened roots. She has worked and socialised almost exclusively with the young since moving away from her mother. Her stepmother. Even her ex-girlfriend. Now here are their spectres, emerging from the shadows in hats and scarves, to remind her of what was and what will, inevitably, be again.

Inside the church, it smells of the solid, ancient things that Wendy doesn't want to admit she loves. Incense and faith, ageing and wood. Already, the hall is full. But at the sight of Marios and Nausicaa, people usher each other aside.

"*Kalispéra*, good evening," they say, in tones that sound at once congratulatory and consoling.

The same people greet Aristos as they might a teenaged boy who had grown a head taller since their last encounter, before nodding with less certainty at Wendy. In single file, they shuffle to the frontmost pew – a row of fold-up seats with standing-height armrests – where a younger man makes way for Marios.

"I'm fine," he hisses, again.

"Marie," Nausicaa pleads.

And he takes the seat.

"Can we really stand here? Aren't we in the way?" Wendy asks.

"It's fine, it's always like this," Aristos says, passing her a candle. "For the ceremony."

"Oh." She lowers it. Then grins, "This is Cyprus . . ."

Again, Aristos smirks. But he does not laugh at her impression of his accent the way he once would have.

Wendy follows his gaze to yet another family that she doesn't know and that she probably won't, and she smiles anyway. The anxiety is radiating off her boyfriend, as glaringly as the light from the Holy Fire – flown in from Jerusalem today, Nausicaa says – and Wendy feels like sharing with Aristos her revelation that it is okay. Here, he is just another one of so many. Isn't it beautiful? Perhaps she is becoming religious. Perhaps she is losing her mind. As the priest recites an ode in the language she still cannot understand, Wendy closes her eyes and lets each eventuality spool out behind them.

Then, a jostling. She turns to see flames springing up towards her, like beacons atop long-ago hills to warn of danger coming. Except that here there are only smiles. Whispers, from stranger to stranger, of *'Christós anésti'*.

"Christ is risen," Aristos translates.

"Christós anésti," Wendy repeats, tilting her candle to light a young girl's.

In turn, the girl smiles and lights her mother's.

When there is a candle burning in every hand, the priest leads them all outside and around the church before stopping in the square out front.

"He is risen, He is not here," Aristos translates his reading.

A wind sends the flames shivering, and Wendy cups a palm to shield hers in step with everyone else. This scene could make it into *Time, Unchronicled*, she thinks. And at once, she ceases to be 'just another one'. She falls out of synch with the people around her, all singing a song to which she never knew the words. Wendy is only another one of any number for as long as it takes her to get the measure. Then she slips back behind her sketchbook or canvas, and into her true form of no one, nowhere. The grey between black and white.

Kashalos comes to her mind on a high note, and for the first time, Wendy feels the vibration in her ears of something like remorse. Perhaps her realisation that this chorus is made up of so many individuals, ringing true. She looks around, at more bright eyes and open mouths than she can count, and she thinks, each person here will go home to their own life. Like in a Kashalos painting, scenes from every one will play out above and below one another with none in particular at the forefront. Not even Wendy's. With this thought, the vibration in her ears turns to a burning, and she lets it. She thinks that perhaps she needed the painter's absence of perspective, to gain some for herself. To see that when she withdraws from here, all the stories she leaves behind will go on unfolding without her. Except Marios's. Wendy glances sideways. Nausicaa will mourn the man and lean harder than ever into her religion. Aristos will go back to his ex-girlfriend or find a new one. Melina will start a family with Petros.

The young girl cries out, losing her candlelight. The girl's mother extends her own candle, and the light is restored.

The priest begins another hymn, and the congregation joins him in singing. People are beaming and linking arms, not one of them lonely. Not one of them free. So many times in her young life, Wendy has feared that art would not work out – and then what would she do? Keep working in bars forever. Give in to starting a family, like everyone else here. These thoughts have made her desperate. But moving to Cyprus, meeting Nikita, discovering Kashalos. These have all been chapters in the success story that she feels sure she will tell, someday. Her candle burns brighter. In its smoke, she sees herself exhibiting *Time, Unchronicled* in Limassol – just a few weeks from now – then flying to Prague and wherever else her Russian friend has connections, as boundless as the sky transporting her.

The priest takes a breath, and the crowd confesses after him.

"It is the Day of Resurrection," Aristos translates, under his breath. "Let us be glorious. Let us embrace one another and speak to those that hate us. Let us forgive all things and so let us cry, 'Christ has arisen from the dead.'"

Wendy lowers her palm, and with one puff, the wind blows out her candle.

Accident Investigation Report

Date: 3 May 2005

Time: 22:13 NZST

Aircraft Type: Fairchild SA227-AC Metro III

Operator: Airwork, NZ

Flight Number: 23

Occupants: 2

Fatalities: 2

Aircraft Damage: Destroyed

Synopsis:

On Tuesday 3 May 2005, Fairchild Metro III ZK-POA was scheduled to depart Auckland, New Zealand at 21:00 h on a freight service to Blenheim, New Zealand. Loading of the freight was delayed and completed at approximately 21:15 h. The crew ordered 570 litres of additional fuel and instructed the refueller to put it all into the left wing tank, rather than half into each tank as per company practice. Refuelling completed at 21:30 h and the flight departed at 21:36 h, without the fuel tanks being balanced.

At approximately 22:12 h, when the aircraft had reached cruise level, the captain instructed the First Officer to open the fuel crossflow valve between the left and right wing tanks. Forty-seven seconds later, the aural alert "Bank Angle" was followed by a chime, most likely the Selected Altitude Deviation warning. The Bank Angle alert was heard 7 times before the Cockpit Voice Recording ended at 22:13 h. During the last 25 seconds of radar data recorded by Air Traffic Control, the aircraft lost 2 000 ft of altitude, and the track turned left through more than 180 degrees.

One witness, who was less than 1 000 m from the aircraft's diving flight path, reported seeing its nose descending after an explosion "like a real big ball of fire". Two smaller fireballs illuminated the falling wreckage and cargo.

The main wreckage field was on hilly farmland 7 km northeast of Stratford. Both pilots received fatal injuries. The aircraft and its cargo were destroyed, with some ground disruption.

TWENTY-SIX

WHEN PETROS ENTERS THE bungalow where he grew up – the door hangs open, as always – he finds his mother and grandparents at the table, with plates of the leftover soúvla that he made them for Easter. Four days old, now. He says yes to his grandmother's offer of a portion, instinctively, and grimaces at its rubbery texture. Without looking at what is on his fork, he can't tell whether it is chicken or pork. Forcing down a half-chewed mouthful, he sits back in his chair.

The clank of Petros's cutlery on his plate is loud, the dining room small and dark. His grandparents keep the shutters down night and day, so there is only the front door to let in the little remaining daylight. A neighbour walks by, waving, and Petros's relatives call out greetings with their mouths full, his grandfather sending a shred of pork across the table. Petros stares after it. He has always found his family home dreary, and – much as he has tried to fight it – embarrassing. It contained no clear authority figure in his youth, being both the house where his mother was raising him and, at the same time, the house where his grandparents were raising her.

Petros steals a sideways look at his mother, dragging a napkin across her lips as the neighbour's footsteps fade. Perhaps that was why he never attached to her in the urgent, absolute way that his friends appeared to their mothers. Panayiota didn't cook or clean as those other mothers did. She stood apart from them in the school playground, showing a great deal more of her legs. Occasionally, she tried to help Petros – with his homework or some other ailment – and collapsed into tears at the first sign of failure. The more she deferred to his grandmother, the more Petros understood that she, Panayiota, was the one most in need of familial care. He compressed his needs until they became secondary, and never learned to accept much womanly comfort. All he knew was to comfort women.

"More soúvla, Petro mou?" his grandmother says, proffering the cellophane-wrapped container.

Petros raises a hand. "I'd better take a look at that light fixture first."

"Ah, nai." Xenia returns meat to table. "Show him the one, Demo mou."

On shaky legs, Petros's grandfather rises and leads the way to a narrow bedroom. Its smell, of leather and jasmine, transports Petros back to the years in which he shared it with his mother. He learned his first profound life lesson, then, that the most outstanding aspects of a person could be the best as often as the worst. It was their context that decided. In this room, Panayiota shone with the youth that frustrated her outside. She became something more like a sister to Petros, twirling around in her few, treasured dresses and swooping over to tickle him, leaping from her mattress to his and whispering gossip into the small hours. The mornings after such nights, Petros watched her brush her long, dark hair in a daze. He thought she was special. The most beautiful woman in the village, with a girlish abandon upon which the sun set only when local men averted their eyes or when Petros's grandmother demanded quiet. Then, reminded of her practical failings, Panayiota turned sullen again.

A pattering as Demos feels around for the light switch.

"Aha," he says, upon pressing it. "You see?"

Petros strains to make out the one single bed that remains in the room, and the chest of drawers hulking in its far corner. Only a flash reflected from the opposite wall alerts him to the ceiling light. Flickering, as his grandparents told him it had been.

"We changed the bulb last week," Demos recounts. "And we'd only just changed the one before that. Teleiósei," he declares the fixture, dusting off his palms. "*Finished.*"

"So, they're burning out, huh? Not just flickering?" Petros asks.

"Nai," his grandfather confirms.

Petros turns the light off and on to little effect.

"It could be loose wiring. You sit back down," he bids his grandfather, "and I'll see what I can do."

Repeating his prognosis as he passes the dining table, Petros steps out into the evening air. Warm and fragrant with pine-scent. He lifts the boot of his car and then the lid of his toolbox, checking it for his torch, screwdrivers, utility knife, wire strippers, electrical wire and wire connectors. Finally, he withdraws his safety glasses. They don't imbue the world with any colour, just make Petros feel as though he is watching it at a remove. Good thing for his family that he is capable and never went further afield. Never took that banal flight to England, to study something airy-fairy or to search for his father. He couldn't have, really, no matter how much he had wanted to. Fortunately, by the time he came to this conclusion, he'd had Melina to soften the blow. Her love was so gentle and restoring, it allowed Petros to believe that his staying in Cyprus was a choice, and not just the compound fate of obligation and fear.

Re-entering the bedroom, Petros pushes aside the thin scrap of a curtain that overhangs the window and wrenches the shutters outwards. An explosion of dust, and he turns his head towards the glass that reflected the ceiling light. It is wall-mounted, protecting a photo of his mother and her older brother, who died the night that Petros was conceived. Panayiota named Petros after him. She was young, then, with hair as long as her slender arms. She is young now, Petros reminds himself, for the mother of a twenty-eight-year-old. But context means nothing to time.

"Entáxei. Fixed," Petros announces, hefting his toolbox out of the bedroom.

"That was quick," his grandfather says.

His grandmother smiles. "Brávo, Petro mou."

"I put in a brighter bulb, also," Petros says, to Panayiota. "Mamá?"

He reaches around the doorframe to switch the light on and off again. Panayiota gives a vague nod.

"Much better," Xenia says. "Now, come and finish your soúvla."

Petros's stomach sinks with his toolbox, but he resumes his seat at the table.

"Where's Melina tonight?" his grandmother asks.

"She's making wedding favours with her kouméra. I think I mentioned, Wendy is an artist? So . . ."

"They're having fun with it."

"Yes, they are."

Xenia's lips stretch into a smile. Across the table, Panayiota's turn downwards.

"She's getting a bit carried away with it all, isn't she? Melina," she says. "I don't remember her going out this much ever before."

"It's nice to see," Petros responds, as though deaf to her bitter tone. "This friendship has meant a lot to her, and I think all the wedding stuff has helped it grow closer."

"She's always been a quiet one," his grandfather says.

"She can be," Petros admits.

"Shy," his grandmother agrees.

He nods.

Beyond the door, darkness has fallen. A breeze is stirring, bringing the smell of fresh soúvla from the local tavérna. Petros shovels in another forkful of his cold, tough leftovers.

"It's coming up now, isn't it? The wedding."

"Yes, the second week of August," he confirms.

"Re, Petro. Why?" his mother complains. "It's going to be so hot."

"Because, Mamá," he says, through his mouthful. "We'll have more time, then. Most of my friends and I will be off work, as will Melina's colleagues, so we know people will come. And we won't have to take much extra time off for our honeymoon."

"Good idea," Xenia says.

"I still think you could have chosen a more interesting destination than Greece," Panayiota grumbles.

"There's nowhere in the world more interesting than Greece," Petros smiles, "or more beautiful. And Poros is a nice, quiet island because there's no airport."

"So, you'll get the plane to Athens?" his grandmother asks.

"Yes, and then a boat. We looked at doing a couple of islands, but the others were expensive. Hydra, especially."

"Hydra is beautiful," Demos chips in. "I met a man from there, once."

"Mia méra," Petros nods, spreading his hands. "*One day,* huh?"

"Ah, Petro," his grandmother sighs. "I wish we had more to give you, to help you. If we hadn't lost Achna . . ."

"Giagiá, I wouldn't expect a thing. Melina and I both work hard," Petros starts.

But his grandparents are lost to the conversation that they always are, eventually, about the village where they lived until 1974.

"We had a beautiful house, didn't we?" his grandmother is saying.

"We did," his grandfather is agreeing.

"With all those potato fields around it. Do you remember, Panayiota mou?"

Petros's mother gives another stiff nod.

"You ran right over them, once, and got a telling-off from the farmer. Didn't she, Demo mou?"

"She did . . ."

Panayiota grimaces as Xenia tousles her hair. Allegedly, before the invasion, the family had owned a fair amount of land. A lemon orchard on the outskirts of Achna, and a plot on the coast between Paralimni and Famagusta. The latter would have been worth a small fortune by now.

"I'll never forget the sound I made when I saw those planes," Xenia says, with her hand on her heart. "The village stank, we'd all wet ourselves. I remember thinking, or wanting to think, that we were marking our territory. Better dogs than cowards, just running scared." With a tut, she drops her palm. "A whole lot of good that did us. We left with nothing, and we were left with nothing."

"There had been warnings," Demos says, "but we didn't believe they'd make it as far inland as us. You don't, until you can smell the death. And it's already too late, then."

Petros bows his head, with – he hopes – enough solemnity for himself and his mother both. She is ripping at the ends of her hair now, exuding a rancour to which he cannot believe his grandparents are oblivious. But this has always been Panayiota's problem, her falling between the cracks. Because she was a child at the time of the invasion, she lost her home but not her house – nor her lemon orchard nor her plot on the coast, she'd had claims to nothing – and yet she had lost everything, people insisted. The poor girl, plunged into womanhood overnight by Petros's arrival in her womb, only to be stunted by his weight in her arms. His childhood preserved hers the way that vinegar did their neighbour's artichoke hearts, turning it evermore sour, until he moved out. Now what is Panayiota left with? No career. No partner. A single child whom she can only watch overtake her. Petros is painfully aware of all this. That his being was both her whole life and the end of it. That she loves and hates him with equal force.

He glances back towards the bedroom, with its photo of Panayiota and her brother. No other man. How like his father does Petros look, now that he is grown? Fifteen years since the man's disappearance from their lives, and he is afraid to ask. As a child, Petros believed it was only the fence around the British Army Base that kept his parents from each other's arms. He can't recall now where he got this idea, whether he dreamt it up, wishfully, or whether it was his grandmother's attempt to shield him from the true nature of his conception. His mother's youth and helplessness, and his father's position of power. Their love was forbidden and more romantic for it, Petros maintained, until he grew old enough to see Panayiota's distrust of men. The way that she averted her gaze, sometimes even from him.

Another split end flies away between her finger and thumb, and he wonders what she is counting off with them. Buried friends. Lost loves. All the private facets of the many lives she never lived. But of course she didn't, Petros wants to shake her and say. A girl incarnate of Aphrodite's island, as beautiful and small and well-placed as it was when that British soldier found her. Of course he invaded her, just as his forefathers – and many others – had the country. It was such an obvious thing to occur that it could have been called inevitable, Petros thinks. And then he hates himself, because what kind of person can think that about their homeland? Let alone their mother.

"The house in Achna wasn't all that special," Panayiota mutters. "And the orchard wouldn't have been worth much."

Demos shoots her a look.

"Well, Papá? You were hardly taking care of it."

"We had lemons every year."

"Fewer and fewer, as I recall."

"You'd be surprised, Panayiota," Xenia maintains. "Even so, it was with our plot on the coast that we really lost out. If we had that now . . ."

"What, we'd be millionaires?" Panayiota snorts.

Petros lowers his cutlery to his plate. Empty, in contrast to the pre-conflict spoils that his grandparents describe, each time as a greater loss. Petros hears almost every refugee talk in this way, as though they were 'someone', before. But how many people can have owned half of Kyrenia? Or Famagusta? How many can have had the single most breathtaking view of the northern coast? It doesn't add up. No sooner than he has swallowed his last mouthful of leftover pork, Petros can recall how juicy the meat was the night he cooked it. Perhaps this is how all mythologies come about, he thinks, by shrouding themselves in the past. Perhaps someday, centuries from now, people will speak of his grandparents in the same breaths as Arachne whom Athena turned into a spider, and Echo whom Hera cursed only to repeat after others. They will speak of Panayiota like Leda of Sparta, who became a mother by the seduction or rape – no one can quite decide which – of a man a different species to her entirely.

As the length of his day descends on him, Petros rubs his hands over his face. There is nothing he can do to change it, much as he would like to for his mother's sake. Nor can he submerge himself back inside the pickle jar to stagnate. His most generous option, he suspects, is to give Panayiota a grandchild. In his mind's eye, Petros can see the happy family that he hopes to start soon after his marriage, the world a better place for having more people like Melina in it. Kinder, more compassionate. Petros reopens his eyes to the glare of Panayiota's bare ring finger. Surely, a grandchild would appease her, act as a branch extending back to her from the life he has grown elsewhere. It wouldn't cast her back into an unwilling cycle, would it? Of stacking wooden blocks and reciting the alphabet, as she had for herself and then for him. He looks at her hair, ends frayed with her pulling at them, and he wonders. How many children must a woman live for before she is free to seek her own purpose?

A car trundles past, shining its headlights over their shins, and Petros stands up.

"You're not leaving, are you, Petro mou?" his grandmother says.

"I think I'd better be. Melina will be home soon and wanting to show me these favours, I'm sure."

"Just keep that between the two of you, will you?" Demos grins, revealing the gaps between his teeth.

"Demo!" Xenia gives him a mock smack. "That's you granddaughter-in-law you're talking about . . ."

"Kalá, Xenia mou. He knows I'm joking . . ."

Rinsing off his plate, Petros smiles. That his grandfather, who has carried injuries since the invasion, can find the humour in passing moments, is a comfort to him. As is any pleasure that Petros can find between his own obligations. His life is one of duty, to his family, his work and his soon-to-be wife. He does little for pleasure anymore, if indeed he ever did. But that is okay. Towelling his plate dry, Petros slides it back into its overhead cupboard. He has never wanted anything more than to serve and be served, in the simple way of a husband-and-wife team with contented members. That is more than any before him were afforded. Yet Melina is not contented. Since their engagement, Petros has grown increasingly sure of this, and the fact that what he once took for her general quietude is something closer to withholding.

"Kaliníchta sas, *goodnight*," he bids his family.

There are kisses all around.

"Call me if that light plays up again . . ."

"We will . . ."

Petros backs outside, waving. He still loves Melina. Still wants her, as he always has. He just needs to know that, apart from all their commitments, she wants him, too.

TWENTY-SEVEN

SHE HAS WORKED THE early shift today, from five a.m., and still she looks dazzling. Her face is made up with flicks of eyeliner and a frosted lipstick that takes Petros back to Christmastime atop Troodos. One smile and he forgets the discomforts of the season upon them, the shirt clinging to his back and the workman's smell contained beneath it. He spreads his arms, and—

"Geiá sou, Agathi," a man bids her, on his way into the bakery.

A colleague or perhaps a regular. Agathi turns to greet him, and Petros is struck with vertigo as he remembers himself. Stupidly tall next to most Cypriots, but none more so than Agathi, whose curves bulge from a squat frame. Her hair is a jet down her back, rippled only where she must have tied it at the nape of her neck. As usual, she is dressed in slim-fitting clothes of all one colour. Tuscan yellow, this afternoon.

Her acquaintance steps through the bakery door, releasing the aromas of fresh bread and coffee, and Agathi offers a plastic cup of the latter to Petros. It cools his palm.

"Sorry," she starts, as her ringtone sounds. She holds her coffee in one hand and plunges the other into her handbag.

"Are you all right?" Petros asks. "Do you want me to take that . . . ?"

"I'm okay. Efcharistó," she thanks him, resurfacing with her phone. "I've got it . . ."

He stands back, only to watch her reject the call.

"All right. Now, geiá sou," she says, stepping, at last, into his arms.

Not fast enough to hide the thrill that flashes across her eyes. Another whiff of the bakery-scent in her hair, and Petros draws back to see a strand glued to her lipstick.

"You've got, a . . ." He motions.

"Mmn, I can feel it." With her hands full, Agathi turns her face up towards him. "Will you get it for me?"

She gives a helpless laugh, and he echoes it.

"Sure . . ."

This is one of the ways in which you stop it from becoming weird, a male–female friendship. At a moment that could otherwise feel charged – Petros leaning closer, taking care to touch Agathi lightly and only on the temple as he drags the hair back from her lips – you throw in a chuckle or an eyeroll. Break the tension. Remind yourselves that you are mates, who share drinks and jokes. Then you move on with a nonchalant 'thanks', just as Agathi is doing. You catch your breath as she steps away. You remember yourself and feel silly or awful, depending upon how much you forgot in your nearness to her. Your other woman. Then you chide yourself, because you haven't touched her, have you? Not like that. So, don't complicate things. Don't implicate her. Don't punish yourself for some imagined crime. Petros smiles. Remember, there is nothing in it. And yet.

"What's going on?" he asks Agathi, as they step out into the road.

She waves her thanks to the driver that gives way – something they never do for Petros alone – and he sticks close to her across the cobbles.

"Eh, the usual. Not much."

"No?"

"No, I . . . What? Why are you looking at me like that?"

"You're smiling. Who was that on the phone?"

No sooner than they have mounted the pavement, the car rolls on past their heels. The Church of Saint Lazarus pushes up from the square before them, and the afternoon sunlight strokes its belltower like the head of a cat.

Agathi opens and closes her mouth. "Éla, Petro mou. Let's not fight, now."

Petros stops walking, mid-step. "It was Aristos."

"We're not talking about it. Not right away, okay?" Lowering herself onto the wall that surrounds the square, Agathi gives him a crinkly-eyed smile. "I want to hear about you first. Tell me. How are things?"

Sitting down beside her, Petros sighs. The wall comes hard to the base of his spine, which aches from his day spent squatting over electrical sockets.

"Things," he repeats, scanning his memories of the last week.

He finds himself avoiding the story of his mother's demanding to join Melina in some kind of wedding-related activity. Any at all, Panayiota didn't care what it entailed, only that August was weeks away. No longer would she be told that there weren't flowers to smell or seating plans to discuss. She was smarter than that. But she was unstable, too, given to weeks of silence followed by fits of shrieking that could be jealous or joyful. She was growing more agitated with every day that the weather turned hotter, so that Petros didn't know how to protect her – whether to agree that she could attend Melina's next dress fitting – except by keeping quiet about her fragility. Bearing it alone, no matter the weight.

"We saw that film," he says. "*I Éfkoli Lia*."

"Ah, *Easy Leah*," Agathi responds, poking a straw into her coffee cup. She offers another one to Petros. "I've heard mixed reviews."

"Yeah," he says, taking it. "I was expecting, you know, the Athens nightlife. The midlife crisis. The romance, of course. But the S&M stuff? Mixed in with the kind of spiritual awakening that this guy was having, supposedly?"

He shakes his head, and she laughs.

"It sounds like a lot."

"It was."

"You wouldn't recommend it, then?"

"Look, no judgement. I don't know what you're into . . ."

Agathi cries out, her straw flying from her mouth.

"Let me assure you," she says. "It's not the film for me, I'm pretty sure."

Petros makes a show of flaring his eyes. "If you say so."

"I do."

"Well, anyway. In cinemas now . . ."

They share a chuckle.

Across the square, pigeons peck around an overlarge cat, and it doesn't move to swipe at them. A child toddles past, pointing, and Petros averts his gaze.

"How was your day?" he asks Agathi.

"Mmn," she starts, lowering her cup again. "Good . . ."

She barely swallows her coffee before launching into a bakery story, widening her eyes for emphasis – of the words 'bread starter' and 'phyllo dough' – and lowering her voice to criticise a new colleague. He is a kid, she says, who has grown up on cheap, mass-produced pastries from the chain that is destroying bakeries like theirs up and down the country. He doesn't understand that bakers should be using their hearts as much as their hands. That their work, done well, is an act not just of creating, but of preserving. Culture. Tradition. Recipes passed down for generations. Agathi's aunts and uncles all emigrated in the sixties, and her cousins do more to honour their heritage – in the community halls of Bedfordview, Johannesburg and the corner shops of Astoria, New York – than almost anyone here.

"Even my boss is talking about 'upgrading' our kitchen equipment. But I like working by hand," Agathi maintains. "Speaking of which," she recalls, aloud, "I did a trial run."

Petros frowns. "Of?"

"Your wedding cake!"

"Ah . . ."

Behind his smile, a sinking feeling. The mention of Petros's engagement is a betrayal, by Agathi, for it is a weight off his mind to think of other things. To forget his fiancée's cold feet and his mother's fixation, and focus instead on his friend's life. Baking. It amazes Petros that such passion can – from the simple ingredients of flour, yeast, salt and water – rise in Agathi's eyes. He never sees its like in Melina's, for anything.

"I hope you'll be happy with it," Agathi goes on.

"Going by everything else you make, I'm sure I will," he manages, though she has made him feel low.

Making comparisons that he never used to, between his fiancée and his friend. He didn't feel like he had to – like he was running out of time, somehow – until Aristos returned to Cyprus. Only in the year since has Petros felt this urgency around Agathi, infecting everything that he used to feel sure of with this constant, low-grade throbbing in his ears like blood.

"Loipón, *now*." Petros lowers his coffee cup. "Talk to me."

"All right," Agathi twinkles, even as she sighs. "What do you want to know?"

"Just, what's going on between you two. How you're feeling about it. I was there the last time he left you . . ."

"Which I appreciate, very much," she says, with a touch to his arm. "But Aristos can't leave me again if we're not together, and he has a girlfriend. I would never go there."

"I know that," Petros says, the aftertaste of coffee embittering his tongue.

A car rolls past them with excruciating slowness.

"Let's walk a bit, shall we?"

Agathi's tone is gentle, her gait familiar. And yet, as they emerge onto the seafront, Petros shrivels.

"So many flights coming in now, for the summer."

"Yeah," he says, noncommittally, as an Aeroflot jet descends towards Larnaca Airport.

Plane-watching is what he does with Melina. It bothered him when, a few weeks ago, she shared their airline-guessing game with Wendy. The same day that she'd had that god-awful doodle scarred onto her shoulder, apparently. Whenever he sees it, Petros wonders why their game doesn't feel so sacred to his fiancée as it does to him. How she could play it with anyone else.

Concrete turns to wood beneath Petros's boots, sending his footsteps echoing down the Finikoudes Beach pier. He lights up with Agathi's smile, in sunset hues, and knows that he is thinking hypocritically. For years, he'd had no trouble compartmentalising his commitment to Melina and his closeness to Agathi. The latter would take up with someone else, eventually. Of course she would – a woman so beautiful and warm – Petros had known that. He just hadn't known that the someone would be Aristos, who had abandoned them both.

Petros pulls up short before the end of the pier. Agathi turns back, her hair blowing into her face.

"I know you disapprove," she starts.

"It's not up to me to approve," he says, over the lapping waves. "I'm not your papá."

"Okay. You worry, then."

"I'm not your mamá, either."

"But you saw what it did to me, having that relationship end with no closure, no explanation. I thought I was going to be with Aristos forever, and I've been alone for eight years."

"Not alone," Petros says, quietly.

Agathi tilts her head. "Not alone, alone. No. You've been there for me, and again, I'm grateful of that. But like you say," she reminds him, sweeping her hair back, "you're not my papá, you're not my mamá. And you're not my boyfriend, either. I haven't felt able to let anyone in like that since Aristos left, and the conversations we're having are helping me to, just, forgive and trust again. He was living with fears that none of us knew about, back then. But he's trying to put all that right, too, talking to his papá and this guy from the CMP . . ."

'You're not my boyfriend'. Did Agathi look mournful as she said that, or was it a trick of the fading light? Forget it. The wind blows up the stench of algae, and Petros turns towards it. This is the other rule to maintaining a non-weird male–female friendship. If ever you sense your teammate – for that is what they are, a person who shares your goal of defending this bond from temptation – slipping, then you must catch them. Subtly, by feigning a wall of ignorance and then waiting a week to call them again. Hopefully, that is enough time to return them to their senses, and you can carry on together as before. The trick is not to embarrass each other by calling out any overlong embraces. It is to repent for them later, in the private dark beside your sleeping partners, before returning to one another fresh-faced.

"Anyway, sorry. That's for Aristos to tell you," Agathi says. "My point is, you're lucky. Melina is lucky. I wasn't, and . . . I don't know." She bows her head, and her hair blows forward again. "I'm not saying I want to be back with Aristos, necessarily, but I want to be with someone. One day. And I think seeing him like this, hearing him out, could help me get closer to that."

"Well, then. I'm happy for you," Petros says. "Not that it matters, what I think."

"Of course it matters."

He spreads his hands, and the ice cubes knock together at the base of his coffee cup.

"I'm your friend."

"Exactly," Agathi says.

"You know what I mean. I'm just looking out for you." He smiles, weakly.

"I do know. And it means a lot," she says, restoring her hand to his arm.

He nods.

And, with a plane descending from the amber sky over their shoulders, they walk back towards the beach.

TWENTY-EIGHT

It is evening when Petros arrives at the house. His child-hood home, once again made a crime scene. His car-door slam resounds. His boots crunch the dust. As he makes for the house, he feels eyes on his back. The village holding its breath, to expend in whispers which – whether of sorrow or malice – will lash like whips and spread like wildfire.

"Éla, Petro mou . . ."

Xenia stands back from the door, her eyes darting over Petros's shoulder. She closes it no sooner than he has stepped inside.

"Is she awake?"

"In and out. Still feeling the sedatives they gave her, I think."

The door to Petros's old bedroom hangs ajar. Beyond it, darkness. He stares into the void, feeling for his grandmother's arm. Upon finding it, he looks at her.

"How's Melina?" she asks.

"Devastated."

Xenia nods, abruptly. "I knew it was a mistake, sending Panayiota with her . . ."

Well, then. Anger rises in Petros, and he pushes it down.

"You can't think like that, Giagiá. We only did what we thought would make her happiest."

Xenia nods again, this time at her feet, and Petros squeezes her elbow. Then he steps forward.

No one talks about the horrors that befall their household – or the horrors that their household inflicts – when they live in a village. Otherwise, all a person's most generous acts put together would not stop the story of their most desperate one from prevailing, even in Dasaki Achnas. People should know better here, having lived through a conflict.

Petros reaches out, and the bedroom door folds away from him.

"Geiá sou, Petro," his grandfather mumbles, eyes downcast.

"Geiá sou, Pappoú . . ."

Demos's touch to Petros's shoulder is like a dying breath. He shuffles out of the room, and Petros takes his place. Then, at a nod from his grandmother, he shuts himself inside.

"Mamá?" he whispers.

The walls shudder.

"Mamá," he says, louder.

Bedsheets rustle as Panayiota rolls over, her body silhouetted in the little light straining in around the curtain. The air is close with her clamminess. Petros wrinkles his nose. The smell makes him want to stay hidden in the dark from all his senses.

As he creeps across the room, Petros feels like the shadow, the absence, that the darkness implies. He recalls the light that existed in this village when he was a child. The community's pulling together, filling in the gaps of members dead and gone. The families here helped each other. He knows they did, by the bonds that Melina's parents maintain with others to this day. But Petros's relatives kept to themselves. What else could they do? Demos crippled during the invasion. Xenia mothering two generations. Panayiota turning madder with every year that she aged but could not grow, past the death of her brother and the birth of her son. And how about him? Petros. The product of rape, or some twisted Stockholm Syndrome in Panayiota? People looked at him with distrust from the time he could walk, knowing that his father was on the base. A British soldier who had, on the one hand, waved the residents of Achna onto his Queen's sovereign soil and stopped any Turks from coming after them, but who had, on the other, expected such unchecked thanks.

Don. That was the name of the soldier, the stranger. Short for Donald, probably, though Petros never heard anyone say that on his occasional trips to the base. His father never took him further inland than Cessac Beach, where the waves and the wind and the planes all roared in their ears, and his fellow soldiers seldom disturbed them. That one syllable was enough, then, to bark at Don across the sand. The thought of it is enough now, to stop Petros in his tracks. As wary of himself as his neighbours were, of his video player and his Air Jordan trainers. As if those things mattered at all.

Petros hangs back from his mother as he did from his primary-school classmates, not approaching Melina until twelve years old. His father was gone. He was distraught. And yet, at last, he had become like so many others in his village. Solidly missing a family member, rather than being both with and without one so conflicting. Melina was the first person that Petros felt he could approach on level footing, never mind the craggy rocks over Cessac Beach. She brought him as much calm as the sea.

"Mamá . . ."

"Mmn . . ."

Petros traces the white bedsheet over Panayiota's shoulder and pictures the white dress that it so incited her to see his fiancée wearing yesterday. He can't find it within himself to feel surprised. She was jealous from the day that he met Melina. Not thirty years old, and bitter as a hag. Petros never complained. He tried to protect her – from his grief and his gladness – by keeping his emotions like secrets inside himself or, at the very least, inside the house. All its residents did.

Their suppressions yellowed and pushed out against the walls, souring the place with death. The smell wafts as Panayiota turns her head, and Petros pockets his hands to stop from clamping them over his nose. He and his grandparents did their best, and still. They were kidding themselves if they thought the village couldn't smell the skeletons, rotting away in their closets. Between their walls. Under their floors. They scrabbled to hide them until grime blackened their fingernails, and they could barely stand upright for their aching bones.

When they did get outside, the sunlight dazed them. They interacted with people strangely, at a remove like in a dream. They kept their vividness for each other, and it was so harsh, sometimes. Melina's softness was everything to Petros. It still is, he finds, as he casts the room into lamplight. His mother groans, and he feels a flare of resentment for the brokenness with which she stopped him from getting out and meeting Melina even younger.

"I wish we were born alongside each other, like eggs in a nest," he used to tell his fiancée, in their tender moments. "I wish we'd never lived a day apart . . ."

Petros blinks his eyes used to the light. He knows now that an abundance of anything – even softness – will only highlight its absence elsewhere. With her blushing smile and her inside voice, Melina turns Panayiota even harsher. It frustrates Petros, too, when he has tracked dirt through the house or spent too much time with Agathi, and his fiancée refuses to raise it with him. She moves on, graciously, leaving him to feel angry and afraid that he is his mother's son. Or his father's, if indeed there was violence there.

Would it help Petros to forgive Panayiota, if he knew that she had suffered to conceive him? In the lamplight, her hair looks ratty and her face aged. He doesn't know. Only that she is lying in bed, recovering from yet another attempt on her own life, because the sight of Melina in that soft, white dress was, finally, too much to bear. What could Panayiota have done but lash out? Petros imagines it, her begrudging Melina a happy wedding day before she realised that in doing so, she was begrudging him – her only son – that happiness, too, and then hating herself. Thinking that she deserved death, both as punishment for her thoughts and as liberation from them. Yes. Somehow, this sequence of emotions – like a staircase spiralling downwards – makes a frightening amount of sense to Petros.

As though just born, Panayiota flicks her eyes ceilingward. They look filmy.

"How are you?" Petros asks her.

"Eh. I've been better."

Her scoff catches in her throat, sending her coughing and shaking her head.

Despite himself, Petros smiles. "You're still in there."

"Yes, well. There's no need to pour salt on the wound."

Their faces are twisted, on the verge of both laughter and tears. Petros cups a hand to his mother's cheek and finds it in a cold sweat.

"You worry me," he whispers.

"Ach, Petro. You know me," she says, turning her head. "I'll be fine."

The air is a shock to Petros's palm. If the past is anything to go by, Panayiota is right. She will be fine. But what about him? He almost lost his mother today, just as he lost his father and his best friend before her. And, just like those others, this almost-loss is not one that he will be allowed to suffer. Don was a Brit, and Aristos a man, so neither of them could have left Petros truly broken-hearted. Besides, when Don departed, Petros had

Melina to look after. When Aristos did, Agathi. Panayiota's instability is, apparently, most difficult for Panayiota herself and – at a push – Xenia. Meanwhile, Petros supports them all, and does anyone ever think of the weight upon him? He withdraws his hand from his mother's pillow. Too big an ask, perhaps. He isn't crying, so he must be fine. Shoulders aching, shirt sticking with the strains and sorrows of so many loved ones. But business is good, and his fiancée is lovely. In a few weeks' time, they will be married and off to Poros. He cannot complain.

"I wish you wouldn't go through all this," he says, instead. "I wish you hadn't . . ." He trails off, for there is nothing left but to wish himself never born.

Panayiota exhales, deeply, before her chest resumes a steadier rise and fall. Petros watches the bedsheet move with it, a mountain sighing in some far-off, snowy place. The silence is dense and peaceful there, he imagines. As a teenager, he thought he could bring one like it back home with him, if he flew off to England and got answers from his father.

"Why did you ruin her if you cared for her? Why were you there for me if you did not?"

For Melina's sake, he has buried this desire. Mostly in anger. But how deep? Looking at his mother, Petros fears that his unanswered questions, his unresolved issues, might never go away. He might find himself incapable of being a father because of some complex about his own. Is that what has driven it all? His eagerness to console Melina since she, too, lost someone from the base, and his resentment of Aristos for becoming another person to leave them for Britain? Petros bites back a sneer. Disgusting, to think that he might have made so many decisions from such a damaged place. They haven't amounted to a bad life. He is not on the street, begging for change.

And yet, he feels ever less sure that he would have any of the things that he does, if he hadn't stayed hurt for so long. His job, of scrabbling for connections that will light up a room. His house, built on the nostalgic foundations of its Larnaca Bay view. His best man Kyriakos, good for a clap on the back and a sombre nod in response to news like this of Panayiota. But Kyriakos will not invite Petros to open up any further – that male charade of respect designed to cover for discomfort – and he wonders why Petros keeps such a close friend in Agathi.

"What's going on between you two? No, but really, maláka?" is the question he will ask.

A mother can take her own life, or die a little more trying. A man and a woman cannot be just friends. All losses are inextricable, interchangeable. All exacerbate and diminish one another. All explain everything and are invalid excuses. Petros's job. His house. His best man, a second choice. His partner, a known entity.

There is a rap at the door.

"Petro?" Xenia's voice sounds.

"Nai, Giagiá," Petros says, standing back from his mother.

"Can I talk to you . . . ?"

"Of course . . ."

He looks, once more, at the ends of her hair so frayed that her pillow bears them up like water.

"Tha epistrépso," he murmurs. "*I'll be back.*"

And, in this case, '*I'm sorry*', '*I hate this*', and above all, '*Be safe*'.

TWENTY-NINE

"Entáxei? *Okay?*" Melina asks.

Petros sees himself through her eyes – arms folded, tense – and clears his throat.

"I'm fine," he says, curtly. "Are you?"

"Yes, I'm okay."

Melina blinks, and her eyeshadow jars Petros. Light swells from the building before them, gilding the many heads cocked and nodding, enthusiastically, in the crowd at its entrance. Most are brown-haired and speaking 'clean' Greek, others blonde and Russian-sounding. Their shirts are clean-pressed, their skirts ankle-grazing. One woman sways with laughter, and her perfume sweetens even Limassol's exhaust fumes. Petros sidesteps her.

Melina gives him a frown. "Are you sure . . . ?"

"I'm fine," he snaps.

She nods and turns her gaze. He reaches after her, regretful, and she feels unfamiliar in her nice dress. Beyond the range of the baby voice that he often talks her around in, with so many strangers in earshot. He settles for smiling at her.

A man looms towards the gallery doors before turning a key and throwing them open. Their glass shudders.

"*Good evening*," the man greets the crowd, in accented English. "*Welcome, all . . .*"

"*Dobryi vecher*, Filipp!" a blonde calls out, over Petros's shoulder.

"Vera!" Filipp smiles. "*Priyatno videt vas . . .*"

He steps back, and the crowd steps after him through the doors, in some dance to which Petros doesn't know the moves. He finds himself swept along, past a table of tepid drinks and up the stairs where the space opens out, to Aristos.

Petros stares at the man, with a fresh haircut and a cocky grin, who resembles his childhood friend again. Surrounded by paintings that are unmistakeably Cypriot, and that give off the same woody scent as those on his father's walls, Aristos looks as though he never left.

"Petro mou," he says.

Petros smiles. All the history between them collapses –

"Arty," another voice sounds.

– And it blows up again, knocking Petros back.

"*Sorry*," he says, to someone over his shoulder.

"*That's okay*," she responds.

Melina, his fiancée, alien with her smooth-brushed hair. Petros looks down to discover a glass of white wine in his hand and wonders why they didn't have beer, or whether he even asked. People fill in from behind him, pointing and murmuring, and he finds himself borne up towards the last person in the world that he wants to see.

"Wendy Price," Filipp introduces her, raising a hand to quiet the crowd, "*is an artist from London, currently working in Cyprus. Tonight, we have the privilege of presenting her debut collection,* Time, Unchronicled *. . .*"

Applause as Wendy strides to meet him. Petros looks sideways – at the people managing it, somehow, with their drinks in hand – before he faces her. Tall in her platform boots, a skirt that falls asymmetrically over her knees, and a T-shirt that is at once overlarge and too short, exposing a blade of her midriff. Petros's eyes slide across it, and he pulls them back nicked.

"*Hi, everyone. Thank you for coming,*" Wendy says, to the room. "*Thank you,* Filipka, *for that introduction. And for having me at your wonderful gallery . . .*"

She looks to the Russian, with none of her usual disinterest. Wendy appears wholly present now, like she is soaking up every moment.

"*I put blood, sweat and tears into this collection,*" she is saying. "*And I mean that literally. A lot of the work – with these paintings, particularly – happened off the canvas. That's what real art is. It's life, it's . . .*" She sweeps a hand around the room, flashing her silver rings. "*Yeah. What you'll see tonight is, like, the tip of the iceberg. Not to take away from it . . .*"

People laugh, as though Wendy is quite charming. But they must have misunderstood, or perhaps Petros has. His eyes are still chasing her gesture, scaling every wall only to slide back down. This can't be her work, can it? This collection made up of the flat shapes that were all Cypriot artists could render for centuries out of their many-times-stormed and down-trodden land, and of the earthy tones drawn from beneath their feet before the British came pouring asphalt roads and the Russians laying marble floors. Petros shifts his stance. He is not an art person, and even he can spot a Kashalos. Surely Wendy is just going to give her introduction in this room before leading them into another decorated with the kind of thorny roses and bleeding hearts that her arms are.

Except, there is no other room. Petros looks from left to right – rocking up onto the balls of his feet, though he is as tall as any Russian here – and when he turns back, it is over. Wendy is smiling, the crowd applauding her again. Filipp is directing them to a table of appraisals from some academic, and around this room they are circling.

Once again, Petros follows the crowd in a daze. An appraisal finds its way into his hand and hangs limp from it. He comes to the first painting – of a girl in tears between snarling parents – and stops. Now what? Petros itches to refold his arms, but he senses that Melina is bursting for such a reason to ask if he is okay again. They are as useless as each other, in this environment. Beach people, tavérna people. Now and then they stretch to the cinema, but that is about as 'cultured' as they get.

"Isn't she talented?" Melina offers, in a small voice.

Petros looks at her. "You've seen these before?"

"Some of them, nai. But in earlier stages, I think," she says, glancing around.

Beyond her, better-dressed attendees signal and submit to parts of the picture that Petros can't see. He tilts his head, yet the glare will not shift from his eyes.

"And you didn't think . . . ?" He trails off, not sure how to articulate his feelings. Only that they are gathering, in a ball at the pit of his stomach.

"Sygnómi," Melina says, to a woman who has stumbled into her.

Vera, from outside. Petros gags on her oversweet perfume. "*Sorry . . .*"

The stench fades with her sharp-heeled footsteps, leaving Petros to blink at his fiancée as though he is the one who has just happened upon her. Melina tucks her hair back to reveal mascara-lengthened eyelashes. She is unrecognisable, talking in a polite, adult voice which Petros realises – because she has sent him off to socialise without her for so many years – he rarely hears.

A phone erupts into ringing, drawing glares from around the room. Petros's. With a jolt, he flips it open, and jolts again to see his grandmother's name.

"Who is it?" Melina whispers, holding his wine.

"Xenia."

Probably calling about Petros's mother, but there is no need to say this. Already, the knowledge is darkening Melina's eyes.

"Kalispéra, fíloi mou. *Good evening, my friends . . .*"

Petros snaps his phone shut just as Aristos reaches them.

"Ariste," Melina greets him, with a kiss on each cheek.

"Melina mou, looking lovely tonight."

"Thank you . . . Well." She gestures around.

Aristos's hand is firmly around Petros's, then sliding back as he follows Melina's gaze.

"You must be proud," she says.

"Yeah." He grins, "She looks great up there, doesn't she?"

"And brave, putting so much of her life into these paintings," Melina goes on, apparently recovered. "She's really poured her heart out, hasn't she?"

"Sígoura, *sure*," Aristos says.

But he isn't looking at the paintings. He is looking at Wendy, eyes bright with carnality. Petros remembers this brightness from their teenaged conversations about girls. Back then, Aristos was all about Agathi. So, he moved on from her. Fine. Except that he didn't. He hasn't. Petros knows – despite Agathi's pleas of innocence – that Aristos is making to get her back. And still, Wendy saunters his way with liquid eyes, blue as the sea over which she came. Petros takes his wine back from Melina.

"*Hi, guys*," Wendy greets them.

"Wendy mou, brávo," Melina says, throwing her free arm around her friend. "*This is amazing . . .*"

"*Thank you . . .*" Wendy tilts her head towards Melina's, briefly, before standing back. "*Are you having a good time? How are you, Petros?*"

Petros gives her a nod, knowing that she has no interest. She only wants to hear more praise of her work, as if she has any right to exhibit it here and presume to host them. To slide her arm around Aristos's shoulders, with the same air of entitlement. And – perhaps most insulting of all – to give off a sheen of self-satisfaction so lustful that Petros's body cannot help but respond. His eyes go to the knife of flesh at Wendy's waistline again, and he hates them. Hates the half of himself that comes from the taller, paler place that she does, undeniably.

Wendy laughs, poking her tongue out between her teeth, and Petros looks down at his hands. Wine in one – he takes a swig – and the appraisal in the other. He decides to read it, just to avoid Wendy's face and his thoughts of his mother. The document is three pages, the first in English, the second in Russian and the third – the third, never mind their where-abouts – in Greek. Petros folds it back.

'A bold young artist, bringing colour to the shadowland between experience and interpretation', it proclaims Wendy, with a sign-off from the Russian Academy of Arts.

Petros glances back up the page.

'Price's debut collection, *Time, Unchronicled*, depicts scenes from her life in London, while paying homage to a painter that she discovered after moving to Larnaca . . . Michael Kashalos, a naive artist known for his depictions of rural Cyprus and its customs . . . Price adds a modern sensibility. Her scenes are sharper, more urban . . . not held back by tradition . . .'

By the time Petros has read to the bottom of the page, it is trembling with his hands. He gulps back the last of his wine.

"*Are you happy with this?*"

His question rings out, stopping his friends mid-exchange. Wendy closes and reopens her mouth. She makes a show of casting around, at the strangers clustered in twos and threes around her paintings, and smiles.

"*I'd say it's going pretty well. Wouldn't you?*"

"*Not this,*" Petros growls, jerking his head at the nearest wall. "*This.*" He whips the appraisal into stiffness and reads, "*'Taking inspiration from Cyprus', 'showing Cyprus how it's done'? No, you're stealing from Cyprus. And somehow, at the same time, you think you're better than Cyprus as well.*"

"*Ach, here we go,*" Aristos laughs, rolling his eyes.

The furrow goes out of Wendy's brow no sooner than it has come.

But Petros isn't finished. "*Forgetting the lessons of her fine art degree and looking instead to the primitive wisdom of the naive?*" he reads.

"*All right,*" Aristos says, reaching for the appraisal. "*Let's give it a break—*"

"*Give me a break,*" Petros sneers, snatching it back.

"Petro," Melina gasps.

People are looking, wide-eyed. Wendy is backing away, evidently wanting no part of this scene. But she drew it, Petros maintains, as surely as she did the others that are strung up all around them. His eyes catch on one of a man in bed between two women, and it seals inside him an ultimate offence.

"*You know what*, Wendy?" he says. "*You're a pretender. And we don't need you here condescending to us.*"

Before Aristos can bundle him away, Petros thrusts his appraisal at Wendy, and it hits her square in the chest. He makes down the stairs, the earthy tones of her paintings sliding past him like rolls of mud after a rain. Then he is out in the evening air, where the sun has set and still its heat rages.

"Petro!" Melina cries out, from the gallery doors.

Petros turns back across the car park, a concrete strip like another lane of the traffic tearing past them.

"What was that?" she asks, starting across it.

"I don't know," he says. "How they can print those things . . ."

She stops, shaking her head. "What was that from you, I mean. What were you thinking?"

A wind blows between them.

Looking at Melina, with her mascara smudged over her eyelids, Petros sees a traitor. His fault, perhaps, for presuming that she would share his indignation. Their mushiness behind closed doors – all their cuddling and their cooing – does not mean that they are aligned. If anything, it might have obscured just how far out of sync they have slipped.

An image flashes across Petros's mind, of Melina dashing from his office as he entered their house. More than once, in recent weeks. He has never asked her why, just held her. Accepted her friendly smile and her chronic lack of desire – never mind the one or two occasions on which she has surprised him – in recent months. He could scoff at her as easily as he could Wendy for running after him out of the gallery. Urgently, as if she would feel so moved to do any more than get into her pyjamas and turn off the light once they arrived home. Meanwhile, Aristos is trifling with two women, both of whom seem to be lapping it up when at least one deserves worlds better. A man who wants her and her alone. Petros unlocks his truck. It all feels so unfair. And silly – if not remiss of him – to care about, when his mother has been so vulnerable.

"Where are you going?"

"Home." He shuts his car door.

"Perímene, *wait*," Melina's voice sounds, distantly.

Starting the engine, Petros pulls up alongside her and winds down his window. She looks so like an orphan, agog at the roadside, that he cannot stand himself.

"Enjoy your exhibition," he says, through gritted teeth.

And he drives off into the night.

THIRTY

He arrives breathless outside her house, as though having run the highway from Limassol.

Everything is wrong. The air is thick in that Larnaca-specific way, his shirt sticking to his back with sweat rather than with the rain of so many romantic comedies. He is gasping for breath when she opens the door. Wrong again, ugly. And what about her? Dressed in boxer shorts and a tank top. Ready for bed – and not as he had imagined.

Her lips part, and a giggle comes from over her shoulder. Roommates. He can hear them chattering away as she slips out onto the doorstep and pulls the door to behind her. Barefoot, frowning.

There are no words. That's one thing they're doing right, isn't it? The gaping. This is when, in films, the man takes the woman's face between his palms and pulls her into a kiss, and she turns rigid with shock before submitting to his will. This has waited so long, it cannot wait any longer. Not long enough for her to recall his engagement to another woman, and certainly not long enough for him to break it off. They must act fast, so that they can plead the heat of this moment later.

Petros steps forward, and still he cannot say it. The phrase he has turned over on his tongue until he has tasted blood, the last few times that he has seen Agathi. And once last year.

A month after Aristos's return, *Troy* had brought the Trojan War – and Ancient Greece, in all its glory – to the big screen. Every night, the people of Cyprus had packed the cinemas. Their part of the world on loan to Hollywood? They had to see it, Agathi said.

It went without saying that 'they' could not mean Petros and Agathi, sitting arm to arm in a darkened room, alone. In accordance with male–female friendship rules, she invited a colleague and used a tactful 'eíste', in place of 'eísai', to tell Petros.

"You" – plural – "should come."

Reluctantly, Melina agreed. But she wasn't at the cinema when Petros arrived, straight from a job in Dromolaxia, to find Agathi. Alone, for her colleague was sick. Ah. It would be just the three of them, then. Petros and Agathi stood in the lobby, feigning interest in the posters for *Shrek 2* and *Harry Potter and the Prisoner of Azkaban* while they waited, knowing that Melina's presence – without the cushion of anyone else's – would expose the oddities of their trio. The closeness between its engaged man and single woman. The coolness between its two women. Petros's popcorn grew heavy in his hands.

Then Melina called, to say that her brother was stuck at work and so she would have to stay in with his kids. Petros felt that buzzing in his ears, like a child in trouble again. But his fiancée only wished him a nice evening and hung up. He stared at his phone.

"Is everything okay?" Agathi asked him.

"Melina's not coming, either," he told her.

He saw the leap of his heart in her face. Even as they exchanged shrugs in shows of disappointment, delight shone from their eyes.

Petros wondered, as the film raged and murmured in turns, whether Agathi, too, was feeling every hair of the distance between them. She grazed his wrist lowering her Pepsi. His arms strained from their sockets, at once sagging and singing with the memory of some profound weight. Imagined, and yet. Petros felt sure Agathi's embrace was the only thing that could relieve him. When it didn't – because they were friends, and he was engaged, and it wasn't to her – he felt that he could do nothing with all his pent-up desire but burst into tears. Kiss her and steal away in fright, or cry and storm off in fury. Those were his only options, he thought. Then the film turned hammy and, thank God, they were restored to schoolchildren, snickering at the back of the class.

As they proceeded back out into the lobby, past a sour-faced usher and an overfull bin, Petros caught the eyes of several strangers. He thought of how he must look to them, like he was on a date. He saw Agathi struggling to get into her jacket and took her bag, savouring her smile. Another small, precious way of saying, 'I love you', without those forbidden three words.

And still, a year and so much feeling later, Petros cannot pronounce them.

Only, "Do you remember that night, at the cinema?"

"*Troy*," Agathi answers.

They share a smile, recalling the melodrama of it. Then, like the city itself, their faces fall.

"That was fun."

"Yeah," Petros mutters, to her doorstep.

How can such joy between two people make them so sad?

A bat swoops low overhead. Petros looks up, nodding. Agathi nods back, though her eyes are over his shoulder. Silence. Then her arms and lips are locked with his, and it is a mess with his squatting and her craning, a mismatch of parts that should tell them to stop.

"Perímene . . ."

Agathi steps inside, closing the door. Petros breathes its woody scent, running his tongue over his lips until all the orange-blossom taste of Agathi is gone and he is listing after her for more. Hearing her voice, in pleading tones.

A murmuring, a shuffling. Then the door is folding away, and Agathi is in Petros's arms again. He is stumbling, blindly, into her living room – no roommates – and then through another door into her bed. More buzzing in his ears, louder now than ever. Can he love this woman if he cannot say the words? Yes, his body assures him. It assures her, too, in a language all its own, that he is helpless but to move in rhythm with. He loves her. Bats outside, draining the life out of blossoming fruit trees. Petros closes his eyes.

He loves her, he loves her, he loves her.

Thirty-One

Petros shuts his car door, and the impact resounds. The stillness pummels him, fist over fist. Above him is the light by which Agathi must be getting ready for the bed that he has just crawled out of. Beside him, the seat in which Melina has ridden since the day he got his license.

Petros averts his gaze. What to do, when you have betrayed the person you love most in the world? Melina will be devastated. But what by? Petros's having cheated on her, or his telling her about it? Surely there is some logic by which keeping this from her is the kind thing to do. The thing that would spare her from wondering what was wrong with her, and why she wasn't enough. Petros knows all too well the pain of confronting such questions. In the year since Melina's withdrawal from him, he has felt crushed to nothing, not knowing what he has failed to give her. From all his trust and love to every cent of every hour of every day he has ever worked. He wouldn't wish that insecurity on anyone, least of all his fiancée.

Then again, there is the honest choice, which he might just be talking himself out of making. Straining to see it as noble and not self-preserving, when he knows that to lie about this would be to cheat Melina twice over.

Petros's breaths come back at him off the windshield, and he lets his door hang open. His mind is a foreign script, impossible to read, his heart incompatible with his behaviour, and yet he cannot say with which he feels aligned. His instinct now is to clean up this mess. But an hour ago, it was to make the mess. How can he say which urge is authentic to the person he is? He has never cheated before, in twelve years with Melina. He could take comfort in that track record. But he can't say that his night with Agathi fell out of the blue sky, either.

Petros looks up, at the glow in her window. In the last eight years, he has cherished his time with Agathi. If he is honest, much as he thought Melina's disinterest in other women strange at first, part of him has enjoyed having this friendship to himself. On the rare occasions when his fiancée has been present – at the weddings and funerals of mutual acquaintances – Petros has left feeling that his exchanges with Agathi were incomplete, somehow. Not once had they crossed physical lines before tonight. And yet an element of their friendship could only exist when they were alone, like a moonflower unfurling to reflect the starlight, until morning broke and it shrivelled again.

A car trundles past, lighting the street, and Petros pulls his door shut again. Going to bed with Agathi has not been his first show of disloyalty. This truth comes upon him with the darkness as the other car turns a corner. He has never been blind to Agathi's beauty. He has thought of her more than once, standing over the toilet in his unlit bathroom with Melina asleep next door. He has felt a part of himself come alive only when she has smiled at him. His friend Agathi, with whom he could share a deeper bond than any two men were capable of. The fatherless boy in Petros needed that. And it has never eclipsed his love for Melina, even in the year that she has seemed as distant as the sun. He has persisted, taking her to places like Cessac Beach where they spent younger, happier days, and holding her close despite her not letting him in. Even in moments when he has wondered what could have been with Agathi, Petros has been unable to forget his commitment to Melina, unable to conceive of a life without her.

He thought that was love, but perhaps it is just loyalty. Not desire but a dependency born of having been with her so long. The trunk of their relationship is like that of an ancient olive tree, solid and gnarled. They have clung to it since they were children. Sometimes, Petros thinks this is beautiful. Other times, pathetic, and he loses respect for them both. There are forests of trees on this island alone, sprouting lemons and carobs and all manner of other fruits that neither he nor Melina has tasted, since they ceased to explore at sixteen. Petros, even sooner. From age twelve, he was set on her. Tonight, his body feels heavy with regret. But whether that is for his years with Melina or his hours with Agathi, for what he has done or what he has not, he does not know.

Overhead, Agathi turns off her lamp, and Petros is back in her bedroom. There is the scratch of her nails, a whisper until he bears down, and she claws at his back. He shivers, newly aroused and already depleted. Then, the darkness. The remembrance. Revulsion. He starts his car.

Winding his way out of the city centre, Petros comes to Finikoudes and drives along the seafront. The rest of Larnaca is asleep, and still the tourists litter this strip. Its bars have closed, turning them out, half naked, to stagger the beach. Even with his windows rolled up, Petros can hear the shrieks of upset and joy. British, he thinks, darkly, as he passes a girl waving her shoes at her boyfriend. In his rear-view mirror, the boyfriend spreading his hands. Petros's lip curling with disdain. The light shifting as the road curves around, and then settling. Petros is nothing like those people, he tells himself. And yet half of him is made of what they are, possessing enough and still wanting more, staking his claim upon everything. He is no better than the rest.

Putting his foot down, Petros speeds past fish restaurants and ice-cream parlours until the apartment blocks turn sparse, and he is alone on the road. To his right, the sea dances. Through his vents, cold air blasts with the noise of a taxiing plane. Light catches the waves, and he sees it, the flight he never boarded and the boy he is no longer, watching the first of many futures climb away. Beside him, Melina when she still had skinny legs and he hadn't failed her yet. When she was someone that he could build a home with, and not the bank to which he was stuck repaying its loan. She was hope. She was promise. He was those same things to her.

"What do you think that one is?"

Quick, before the plane turned and the sun caught its tailfin.

"Mmn . . . Cyprus Airways?"

"I think Aeroflot."

The rocks of Cessac Beach pressed warm beneath their backs. It didn't matter who was right, only that they were together.

"British Airways . . ."

Melina said that Petros had the sky in his eyes, and he thought it was the best compliment he had ever received. A piece of his father that he had held on to, perhaps by gazing so desperately after the man.

Petros didn't understand anything then. Perhaps that is what he mourns, not a younger version of his fiancée so much as a naiver one of himself. Between the roaring of the air conditioning and the glinting of the sea, he glances from the road to the expanse past his right shoulder and is certain of the children they were, just over the crest of the years. He pulls over. He is going to wade into the water, to hoist himself and Melina out dripping and escort them back to the innocent past. His feet sink into the sand. A wave washes over his shoes, its cold startling.

Petros steps back. Drying his eyes, he sees nothing but the sea, rolling in and out in the rhythm that it does, unstoppably. He sinks back into his car seat. Life is an accumulation of choices. For years, Petros has been so concerned with making his 'good' that he hasn't considered whether or not they have felt right. Now he has done something bad, and he feels no better. Where can he go to start over? He has come to the edge of his island, his world, to discover. There is nowhere. Whatever you do, life goes on, and you can only go with it. Wave after wave, eroding your shores. They are deafening. He gets back on the road.

At home, another lit window. His heart seizes. Melina is awake. And back in his office, Petros realises. On shaky legs, he approaches the door.

When he steps inside, there is the sound of scuffling – the office light pinging off – and then his fiancée descending the stairs. Petros braces for tears or anger, but Melina's face looks twisted. Guilty, he thinks. He must be projecting.

"Geiá," she says, from the bottom step.

"*Hi,*" he echoes.

They stare at each other, the living room large between them.

"How was your night?" she asks.

The words stick in his throat, and he nods.

"How was yours?"

She nods, too, lowering her foot to the floor.

He turns to shut the door, and the memories of all their years spent dreaming and working towards it – this wood in this frame, the excitement they'd shared the first month they had been able to save some money, and the lifestyle magazines they had read in their rental apartment above a coffee shop whose grinder had shaken their cupboard doors – rush inside.

"Moráki mou," Petros says, covering his face with his hands. "*My baby . . .*"

Melina is by his side when the first sob breaks, holding him and telling him that everything is all right.

"No, it's not."

"But it will be, whatever it is . . ."

"It won't."

"Petro . . ."

"I mean it," he says. "You wouldn't be saying that if you knew."

Roughly, he swipes at his tears. Melina takes a step back from him.

"So, don't tell me," she says.

He shakes his head. Her face is set, her lips pressed firm. And still, there is that look about her, like the fear that was twisting her face has pooled in her eyes.

He has to tell her. "I've done things . . ."

"As have I."

He blinks.

"That doesn't change the fact that you're the best friend I've ever had. The only one, in many ways. Nothing changes that," she says.

He takes her by the shoulders.

"I love you," he says, with more fervour than ever before.

"I love you," she croaks, with just as much feeling.

Perhaps this is what they have needed all along, Petros thinks. An injection of uncertainty, to protect them from complacence. He knows already that this won't be enough to sustain their future. But somewhere, in the woman before him, is the girl from the sea. The girl with whom he grew up, and from whom he learned what love was, and for whom he has been everything

– as well as not enough, somehow – and who has been everything to him. Without her, Petros would not know himself. The understanding that he wants to – it is past time – creeps over him, and he holds her tighter. Just for this moment, while he still can. He breathes the cooking scents caught in her hair and thinks of the children they were. So open. So endless. It is to them that he and Melina owe this wedding, the people whose once upon a time deserves its ending at the altar. Whether they live happily thereafter will be for another story.

Cupping Melina's cheek, Petros whispers that he loves her for the fifth or sixth time. She whispers it back. Tears stream from their eyes, wetting their kiss and blurring his vision so that he must fumble for her hands.

"I'm sorry."

"I'm sorry."

"Let's get married."

"Okay."

Their laughter comes spluttering and breathy.

"But I think, once we get to Athens," Petros says, with a sniff, "I need to go and look for my dad."

He dries his eyes to see Melina smiling, as though she has been waiting to hear this for some time.

"I'm glad for you," she says. Then, "Actually, I think there's someone I need to find, too."

Petros could – perhaps he should – ask her who. Instead, he reaches once more for her hand, and they guide each other upstairs to bed.

THIRTY-TWO

ON THE FIRST SUNDAY of August – his last as an unmarried man – Petros awakens to the ringing of church bells and an absence in his bed. Melina has stayed overnight in Dasaki Achnas, where Petros, too, will prepare for their wedding in his childhood home.

The place is just as he left it, with the dining table pushed to one side and the chairs arranged in a semi-circle. His grandmother is already crying, his grandfather standing by Panayiota. Then come Petros's friends, Kyriakos with a clap on the back and another boy with whom he shared army barracks, and several others from school and his time spent running that souvláki bar. This is the first time that Petros has allowed any of them to meet his family – for good reason, he thinks – yet he feels none of the shame that he had anticipated. Only gratitude that everyone around him is alive and well to see this day.

A band comes with violins and lutes, playing folk songs to which everyone dances and clinks zivania glasses. Then it is time for Petros's last shave. His friends cheer him into a seat in the centre of the room and fall quiet as he takes it. Landing with him, the realisation that life is about to change.

"How are you feeling?" Kyriakos asks him.

Petros's smile quivers, and he breaks out into tears.

"Sorry . . ."

The room flinches, but Petros can no more compose himself now than he could after his night with Agathi. It was like he came uncorked, then, and he has been pouring out a lifetime of bottled-up emotions in the weeks since. His grief. His joy. His fear. What if Agathi talked, and people decided that he didn't deserve Melina?

"That's the nice thing about a marriage." Melina's words, washing over his ears in the gentlest waves. "It's only up to the people in it."

Petros's friends are making to console him, with muttered clichés and attempts at humour, when the last of them arrives.

"Ariste," Petros greets him, with a smile.

"Sorry I'm late," Aristos says.

"No need to apologise."

Petros has forgiven him everything, since he himself messed up and learned the value – the necessity – of absolution, the lifebuoy that a second chance can be. At the look that passes between them, Kyriakos offers Aristos the razor with which he was about to shave Petros's chin.

"Are you sure?" Aristos asks him.

A moment later, he is leaning as close to Petros as when they were teenagers.

When the groomsmen arrive at the church, half of Dasaki Achnas is there to meet them. The village that eyed Petros with suspicion for years, apparently won over by his commitment to one of its most beloved daughters. He smiles, wanting more than anything to be worthy.

Melina arrives on foot, beautiful in her flowing dress. As is customary, Petros invites her to take his arm and go with him into the church. Their niece and nephew precede them as bridesmaid and pageboy, and the joy that appears on their loved ones' faces is like something out of a fairytale.

There is the swapping of their stefana, their *crowns*, three times – which Wendy almost messes up, getting the ribbons tangled – the exchange of their rings another three times, and the Dance of Isiah around the sacramental table. Then Petros and Melina are married. Kissing, soaking up the applause, and parading out into the afternoon sunlight for their first photographs as husband and wife.

Their colleagues and more distant relatives mill around the side of the church, while Petros and Melina pose out front with various combinations of their parents and wedding-party members. Beyond the cameraman, Petros sees Agathi hurrying towards her car, and his instinct to call after her dies with the next camera flash. She has the cake to attend to, he tells himself, restoring his smile. Besides, what other place was there for her today? She wasn't a close enough friend for Melina's dressing ceremony, and not a male enough one for his.

The cameraman directs the kouméra to stand beside Petros, and Wendy does as he says without waiting for a translation.

"*You must know all about our wedding traditions, from studying Kashalos,*" Petros supposes, aloud.

Wendy snorts. Then says, "*You know, I didn't write that appraisal.*"

"*I know. I'm sorry, I shouldn't have thrown it like I did.*"

"*It's cool.*"

She gives him a sideways glance before the photographer calls her gaze back.

"*Actually, I don't know if Melina mentioned, but a couple of local papers picked that up. Filipp says my exhibition has had way more footfall since then, so. I almost feel like I should thank you.*"

"*Almost, huh?*"

The photographer lowers his camera, and Petros turns sharply to Wendy.

"*They didn't print my name, though?*"

"*No,*" she assures him, with a satisfied smile. "*Only mine.*"

With all the church photos taken, they get in their cars and regroup at a seaside restaurant for dinner. The room is set up with long rectangular tables and a modest space for dancing. Petros and Melina make for its centre, to the sounds of claps and cheers. She laughs, helplessly, in her struggle to cut the cake. A doukissa, tough with biscuit shards and from setting in the fridge. Petros catches Agathi's eye, just in time to shoot her a smile before Melina's knife hits the plate. More applause sounds, and then a forkful of cake is in Petros's mouth, cloying with cocoa power and condensed milk.

In a quiet moment after their meal, when Petros has wormed his way back around to Aristos, he asks the question that his friend ordered him not to, ahead of this evening.

"How have you been, since the funeral?"

Aristos's father's – a long time coming and then, suddenly, last week.

"Not now, Petro mou. It's your wedding day."

"And you're my friend."

Aristos nods, gratefully. "That confession he gave . . ."

To the Committee on Missing Persons, as Marios lay dying.

"I've felt proud of him, these last few days. Like I can let people in again, after all this time . . ."

A squeal from the dancefloor, where Wendy – visibly drunk already – has dragged Melina. The latter twists, clumsily, and Petros gives a tender laugh. Wendy turns her head. In response to her nod, Aristos waves as he might to a loose acquaintance. He is displaying none of the desire that he was the night of Wendy's exhibition opening, nor any of the bravado that he boasted as a teenager. Instead, an air of calm. The capability that he will need to manage his father's estate, first in Athens, then in London, and then back in Larnaca.

Excusing himself, Petros slips out into the night air, tinged with cigarette smoke and something not unlike orange blossom.

"So, how was she?" Agathi's voice sounds.

Petros's shoes crunch the sand.

THIRTY-THREE

They arrive at Larnaca Airport in good time, having driven through the sunrise. When they reach their gate, the sky is a clear blue. Petros gazes out the window at it until a yawn blurs his vision.

"Oríste," a woman's voice sounds. "*Here.*"

He blinks her into focus, proffering a bottle of water. Melina, the girl to whom he has just honoured his lifelong commitment. Between them stand the two carry-on suitcases that they changed their booking to include, rather than a shared one for the hold. Petros's smile fades, and he takes the water.

"Efcharistó," he thanks Melina.

The woman without whom his future is a complete unknown.

He tips his head back and drinks until the bottle shrinks inwards, its cracking sound obscuring the "final call" of an overhead announcement.

"Are you okay?" Melina asks.

"Fine," Petros says, as he lowers the bottle. "I just thought I heard . . ."

A passenger assistant calls them for boarding.

They file onto the plane, to seats chosen at a time when they had still poured over such details together. It wasn't only the cloudless sky or the Aegean Sea, studded with Greek islands, that they had wanted to see, but the view over a Boeing-737 wing.

"Do you want the window seat?" Petros asks.

"Don't you want it?"

"Go ahead."

"If you're sure," Melina says.

Taking a breath of the kerosene-soured air, Petros hefts their suitcases up into the overhead lockers and ducks into the middle seat. His wife thanks him, warmly, sliding a book into the seat pocket before her. *Boy Meets Boy*, its cover reads.

"Sorry," a flight attendant says, squeezing past.

Petros watches her weave to the front of the plane where a second crew member waits, smiling like a person in love. He is one, Petros realises, as the two of them exchange bright-eyed looks. The girl with the oversweet perfume and the boy with the baby face. Love's next incarnations.

People go on shuffling past with their bags, then cease to. The aisle is clear, the cabin-crew couple anxious-looking. The girl leans out the aeroplane door, while the boy murmurs into a radio, until a final two passengers come striding in. Petros touches Melina's wrist, and she catches her breath.

"What are they doing here?"

"You know, I thought I heard his name called in the airport, but . . ."

The door slams shut.

"Kyríes kai kýroi," a third crew member says across the tannoy, "*ladies and gentlemen.* A warm welcome aboard this Helios Airways flight to Prague . . ."

"Prague?" Melina echoes.

". . . via Athens . . ."

"Ah," she breathes.

Petros, too, slumps back in his seat.

"I'll be your cabin manager . . ."

"It's a connecting flight. She must be going all the way to Prague, to see that gallery owner," Melina says, of the girl coming down the aisle.

The girl rummages for space in an overhead locker, with cropped, bleached hair and silver rungs laddering her ear. The man behind her is short, his hooked nose and heavy brows unmistakeable. There is a kerfuffle as they compare tickets, a rustling of papers and a shifting of feet, before the apparent realisation that they will be sitting just across the aisle from one another. A happy accident, it would seem.

"Ariste," Petros calls.

His friends, and several blank faces, turn towards him. He raises a hand.

"Petro," Aristos beams, over the back of his seat. "I wondered if I'd find you here. Geiá sou, Melina mou, hello. How's married life?"

Melina gives him a nod. "The same. With better photos," she adds.

The surrounding strangers join her in smiling. Everyone loves a wedding, much like the ten- and twenty- and thirty-year anniversaries that come later. Causes for congratulations, even if every one of those years has been fraught or hollow. Other married people forget, wilfully or by some temporary amnesia, what they are clapping for. Another two people signing away their freedom to choose one another each day. Brávo. Another two people vowing to stay the dissatisfaction and regret that has come to all those before them, on some front or another. They cling to the notion that a shared life is an ideal one. It must be, for someone. Otherwise, what have their efforts – to maintain a relationship that, whether due to ill-health or money troubles or wandering hearts and hands, has caused them as much pain as pleasure – been for? Surely, some couple has achieved it. That rare thing called happiness. Perhaps that couple is Petros and Melina. Why not, if only for the moment in which this tube of a hundred and twenty-one strangers is smiling upon them? He opens his palm, and she laces her fingers through his. They fit perfectly but for the ridge of her wedding ring.

"Na zísete," Aristos says, congratulating them once more.

The cabin manager hangs up her radio and comes clomping down the aisle, instructing him and Wendy to sit down. She looks from side to side as she goes, ensuring that everyone has their seatbelt fastened. Only when she reaches Petros and Melina does she stop.

"Kaliméra, *good morning*. Can I see . . . ?"

They raise their arms.

"Thank you," the cabin manager says. Then smiles, "You're just married?"

They nod.

"Congratulations," she coos. "I'll have my wedding, too. Next month."

"Ah. Well, congratulations to you . . ."

Petros feels the smile remain, vaguely, upon his face as the cabin manager's footsteps fade down the aisle. Perhaps she is the one about to say 'I do' to true happiness, with whomever her fiancé is. Perhaps they have discovered the secret. Why not?

At a reminder from the cabin crew, Petros holds down the 'end call' button on his phone. Just before the screen goes dark, it shows the time changing from 07:59 to 08:00. He slides his phone away, satisfied that he has never felt such a perfect sense of one chapter ending and another beginning. They are rolling towards the runway, the water coming into view beyond Melina's window. Petros nudges her, and she looks outside and then back at him. She is smiling, her face framed by the blue oval of sea and sky. A picture of her and Petros – and Aristos and Wendy, and who knows how many others onboard – where they were always meant to be. Free of the feeling that it is all they can do to watch planes full of other people come and go. For at last, they have boarded their own.

As the engines fire up towards take-off, Melina lays her head upon Petros's shoulder. He leans his head upon hers and, temple to temple, they close their eyes.

Accident Investigation Report

Date: 14 August 2005
Time: 09:03 UTC
Aircraft Type: B 737-31S
Operator: Helios Airways
Flight Number: 522
Occupants: 121
Fatalities: 121
Aircraft Damage: Destroyed
Synopsis:

On Sunday 14 August 2005, Helios Airways flight 522 departed Larnaca, Cyprus at 06:07 h for Prague, Czech Republic via Athens, Hellas. The aircraft was cleared to climb to FL340. As it climbed through 16 000 ft, the captain reported a Take-Off Configuration Warning and an Equipment Cooling System problem. Communications between the captain and the operations centre ended as the aircraft climbed through 28 900 ft. At an altitude of 18 200 ft, the passenger oxygen masks deployed in the cabin. The aircraft levelled off at FL340 and continued on its programmed route. No further radio calls to the aircraft were answered.

At 07:38 h, the aircraft entered the KEA VOR holding pattern over Athens International Airport. At 08:32 h, during its sixth holding pattern, it was intercepted by two F-16 aircraft of the Hellenic Air Force. One of the F-16 pilots observed the aircraft at close range and reported that the captain's seat was vacant, the first officer's seat was occupied by someone who was slumped over the controls, the passenger oxygen masks were dangling, and three motionless passengers were seated wearing oxygen masks in the cabin. At 08:49 h, he reported a person not wearing an oxygen mask entering the cockpit and occupying the captain's seat. The F-16 pilot tried to attract his attention without success.

At 08:50 h, the left engine flamed out due to fuel depletion and the aircraft began descending. At 08:54 h, two MAYDAY messages were recorded on the CVR. At 09:00 h, the right engine flamed out at an altitude of 7 100 ft. The aircraft continued descending rapidly and impacted hilly terrain at 09:03 h in the vicinity of Grammatiko village, Hellas, approximately 33 km northwest of Athens International Airport.

The 115 passengers and 6 crew members on board were fatally injured. The aircraft was destroyed.

Epilogue

They take a taxi from Kolonaki. This is where they are staying, in the Saint George Hotel, because Aristos's father used to
own an apartment in the area. It should have passed to Aristos,
along with the rest of Marios's portfolio. Instead, it went to
Nausicaa – the woman Agathi had come of age believing that
she would one day call mother-in-law – who lost Aristos some
eight years after Agathi had. Nausicaa had buried her husband
that same month, and she had no other children. She took her
own life.

What happens to things when there is no one alive to inherit
them? Marios's apartments cannot all be full of ghosts. And
yet, as her taxi weaves through the highest inhabited streets on
Lycabettus Hill, Agathi finds herself peering up into the few
windows with their shutters open. She glimpses an ankle flash
past one, and a man on the phone in another. The rising sun
glares down the street and, like a child rebuked, Agathi drops
her gaze.

"Eísai entáxei?" her husband asks, squeezing her hand.

"I'm okay," Agathi smiles, as reassuringly as she can. "Esý?"

Jason nods one too many times before saying, "Nai. Yeah, I'm okay."

Their taxi takes a right turn, and Agathi leans into it. She keeps her eyes open until Jason's lips are on hers, acquainting herself with his face as though for the first time. She knows the grief that has etched itself into his under-eye lines, and the transnational love story behind his high cheekbones. She hopes she has contributed to the joy recalled in his crow's feet. But the better you know someone, the worse they can shock you. Or so Aristos, her first love, taught her in life. From his death, Agathi learned to take no one she loved for granted. Not just to look at her husband, but to stand back and see him. Not to let fall her arm over his, but to hold him with feeling.

Sitting upright, Agathi tightens her seatbelt. She withdraws her hand from Jason's, momentarily, to remind herself where her body ends and his begins. To better appreciate them both, in much the same way as she has come to their daughter and son through her alone time with each of them. Another turn as their taxi clings to the hem of the hillside park where Aristos never took her, and Agathi fights to maintain her posture. But of course she is grieving, for Petros and Melina – even Wendy – as well as Aristos. All four were towering figures in her life before theirs ended, that terrible day nineteen years ago. Agathi can't believe all that time has passed. Before she knew of the husband and children she would go on to have, she struggled to fathom how she would survive it. But then she realised that, in many ways, she had been grieving for a long time already.

There is a purity to mourning something that you wanted and never had. An almost heightened sense of loss, for you are left with the idea untarnished. You haven't watched it turn thin and feeble in the final throes of a terminal illness. You haven't grown jaded as it has slacked and ceased to be worthy of your love. In your dreams, this thing has been perfect. And if it is gone from reality before you can grasp it, you will never wake up. That was how Agathi felt when Aristos left for London. Comatose. They had been too young to move in together and start bickering about his socks on the floor, or to have children and fight over whose turn it was to tend them each night. As far as Agathi was concerned, long after he had broken her heart, marriage to Aristos would have been blissful. She was twenty years old, and she had lost the love of her life.

When she could cry no more, she turned towards anger. It felt easier to hate Aristos than it did to miss him. And so, Agathi decided that his swagger was not winning but brash, his looks not good but devilish. She developed a complex relationship with God, questioning why he had taken her love when she had waited until she was sure that Aristos would marry her before giving herself to him physically. Had she been too Christian for her boyfriend, or too heathen for the Father? From whom was this punishment? Eventually, Agathi grew weary of the darkness in her heart and returned to Saint Lazarus's Church. The congregation welcomed her back. They made good and assuring contacts for her, and she made Easter and Christmas breads for them.

What rose from there was Agathi's love of baking. The sense of order that it required and taught her, in equal measure. Baking was a science – unlike cooking, which could be slapdash and variable, it took precise, step-by-step consideration. So long as she got her quantities right, Agathi could not go wrong. This reassured her so much that she spent all her time in the kitchen, until her mother suggested that she enrol in a pastry-chef course. From the first class, it made sense. Agathi at the scales, weighing out every egg before she committed to breaking it open, as she had failed to do earlier in her life. Never again would she throw anything into a pan just because it looked right. Her portokalópita became renowned. She got a job a week after her diploma.

She still grieved for what could have been with Aristos – she had never imagined anything else – but she built a life for herself. A house share with two roommates, a standing Sunday-lunch date with her family, and frequent coffee breaks with Petros. Then Aristos returned, with his bravado gone and his face changed. Longer, with less baby fat and closer-cut hair. Agathi was shocked by his vulnerability, unsure what to say when, after several meetings, he asked her if she still loved him. The answer was yes – of course she loved Aristos – but which version of him? The one she had been with as a teenager, the one who had come back to her as an adult, or some fictionalised account of him that she had held on to in between? She told him that she needed to think about it.

Meanwhile, there was Petros, who had proven himself to be her true constant. Agathi was grateful for his support and jealous of the life that Melina shared – and, Agathi thought, took for granted – with him. She had often looked upon his displays of emotional availability and devotion, and wished that she could have seen their like from Aristos. Did that mean that Petros would have made her happier? Agathi thought she would know if she slept with him. It was an awful thing to do – utterly unlike her – but a necessary one. Despite herself, she enjoyed the warmth of his skin and the whisper of his breath. She looked at him afterwards, across the tangle of her bedsheets, and thought, yes. This could be something. But it felt like a window's glimpse at the twilight hour. Like, before long, someone was bound to pull the blinds and shut her out. It just so happened that the someone was not Melina, in the end.

Melina made a wonderful bride, one of those who looked as though she had been destined for her dress. Agathi cried, telling her this. She felt so sorry. Melina squeezed her hands and told her, with unmistakeable meaning, that it was okay. Catching her breath, Agathi looked to Petros, who averted his gaze. It wasn't until later, when they met outside, that he placed a hand on her shoulder. Agathi was still feeling the ghost of it when Aristos appeared.

"It's over."

"What?"

"Bettween Wendy and I, it's over," he said, fumbling for his cigarettes. He lit one. "Take me back."

Agathi stared at him, the warmth of the night closing in on her.

"Ariste . . ."

"Please, Agathi mou. It hasn't been the same with anyone else."

She watched the ash build up at the end of his cigarette, how easily he tapped it off. Tears bloomed in her eyes.

"How can I trust that you won't make me fall in love with you—"

"I hope I will."

"– and then leave me, the way you did last time? Just fly away and not come back?"

"Never again," he promised.

He gave her a single, light kiss. They agreed to talk when he was back from Athens.

And, two days later, she saw the tailfin of his plane torn off and upended on that mountainside, Helios's golden face gazing up at the sky from which he had plummeted. The image was inescapable, all over the news and the insides of Agathi's eyelids. She screamed and cried and cursed Aristos for breaking his promise a second time, hurling insults at her television screen to provoke some response. There was none from Aristos, none from Petros, none from Melina and none from Wendy. Only silence, ringing in Agathi's ears for months.

Then, the one-year memorial service. Agathi stared at the gaunt faces of her fellow attendees, wondering who had blackened their eyes and how it was possible to feel so cold in August.

She spoke to no one, until the third year when a boy about her age approached her. A man, really. Her gaze sank into the lines threatening his forehead, and she knew that time had not stopped for her grief, either. Girlhood had passed her by.

The man told her he had lost his sister in the crash, and that she had looked a little like Agathi. Then he asked if Agathi wanted to get a coffee with him.

"Because I look like your sister?" she replied.

They chuckled, her with a hand hovering over her mouth and him with a hand hanging over his eyes, until the guilt took hold. They shed a few rapid tears before composing themselves, quickly, as people in mourning must learn to. Then the man said that his name was Jason.

They took things slowly at first, each afraid of gaining another loved one to lose. Jason talked about his Czechoslovakian father, an employee sent to his country's first Embassy in Cyprus in 1964. He talked about his return to Prague when Turkey invaded ten years later, with his Cypriot wife and their baby daughter. Jason had been born there and lived a back-and-forth life until choosing Cyprus for himself as an adult. His sister had been on her way home from visiting him when Flight 522 crashed. The guilt was crushing. And yet, he talked so fondly of the woman that Agathi came to feel as though she, too, had known her. As though Jason's love was a force that knew no finality. Their affection for each other became undeniable.

Life took over from death. There was a wedding, a baby girl and then – with some extra help, because they were older – a baby boy. Those babies are on the cusp of adolescence now, and so different that Agathi can scarcely believe their relation, sometimes. Renata, named for Jason's late sister, is quiet and studious. Nothing like the mischievous, musical woman who would have been her aunt, Jason confesses. Agathi understands his struggle. Their son Panos – named what Petros claimed his would have been – is boisterous and can be impatient. Because, Agathi reminds herself, he is not Petros's son. A few years from now, he will cease even to be hers in such an immediate, practical sense. Both children will stand to pilot their own planes through life. They are already eyeing up the seatbelt signs, Renata talking of universities in France, and Panos of football teams in England. When the time comes, Agathi and Jason must be ready to wave them off, smiling.

And so, here they are, unable to go any further into the future without first laying to rest the past. Their taxi speeds along the coast, and its driver talks of the messenger who, over two and a half thousand years ago, ran this road from Marathon to Athens with news of Greece's victory over the Persians. The first marathon. The road winds up over a mountain range, and he talks of the fire that, just weeks ago, ripped across it and into Athens's suburbs.

"Panagía mou," Jason murmurs.

Agathi follows his gaze out the window, to the hills rolling, blackened and ash-topped, for miles. History is all around them, she thinks, as well as inside them. It is a force both to act upon and to be impacted by, inescapably. She had a similar thought on the plane – flying the same route that her loved ones had, nineteen years earlier – as it climbed through what looked like eighteen thousand feet. So, she thought, this was around when the oxygen masks would have dropped. And how long would their supply have lasted, fifteen minutes? She leaned her head back. This, she thought, was around when the plane would have gone to sleep, thus becoming a 'ghost flight'.

Winding up from Marathon – a smaller town than Agathi had imagined – the taxi comes to a lusher, quieter mountain range, untouched by fires or other cars. The road jerks steeper, and she grips Jason's hand.

"Don't worry," their driver chuckles, revving the engine up an almost vertical dirt track.

Agathi's stomach lurches. She jumps out the moment they stop, beneath a small, sand-coloured church. A cross tops the roof – thin enough that Agathi thinks she could snap it – beneath a vivid blue sky. Bricks underfoot. Tall, narrow windows. Agathi tries the doors, to no avail. Stepping closer, she peers inside to see rows of wooden chairs and a half-full bottle of water. The latter brings tears to her eyes. This is the most remote place she has ever stood, with only the sound of the wind and the smell of the earth. And yet here is this ugly, polluting sign – leftover from the memorial service held each year – that it has not been forgotten.

Coming back around the church, Agathi finds her husband before a stunning view. She comes up beside him, and a warm wind takes her breath away. All around them are green-covered mountains. Below, a dam and then the sea, as blue as the sky.

"If this was it," Jason manages. "If this was the last sight they ever saw . . ."

His words catch in his throat, and Agathi takes his arm. Of course, everyone but the flight attendant who crash-landed the plane here lost consciousness long before they reached their final resting place. Jason must know this. He has watched all the footage that Agathi has, as desperately. But what no cameraperson ever gave them was the gift of panning around. Agathi looks back, just to check that the church is still there. For not once – on the news or on the internet or anywhere else that broadcast the crash – has anyone thought to say, look. There was horror. There was death. But there was beauty, too. For all the smoke, a mountain breeze. For every body, a forest of trees.

Agathi looks down, to the memorial shrine at her feet. Stacked around it like gravestones are photographs, crosses. Even a toy airplane. With a sob, Agathi leans into her husband's shoulder. So many young faces, and inscriptions in marble.

'Kaló taxídi', one of them reads. 'Safe travels'.

The last words you say to someone before they wave you goodbye and turn away.

Acknowledgements

Thank you, as ever, to my friend and cover designer Mark Ecob, for emboldening me to publish my first book and for bringing this third one to life so beautifully. Thank you to my editor Edward Wall, for immersing himself in this story and helping me lift it to entirely new levels.

Thank you to the Moons and to the Archies, for their extraordinary support while I was struggling through my first draft, among other things.

Thank you to Alexandros Chronides, Julie Fitch, Logan Govier, Charlotte and Marcus Pierce-Smith, Eleni and Kyros Savvides, and Jacopo Tarello, for their friendship and insights throughout this process.

I am grateful to the authors of the following publications: *Aircraft Investigation Report: Helios Airways Flight HCY522 Boeing 737-31S at Grammatiko, Hellas on 14 August 2005* by the Air Accident Investigation & Aviation Safety Board (Hellenic Republic Ministry of Transport & Communications, 2006); *The LGBTI Movement in Cyprus: Activism, Law, and Change Across the Divide* by Okan Bullici, Enver Ethemer, Costa Gavrielides and Nayia Kamenou (Friedrich-Ebert-Stiftung, 2019); *Beneath the Carob Trees: The Lost Lives of Cyprus* by Nick Danziger and Rory MacLean (jointly published in 2016 by Armida Publications and Galeri Kultur Publishing, in association with the Committee on Missing Persons in Cyprus); *Refugeehood and the Postconflict Subject: Reconsidering Minor Losses* by Olga Maya Demetriou (State University of New York Press, 2018); *Aircraft Accident Report: Crash During Landing T R S Executive Airlines (doing business as American Eagle) Flight 5401 Avions de Transport Regional 72-212, N438AT San Juan, Puerto Rico May 9, 2004* by the National Transportation Safety Board (National Transportation Safety Board, 2005); *National Transportation Safety Board Aviation Accident Final Report* by the National Transportation Safety Board (National Transportation Safety Board, 2005); *Aviation Investigation Final Report* by the National Transportation Safety Board (National Transportation Safety Board, 2006); *The 2002-04 Annan Plan in Cyprus: An Attempted UN-Mediated Constitutional Transition* by Neophytos Loizides and John McGarry (Forum of Federations, 2019); *Tetralogy of the Times: Stories of Cyprus* by G. Philippou Pierides (Nostos, 1998); *Aviation Occurrence Report: Fairchild-Swearingen SA227-AC Metro III ZK-POA, Loss of control and in-flight break-up, near Stratford, Taranaki province, 3 May 2005* by the Transport Accident Investigation Commission (Transport Accident Investigation Commission, 2006).

I am grateful also to Andreas Hadjiloucas, Catherine Louis Nikita, and Natasa Theodorou at the Costas Argyrou Museum for coordinating the wonderful *Kashalos: From Light to Shadow* exhibition.

Very special thanks are due to Matthew Phillip Long, for more encouragement and re-readings than I fear I can ever repay him.

To my parents, Giorgos and Jennifer, for keeping me healthy and persevering.

To Max, for everything.

And, of course, thank you to every reader who makes what I do possible. If you enjoyed *Ghost Flight*, you can discover my other books and sign up to hear about new releases on my website.

www.ingramcontent.com/pod-product-compliance
Lightning Source LLC
Chambersburg PA
CBHW030939120726
47906CB00002B/635